SET
TO KILL

a mystery novel
by
Arthur Marx

[signed] Arthur Marx

Barricade Books, Inc.
Fort Lee, New Jersey

Published by Barricade Books Inc.
1530 Palisade Avenue
Fort Lee, NJ 07024
Distributed by Publishers Group West
4065 Hollis
Emeryville, CA 94608

Copyright © 1993 by Arthur Marx
All rights reserved. No part of this book may be reproduced, stored in a retrieval system, or transmitted in any form, by any means, including mechanical, electronic, photocopying, recording, or otherwise, without the prior written permission of the publisher, except by a reviewer who wishes to quote brief passages in connection with a review written for inclusion in a magazine, newspaper, or broadcast.

Printed in the United States of America.

Library of Congress Cataloging-in-Publication Data

Marx, Arthur, 1921– .
    Set to kill / Arthur Marx.
      p. cm.
    ISBN 0-942637-80-1 : $17.95
    I. Title.
PS3525.A7737S46   1993
813'.54—dc20   92-33271
                                                   CIP

0 9 8 7 6 5 4 3 2 1

To Lois, who has everything.

One

There are two kinds of Hollywood writers—the "what's new" writer—he doesn't write anything, he just phones his agent every day and asks him "what's new?" meaning, "did you get me a job yet?" And the "writing" writer; he does what a writer is supposed to do—he sits down at a typewriter and writes something his agent can sell.

> M. C. Levee, famous
> Hollywood agent of
> the thirties

For the better part of Tuesday, Gabe Steele sat at his desk in his small, untidy furnished apartment, chain-smoking cigarettes and waiting for a call from his agent. Intermittently he tried to think of a fresh idea for a screenplay or television series, but he found it hard to concentrate with so many unpaid bills staring at him from the top of his cluttered desk.

As the rays of the midafternoon sun started to slant into the room through the dusty Venetian blinds behind Gabe's chair, warming the back of his white terry robe, he glanced at his wristwatch. Three P.M. A week to the minute since he had last spoken with his agent, who had promised to get back to him within twenty-four hours ("Cross my heart, babe!") with news of a television writing assignment he was "hot on the trail of."

Suddenly cognizant that another week had flown by without any income, Gabe did something he vowed he would never do: he picked up the phone on his desk and punched out Lou Gershwin's number, thereby joining the ranks of the countless "what's new" writers all scrambling for jobs in the Hollywood marketplace.

Gabe hated to degrade himself by being the initiator of the call, especially when he knew from twenty years of experience in the business, that if his agent had a job for him, *he* would phone Gabe. But these were desperate times; they didn't allow him the luxury of patience. Except for a couple of small residuals, Gabe's income had dropped to practically zero in the first four months of the current year; the bills from all his charge cards were piling up at an alarming rate (how long could he get by with just paying the "minimum"?); and Marge's lawyer had phoned him twice in the past ten days to dun him for back alimony payments.

Of course, even before his split with Marge, he had been aware from friends who'd gone through the travail of shedding a wife that divorces were expensive, especially in a community-property state like California.

As he waited for Gershwin's secretary to answer the phone, Gabe's pride nagged him to hang up before he was connected. He could guess what Connie was going to say to him, anyway—that Lou was on another call, and he'd have to get back to Gabe. He might as well save that humiliation and also the price of a phone call from Pacific Palisades to Beverly Hills. In his financial condition, a dime saved was a dime earned that he wouldn't have to give Gershwin ten percent of.

However, Connie picked up on the other end before Gabe could put the receiver down. Remarkably, she didn't give him the usual stall after he had identified himself.

"Oh, sure, Mr. Steele," she said in a friendly voice, "I'll put you right through. He's been wanting to speak to you. He asked me to remind him."

Well, that was encouraging. The cigar-smoking little weasel must have landed something for me, thought Gabe, otherwise he wouldn't have asked Connie to remind him to call.

"What can I do for you?" asked Gershwin cheerfully, after the two had exchanged the usual insincere *hello-how-are-yous*?

Gabe felt a sudden sinking sensation in his gut. For those weren't the words of an agent who had work for him. "You were going to get me an assignment," Gabe reminded him a little apologetically. "You said you knew a show that was interested in me."

After a long pause, Gershwin intoned, "Oh, yeah. 'L.A. Law.'" He cleared his throat. "Well, babe, that didn't pan out."

"I'm not 'babe,' I'm Gabe."

"Excuse me, babe, of course you're Gabe. Anyway, I spoke to the story consultant. They're full up for this season."

"What about the other suspense series?" prodded Gabe. "'Mrs. D.A.' and 'Death Squad'?"

"Everyone's waiting for a pickup before they give out any more assignments," replied Gershwin evasively.

"I don't believe it," Gabe fired back. "They're all successful shows. There's no question of pickup. Now what's the problem? I have more credits than most people in this town."

Another long pause and then Gershwin said, "I have to level with you, Gabe." Chilling words that never failed to send a shiver of despair down Gabe's spine. "I've got a problem selling you."

"How can that be? All my scripts have been produced. One was nominated for an Emmy. I'll stack my reputation in this town against anyone's."

"Don't have to tell me. If I were a producer, you'd be my head writer," stated Gershwin. "The problem's nothing to do with your work. It's the grey hair. All the guys in charge of shows today look like they just got out of kindergarten. They see a middle-aged guy like you walk in, and it's an immediate turnoff. As much as I hate to tell you this, they're hiring people their own age."

"You mean at the age of forty-three, I'm all washed up?"

"The networks are trying to appeal to an under-thirty audience. They think young writers are the answer."

"What bullshit!"

"Sure, it's bullshit, but it's a fact. Hopefully it'll turn around."

"When?"

"How the hell do I know? Everything goes in cycles in this business. Next year they'll probably realize what garbage they're putting on the tube and go back to the experienced writers again."

"Next year! What am I going to do to eat now? I've got bills to pay—and alimony."

"Look, Gabe, I know it's hard to accept," said Gershwin in a condescending tone. "But I'm not making the rules, which is why I tell all my clients when they're making it to save their money and stop spending it on drugs, fancy cars, and cellular phones."

"I don't do drugs, and I drive a three-year-old motorcycle."

"Maybe that's your problem—you don't look successful enough," retorted Gershwin. "Anyway, I hope you saved your money."

"Well, if no one'll hire me, I guess I better come up with a series idea of my own."

"I don't know if that'll do you any good, either. If you're not on the list of desirable writers, they'll either just pay you bupkes for the idea, or else they'll steal it from you."

"You mean there's actually a list?" exclaimed Gabe, trying to fight back a sense of panic.

"Well, no one on the outside has ever seen it," equivocated Gershwin, "and the networks all deny it if you ask 'em about it, but the word around town is there definitely is such a list—the white list—and if you're not on it, you'd better be prepared to spend the rest of your life in your rocking chair telling your grandchildren about the good old days."

"Jesus!" exclaimed Gabe. "If that's really the case, this is as bad as the Hollywood Ten blacklist days. Maybe even worse. Because there are more of us with grey hair now than there were Communists then."

"I agree," said Gershwin. "It's tough."

"Those bastards at the networks ought to be exposed," muttered Gabe. "Maybe a class-action suit is called for by all the older writers."

"That's why the networks are playing it so close to the vest," explained Gershwin. "If the list ever got out, the networks could be in for a lot of trouble. But so far even the Writers Guild can't come up with any hard evidence that a list actually does exist. All everyone knows is that you can't sell a writer over forty, unless he's Neil Simon or Bob Towne."

"This is dreadful," said Gabe, with another sinking feeling in his gut. "What's a guy supposed to do—stop living?"

"Don't kill yourself yet," advised Gershwin.

"What's to live for if I can't make a living?" asked Gabe. "Even my unemployment insurance has run out."

"Well, if you come up with something really sensational, some high-concept idea, that is, maybe I can sell it . . . if you want to put another name on it or find some kindergartner to share the credit with you."

"Well, I have one great idea, I think," said Gabe. "It's about—"

"Can't hear it now," Gershwin interrupted him. "I got a client waiting on the other line."

"What am I—chopped liver?" retorted Gabe, defensively.

But Gershwin never heard it. He'd already hung up, banging the receiver down so hard that it nearly broke Gabe's eardrum. In retaliation, Gabe banged his receiver down harder, not that Lou was able to hear that, either, but he had to take his frustration out on something, even an inanimate object. Following that, he lit another cigarette and sat quietly for a moment, smoking and contemplating a gloomy future.

Judging from that phone call, Gabe had three options:

(1) Dye his thinning grey-streaked hair black.

(2) Fire Lou Gershwin and get a new agent.

(3) Go to the Racquet Club and work some of his hostility off on the tennis court.

Since it would fool no one to change the color of his hair, unless he also sprang for a face job to remove some of the lines which creased his forehead and were beginning to form crow's-feet at the corners of his eyes, and one Hollywood agent was as good as another when you were being blacklisted because of your age, Gabe opted to spend the rest of the afternoon at the Beverly-West Racquet Club, even though he was slightly embarrassed to show his face there with his monthly bills three months in arrears. However, no one was likely to bring that up if he didn't make himself too conspicuous as he passed the manager's office on his way into the clubhouse.

Consequently, he decided to risk it. A couple of stimulating sets of singles in the sultry smog-laden spring air would either kill him at his advancing age or rev up his flagging spirits, either of which he'd settle for in his present frame of mind.

Two

The Beverly-West Racquet Club was approximately a twenty-minute ride from Gabe's apartment by motorcycle, a mode of travel forced on him in the divorce settlement by an avaricious wife, who got custody of the BMW, and which this afternoon, after his disheartening confrontation with Lou Gershwin, seemed completely incongruous with the senior citizen image of him most of the production heads in town apparently had. "The assholes," muttered Gabe with a tinge of bitterness, as he recklessly weaved his bike in and out of the dense Sunset Boulevard traffic. If only they could see me now: helmetless (why save your head if the rest of your body is smashed to bits?), thinning grey hair flying in the breeze, suede jacket, Calvin Klein blue jeans, goggles, and Western boots. If that's the look of someone too old to write for television, then Madonna is the queen of England.

Arriving in front of the Beverly Hills Hotel, Gabe turned his Honda 700 south down the palm-lined Beverly Drive, crossed Santa Monica Boulevard to Burton Way, turned left again past the city hall, and then headed east into Beverly Hills' little known factory district.

The Beverly-West Racquet Club was on the dividing line between Beverly Hills and West Hollywood, tucked in between an eight-story condominium on its east and a Bekins Van and Storage warehouse and small-parts machine shop on its west.

It wasn't the largest club in Los Angeles nor did it have the most up-to-date facilities. It only had seven courts, a small swimming pool, and 150 members, and its two-story, Spanish-style clubhouse was fairly ancient, with plumbing that needed replacing, for it had occupied the same ten-acre parcel of land for more than sixty years. Nevertheless, it was considered by the "in" crowd to be the most desirable place in Southern California to bat a tennis ball around. As testimony to this, there was a long waiting list of people anxious to part with forty thousand dollars for the privilege of playing here.

Gabe had been a fixture at the club since his father had treated him to a membership when he was a fourteen year old promising tennis star.

And although he had given up serious tournament play to go to work after winning the state NCAA championship in 1971, he'd always maintained his zeal for the sport and kept in shape by playing not less than four times a week. Consequently, he was still one of the top singles players in the city and could hold his own, at least for a couple of sets, among the club's present crop of aspiring Andre Agassis and Stefan Edbergs.

As a result, Gabe was looked up to by most of the members of the club, even though the majority of them were far more successful in their chosen professions than he was. The membership consisted mostly of prominent Beverly Hills doctors, lawyers, judges, bankers, businessmen, entrepreneurs, and their families, with a sprinkling of film and TV actors and executives thrown in to give it a little glamour. There was even a rabbi on the club roster.

Most of the members drove Rolls Royces and 560 SLs (except the rabbi, who drove a Seville) and lived in million-dollar homes in Beverly Hills and Bel Air (except the rabbi who lived in a five-hundred-thousand-dollar home in West L.A.). But none of them could hit a backhand down the line or serve an ace when it really counted. Which made Gabe a person to be envied.

Gabe parked his Honda in an empty space up the street from the clubhouse entrance, chained it to the post of the parking meter, slid a quarter in the slot, and then headed down the sidewalk beneath a lavender bower of Jacaranda trees in full bloom.

As his long loping strides carried him down Jacaranda Drive towards the club's front walk, Gabe noted that there wasn't another empty parking space on either side of the street—a sure sign that most of the late-afternoon regulars were probably out on the courts already. A small wooden plaque on the front door of the club stated in gold-leaf lettering:

BEVERLY-WEST RACQUET CLUB
Members Only

Gabe suddenly felt so eager for a game of tennis—even the worst kind of tennis—that he momentarily forgot about being inconspicuous as he pushed open the heavy oak door by its polished brass handle and stepped into the clubhouse. The hard leather heels of his boots made a loud, clicking noise as they hit the polished parquet floor of the club lobby, which was separated from the manager's office by a glass panel. Directly behind the glass, at a combination desk and phone switchboard, sat the club's receptionist/bookkeeper, Jenny Ho, a mix-blooded Hawaiian girl of about twenty-five, who, in a sleeveless Tahitian-print summer dress, looked as if she had stepped right out of a United Air Lines commercial. Jenny was a knockout, in Gabe's male chauvinistic opinion, not tall, but beautifully proportioned, with shiny black hair, almond-shaped eyes, pearl-white teeth, and very kissable-looking lips.

Despite Gabe's desire to get by the club office unnoticed, he couldn't resist stopping at the window to smile at Jenny and ask her how everything was going.

"Just fine, Mr. Steele," she replied, returning his smile with one of her own that exuded more sex appeal than she was probably aware of.

Even though there was a club bylaw prohibiting members from dating employees, Gabe was tempted to break it and ask her out and probably would have if at that moment the imposing figure of the club's president, Jock Kornfeld, hadn't suddenly loomed up in the doorway to the manager's office behind Jenny.

A tall, dynamic-looking man, about ten years Gabe's senior, with alert black eyes and a congenial smile when he wanted to turn it on, Kornfeld was the type you automatically assumed was an executive of some kind, even though you knew nothing about him. The way his clothes fit his broad-shouldered slightly overweight body, you figured they had to have been custom-made (and they were). His full head of wavy grey hair had obviously been "styled" to fit the current trends. And even in such sporty surroundings as the Racquet Club, he always showed up in a suit (a beige gabardine one today), tie, and shirt with French cuffs and gold-and-diamond links.

As their eyes met fleetingly, Gabe felt uneasy about the way Kornfeld was staring at him—as if he were aware of his past-due account and was about to take action on it.

In an attempt to avoid a confrontation at this time, and wanting to kick himself for stopping to flirt with the receptionist, Gabe quickly turned his gaze away from Jock, muttered "See you later" to Jenny and bolted towards the door to the living room beyond the lobby. But he'd only managed to put a couple of steps between himself and the office when Kornfeld's loud voice stopped him in his tracks. "Wait up, Gabe, I want to talk to you."

Oh, God, this is it, thought Gabe. They're going to invoke the "three-month rule" on me. ("Any member who falls more than three months behind in his dues will automatically be suspended until he makes good his debt.")

"Can't it keep?" asked Gabe, turning diffidently back to Jock, who was now standing in the open door to the manager's office, beckoning him. "I'd like to line up a game for myself before it gets dark."

"The sun won't set for another two hours,"

Jock assured him, glancing at his diamond-studded gold Rolex. "This won't take long."

Taking a step towards Gabe, Jock put a firm hand on his forearm and pulled him into the manager's office.

Shit! thought Gabe. This club must really be desperate for money if it has to sic the manager and the president on me!

But as Gabe glanced around, he realized the manager wasn't in his office; just Jock and himself.

Dropping into the manager's chair, Jock stuck a cigarette between his lips and lit it with a gold Dunhill lighter.

"Where's Mr. Fisher?" asked Gabe, hoping to keep Jock's attention off his insolvent condition by inquiring about the manager.

"The board of directors and he had a little row last night," explained Jock. "Fisher quit. He's already cleared out."

Gabe whistled. "Must have been more than a little row to make him do that. I thought he was planning to settle down here for life."

"The guy's paranoid—what can you do?" said Jock, blowing a smoke ring across the desk at Gabe. "All the board asked him to do was put his ear to the ground and try to discover who's been breaking into the lockers, and he took offense at it."

Jock was referring to a series of unsolved petty

thefts that had intermittently plagued the men's locker room for over a year now. A member would return from the courts to find anything from a gold watch to a couple of hundred dollars in cash to anything else of value missing from his locker. Since it didn't happen very often—indeed it had been more than a month now since the last theft—and it was easy enough to prevent a loss simply by carrying your valuables onto the court with you (which Gabe always took the precaution of doing), it wasn't a major calamity to the membership. But in an allegedly high-class club such as the Beverly-West, where it cost an arm and a leg to get in, and every potential member had to be screened as thoroughly as a candidate for the U.S. Supreme Court before being accepted, it was an aggravating thing to have to live with.

"Why in hell should he take offense at that?" asked Gabe.

"Beats me," shrugged Jock. "All we told him was that we thought it was the manager's responsibility to try to get to the bottom of it. And he blew his stack and said, quote unquote: 'I'm no Sam Spade; I'm a manager. If you want to catch a thief, call the cops.' And when we told him we preferred not to bring outside attention to the problem because it would be bad for the club's reputation, he just snarled, 'That's not what I'm getting paid for,' stormed in here, cleared out his desk, and walked."

"Maybe he's the thief," suggested Gabe. "He had a pass-key to the lockers."

"No way. He's so honest, he doesn't even believe in tax shelters."

As Jock paused to take a drag on his cigarette, Gabe squirmed in his seat uneasily, wondering when he was going to get around to mentioning his bill. It didn't seem possible that Jock had called him in just to talk about the thefts or the departed manager.

"Anyway," Gabe finally said, anxious to get the unpleasant confrontation over with, "what did you want to talk to me about?"

"We're talking about it," replied Jock.

"We are?" Gabe was puzzled.

"Yeah, champ, we are."

"Oh, I get it," said Gabe, somewhat relieved. "You think because I write detective shows that I can find the thief."

"Well, if you could, the members would greatly appreciate it," said Jock, "but that's not why I'm talking to you." He waited, as if for dramatic effect, before saying, "I've been instructed by the board to ask you to take over the managership."

"Me!" exclaimed Gabe, amused.

"Why *not* you?" said Jock, with a chuckle. "You know tennis like a pro; you know all the members; and who's as familiar with the day-to-day workings of the club?" He mashed his cigarette out in an ashtray. "Certainly not some total stranger we'd bring in."

He had a point. Of all the club's members, Gabe was the only one who'd been there through all its various management regimes, including this present one, in which the members, tired of uncaring private ownership, had assessed themselves in order to raise enough money to buy the club, or at least to make a down payment and assume the mortgage. Now the club was run by an elected board of directors and a president, with the manager having to answer to them. He had no autonomous authority of his own and was mainly there to implement the board's policies.

Gabe had also served a couple of terms on the board of directors. As a result, he had an awareness of just about everything that went on at the club; also an intimate knowledge of most of the members' personal lives, idiosyncrasies, and problems. He knew which ones were rich and which ones were pretenders; which ones were sick and which ones were healthy; which ones loved their kids and which ones were disgusted with the way they were turning out; and which ones cheated on the court and which ones cheated on their wives, and that included the club's esteemed president who was seated across the desk from him, waiting anxiously for his decision.

Gabe also knew that although Jock was the head of Giverny Cosmetics and was considered to be a very successful businessman in his own right, he'd never have had that position in the first place if his wife's father hadn't given it to him for a wedding present.

So as much as Jock might have wanted to leave his wife for a young bimbo, he'd never do it for fear of losing his four-hundred-thousand-a-year position with his father-in-law's company.

Still, did an intimate knowledge of the follies and foibles of most of the membership qualify Gabe for the managership? Certainly his Bachelor of Arts degree from the UCLA School of Cinema Arts didn't. Moreover, he was no businessman and never would be. He could barely keep his checkbook straight.

"Well, what do you say?" persisted Jock, studying the gold-and-diamond wedding band that ornamented his wedding finger. "We're prepared to guarantee you twenty-five grand a year, ten percent of the ball concession, and the manager's quarters rent free. Of course there'll be a thirty day tryout period in case either side wants to change his mind."

"Why me instead of an experienced manager?" asked Gabe.

"Frankly," said Jock, "we're sick of the kind of managers we find in the general marketplace.

Ex-hotel managers, ex-restaurant maitre d's, ex-ship stewards who no longer want to go to sea. Half of them I wouldn't trust farther than you can throw a piano, and none of them know a fucking thing about tennis or how to get along with a membership like ours."

"Your offer's very flattering," replied Gabe, "but I'm a writer. Why would I want to take on the headache of dealing with this spoiled group?"

Jock shrugged. "I don't know. I just had an idea things weren't going too well for you in TV these days."

"What makes you say that?" snapped Gabe, taking offense even though it was true.

"Just a shot in the dark," said Jock, with a sly grin. "You usually pay your bills on time, but at last night's board meeting, it came up that you're about to be 'posted.'"

Gabe squirmed uneasily in his chair. So Jock *did* know about his delinquent bills; they just weren't the main reason he called this meeting. "Well, I have been running a little short of cash lately," admitted Gabe, avoiding Jock's penetrating stare. "TV's a funny business. It goes in cycles. One year you're doing great, the next year you can't get an assignment. It's the nature of the business. And then there's my divorce. But I'm not worried. I've been through dry spells before."

"Oh, I understand show biz," smiled Jock, trying to sound hip. He drummed his well-manicured fingers on the desk top. "I'll tell you what we're prepared to do if you'll give it a try. We'll sweeten the package. We'll wipe out your debt to the club. And who's to say you can't continue being a writer? If you get an assignment, you can knock out your TV scripts when you're finished with your work. At the same time, you'll have the security of knowing a check will be coming in every week, plus a free place to stay. The manager's apartment's pretty nice since we've had it redecorated."

"What exactly would be my duties?" asked Gabe, wavering.

"Nothing that'll strain your brain too much, I guarantee you that. You open the club at eight in the morning for the Early Birds and stick around until closing. You'll have to supervise the help, approve the daily menus, make sure nobody sneaks any guests in without registering them, and see that the clubhouse is kept clean and the courts washed down at least three times a week. You'll have to compose the club announcements and be responsible for the mailings to the general membership. The cook will make out his own supply lists, but you'll have to authorize the actual purchases of food and liquor. You'll see that the bills are sent out the first of the month, and you'll see that members pay them on time and see that the three-month rule is strictly enforced and keep the junior members out of the cocktail lounge and cardroom."

"That's all!" exclaimed Gabe, in mock astonishment. "Don't you want me to do windows?"

"No," smiled Jock, "but you will be expected to fill in in tennis matches when the members are short a player. That's something other managers haven't been able to do because they weren't tennis players. That's why the board jumped when I mentioned you for the job. We've always wanted a playing manager."

The more Gabe thought about it, the more the managerial job appealed to him. After all, what was so great about being a TV writer? You worked for a couple of weeks, and you lay off for a couple of months. The status part of the job was zilch and the insecurity impossible.

"Okay, I'll give it a shot," Gabe finally answered. He was trying not to sound too eager, but underneath he was thrilled. "But just remember, I'm no Sam Spade, either."

Kornfeld started to stand then immediately dropped back into his chair. "There's one thing about that situation you might keep in mind, though," he added.

"What's that?"

"The other afternoon seven hundred and fifty dollars disappeared from the gin table when the cardplayers were settling up."

"Disappeared? How could it with everybody sitting there?"

"That's the mystery."

"Who was in the game?"

"The regulars: Herb Gross, Bill Nerney, Bunny Parker, Marty Engels, Harold Robinson, Dr. Meyerberg."

"You think the locker-room thief could be one of the cardplayers? They're all pretty well fixed, aren't they? And they play for high enough stakes."

"Well, I just heard that Marty Engels' store, The Toy Menagerie on Rodeo, filed for Chapter 11 the other day. And he owes the club a bundle. It's conceivable he could be having cash-flow problems, don't you think?" ventured Kornfeld.

Gabe shrugged. "If he's got a store that's going belly-up on Rodeo Drive, I doubt if what he can steal from a locker is going to be much help to him."

"Well, you never know," said Jock. "Anyway, keep your eyes and ears open if you're serious about taking this job."

"Yes, I'm serious."

"Great! I knew you wouldn't disappoint me, champ." Jock's tanned face broke into a broad grin as he leaped from his chair, grabbed Gabe's hand, and started to pump it up and down vigorously. "Boy, wait till I tell the board I talked you into it. This is the greatest thing that's happened to the club since Donna McCleary started sprouting tits."

"Not to change the subject," grinned Gabe, "but now that I'm manager, what do I do first?"

"Well, for starters you can play me a couple of sets of tennis right now, and show me what's wrong with my backhand. I've lost all confidence in it, and I want to get it back before my next ladder match. Then tonight or tomorrow morning give these people a ring, and tell them that the board voted them in for membership last night." He handed Gabe a slip of notepaper with the names "Aaron and Jan Wexler" scribbled on it in his large looping hand, along with their phone number.

"Do I know them?" asked Gabe.

"They've been my guests over here a few times," said Kornfeld. "Wexler's my lawyer on tax matters. He's saved me a bundle with Uncle Sam. And Jan's a doll and really built. She used to dance topless at the Lido in Vegas. It gave me a hard-on that wouldn't quit. Well, enough club business for now." He laughed, put a fatherly arm around Gabe's shoulder, and steered him towards the steps to the men's locker room. "Let's suit up. I need to sweat a little."

Three

The exercise, together with the new job, made Gabe feel better about himself again. He even had a good appetite after working out with Kornfeld for an hour and a half and spending another twenty minutes relaxing in the sauna. So after showering and shaving and getting back into his street clothes, he stopped off at the Hard Rock Cafe, just around the corner from the club, for a beer and his favorite dinner of barbecued ribs and french fries, before going home to his apartment to pack.

With two months still to go on his lease, and no guarantee (the way things had been breaking for him lately) that he'd be any more successful as a manager than he'd been as a writer, Gabe decided to take only those things he'd be needing most—clothing, toilet articles, his word processor, TV set, and a few books. But he chose to leave his larger possessions—two steel filing cabinets containing all his scripts, a wall full of books, his kitchen equipment, his skis, and a couple of oil paintings he loved—in the apartment until he knew what his future would be.

Even so he still had to rent a U-Haul truck to make the move the next morning, for there was no way he could carry two suitcases, a TV set, and a word processor on a motorcycle.

It was such a beautiful morning, however, that Gabe felt uncharacteristically optimistic about the chances of making good at his new job as he finished loading the truck around ten o'clock, locked up the apartment, and drove into Beverly Hills. It was the kind of spring day that always lifted his spirits. Bright sun, a blue and cloudless sky, and a faint perfumy smell of orange blossoms in the air. It was a smell that reminded Gabe of springs of long ago and evoked feelings of nostalgia for his youth. Spring had been the time when the tournament season officially began; the time for forgetting last year's losses and mistakes on the tennis circuit and anticipating important new victories sure to be yours during the coming months if you got a few breaks.

The feeling remained with Gabe all the way to the Racquet Club. There he parked the U-Haul truck in the loading zone in front of the clubhouse and hurried up the tulip-lined walk to get someone to help him carry in his things.

Arriving in the foyer, Gabe could sense that

the club was already alive with midmorning activity. From the surrounding courts came the familiar sounds of ball against gut, and the strident voices of the players in a women's doubles match shouting, "Nice shot, Martha," and "Oh, shit!" From the living room beyond he could hear the roar of a vacuum cleaner and smell the odor of furniture polish as the cleaning crew went about its morning chores. And to his right, he could see Jenny Ho at her post at the reception desk, sipping a cup of coffee and looking not quite awake yet, though not any the less attractive.

Jenny perked up as she noticed Gabe, in grey slacks, white shirt under a pink pullover sweater, and tan loafers, smiling cheerfully at her from the other side of the glass. As always she was glad to see Gabe, for not only was she turned on by his looks, but he never treated her like an employee as so many of the other members did. This morning she was especially happy to see him as it suddenly dawned on her that from now on she would be sharing the office with Gabe instead of the officious, pot-bellied Mr. Fisher, who was all business and square as an ice cube and just as cold.

Gabe was just her type. Tall, without an ounce of excess fat on his frame, and legs that were terribly sexy, especially in tennis shorts. He had a good sense of humor and a kind and intelligent face. Not exactly a handsome face but very masculine: large straight nose, strong mouth, nice lips, and a haircut that didn't look like the product of a Beverly Hills hair stylist. In fact, though he dressed nicely, he always managed to avoid that "Rodeo-Drive-chic" look, with the Gucci loafers and the Louis Vuitton tennis racket covers and carryall bags that so many of the members affected.

"Morning, Mr. Steele," exclaimed Jenny, with a warm smile. "Welcome to your new job."

"Thanks, Jenny." He waved 'hi' to her through the glass. "Now that we're coworkers, you can call me by my first name."

"Okay, Gabe." She grinned at him, pleased with the message he was sending her.

"Anything going on I should know about?"

"Just a call from the 'pres' saying I should remind you to phone the Wexlers and tell them they are officially in, if you haven't already done so."

"No, I've been too busy moving. Remind me to call them just as soon as I move my junk upstairs. Right now, see if you can rouse somebody to come outside and give me a hand."

"I'll buzz Tony," offered Jenny. "He's not busy."

Tony Mendiola was a Filipino of indeterminate age who had been on the club's staff, doubling as handyman and busboy, and sometimes even "fry cook," longer than any other employee. His nearly all-white hair attested to that.

Gabe had just opened the tailgate of the U-Haul truck when Tony's diminutive figure appeared at his elbow in a white jacket.

"You want me, Mr. Gabe?"

"Give me a hand, will you, Tony? I'm moving into the manager's quarters."

It took a moment for the full meaning of that to register on Tony's dark-complected face. When it did, he broke into a fourteen-karat grin. "You going to be the new manager?"

"Yeah, Tony. You approve?"

"You bet, Mr. Gabe." He hugged Gabe warmly then sprung onto the tailgate of the truck with the agility of an Olympic gymnast and started passing Gabe's belongings down to him.

The manager's apartment was located on the second floor, in the rear of the clubhouse, and featured a commanding view of the alley, a row of trash cans, and some of the parking stalls belonging to the neighboring condo. The place itself consisted of a fair-sized bedroom, a small sitting room with a stone fireplace in one corner, and a tiny bathroom trimmed in Mexican tile. The place had recently been done over by one of the members' wives who had somehow persuaded the board that she once had been a professional decorator. In Gabe's opinion, Gloria Holtz should never have returned to decorating. While the architecture and decor of the rest of the clubhouse was Early-California Spanish, she somehow had seen fit to do the manager's quarters in early Howard Johnson. It was a symphony in formica. There were even cigarette burns on the formica nightstand beside the queen-sized bed. However, the mattress was firm, the black naugahyde sofa in the living room adequate, and the rooms themselves bright and cheerful, so he supposed he had no right to be critical. At least it was free.

Despite its tacky decor, his new digs had certain advantages over the large ranch-style house in Brentwood he had once shared with Marge, and which he had turned over to her in the settlement. The main one being that living alone was a lot more cheerful and pleasant than having to listen to her constant carping about the fact that he either had his head in a book or bent over a typewriter and that he never came up for air except to play tennis, which, she claimed, he'd rather do than be with her. This wasn't exactly the case, but there was a grain of truth to the accusation, especially in the years when their marriage started to deteriorate.

It may have been true that opposites attract, as it was in his and Marge's case, but once the attraction became old hat, all that was left was two people with diametrically opposed ideas of what constituted living. She liked to loll around in bed until noon, while he was an early riser; she preferred breakfast in bed to sex in bed; and she refused to ruin her figure by having kids.

Moreover, she hated athletics and any kind of strenuous exercise. Her idea of a long walk was from the house to her BMW. And she was always accusing Gabe of being an "incurable jock," as if he still had an insatiable and adolescent craving for "the thrill of victory" and "the agony of defeat." This was an exaggeration, of course, but Gabe was willing to concede that it was important to him, after sitting at a desk all day, to get out in the fresh air and sunshine and clear his head of story headaches by running after a little white pellet for a while. Marge just couldn't understand a man's need to get out with other men and play "hard" after work. She claimed that time spent away from her on a tennis court was an indication he didn't love her. It was a never-ending battle. Things finally reached a stage where he believed she was actually more jealous of his tennis playing than she would have been had he been spending his afternoons in bed with another woman.

Her attitude eventually did drive him into the arms of a girl who worked in the perfume department at Neiman Marcus. This affair didn't last much longer than it took for the odor of the men's cologne she sold him to wear off, but when Marge found out about it, she finally had sufficient grounds to put a merciful end to a marriage that never should have been.

Within the hour, Gabe was moved in and sitting at his desk in the manager's office, about to assume his duties.

"Okay, Jenny," he called to her through the open door, "try the Wexlers for me, will you?"

"Coming right up."

As he watched her respond to his order, Gabe had the strangest sensation that being manager of a club was a little like being the captain of a ship. All he had to do was bark out an order, and the people under him swung into action. He'd never been in charge of anything or anybody before, and to his amazement, he found he liked the feeling.

"Want to pick up for Mrs. Wexler?" Jenny called out. "I've got her for you."

Gabe straightened up in his chair and put the receiver to his ear. "Mrs. Wexler, this is Gabe Steele."

"Who?"

"Gabe Steele, manager of the Racquet Club. I thought you and your husband would like to know you've been accepted for membership. So welcome aboard. You are now free to use the club anytime you want."

"Oh, wow! That's neat," exclaimed Mrs. Wexler. "I'm going to phone Aaron at his office right now and tell him to cancel all his appointments this afternoon and come over to the club and play with me. Thank you so much, Mr. Steele. I don't know how to repay you."

"Just pay your bills on time," chuckled Gabe.

"Don't worry," she said, "my husband's a nut about that."

Gabe was still chuckling as he put the receiver down.

"What's so funny?" asked Jenny.

Gabe told her about Mrs. Wexler's almost manic reaction to begin accepted for membership and added, "I wonder how long that'll last."

"What do you mean?" asked Jenny.

"Her enthusiasm," explained Gabe. "That's Stage One in the Diary of a Beverly-West Racquet Club wife. I've made a study of it—in fact, I've lived it. In the beginning, the wife is as happy as a little puppy to be a member of the glamorous Beverly-West Racquet Club. She's real gung ho about playing tennis every chance she gets. She's seen Steffi and Martina play on TV, and she thinks it'll only take a few lessons to be able to play like them. So she takes lessons when her husband's at work; she has lunch here; and she comes here on weekends with her husband. But soon she discovers that all clubs are basically the man's play toy and that women are second-class citizens, who are only allowed to use the courts when the men aren't on them. Their husbands don't like to play with them because they're not as good as the men, and other men won't play with them unless they're on the make.

"Stage Two: The wife, realizing she'll never be another Martina, loses her enthusiasm and starts showing up at the club less and less. At the same time, she resents her husband enjoying the club and being able to get into good games when no one will play with her. So she starts a campaign to keep hubby from going there so much and making her a tennis widow. She demands that he spend more time with the family on weekends. Go on picnics or to the beach or take her to museums and art shows. He hates museums and art shows because you can't work up a sweat looking at a painting. But it's either do what she wants or no sex. So they work out a compromise—he'll go the museum-art show route with her on Sundays, if she'll let him play tennis on Saturday mornings and weekdays after work.

"Stage Three: The detente lasts a couple of years at most. By then her husband realizes he'd rather play tennis than have sex with her—the pleasure lasts longer, for one thing—so he goes back to playing tennis whenever he feels like it, and if she doesn't like it, she can lump it. If she loves him enough, she'll put up with this treatment. If she doesn't, she'll just suffer in quiet desperation until she finds a guy who'll spend some time with her, which will probably end in an affair and eventually a divorce. And if the husband's lucky, he'll get to keep the club membership in the settlement. End of story."

Jenny, who had sat giggling through most of Gabe's monologue because she recognized the truth of it, did a sudden switch when he concluded and came to the defense of her own sex.

"Aren't you being a little chauvinistic?" she said, in a chiding tone.

"Of course I am. But the story's pretty universal just the same. It's as old as the world itself. Just substitute golf or football or maybe even discus-throwing for tennis, and it still fits. Most men love sports, and women would rather play with dolls."

"Oh, come on," insisted Jenny. "Some of the wives around here enjoy playing."

"They're the exceptions—maybe twenty out of a hundred-and-fifty wives play regularly. And most of them only play because they think it's chic, or they're bored sitting around the house, or they have a pretty tennis outfit they want to show off, or they want to keep an eye on their husbands."

"You are a cynic," she laughed.

"How about you, Jenny? Are you into sports, or wouldn't you rather play with dolls and babies?"

"I enjoy swimming, and I can handle a surfboard pretty well."

"Of course you would. You're from Hawaii. But do you really enjoy the physical exertion, or do you prefer just lying around in the sun in a bikini?"

Jenny laughed. "Guilty as charged."

Their conversation, which Gabe found he was enjoying, was interrupted by the arrival of the mailman, who opened the door to Jenny's office, handed her a bundle of envelopes and departed, exhorting her to "have a good one."

Jenny looked through the envelopes quickly then handed them to Gabe.

"For me? How nice!"

"Anything you don't understand, give a yell," she said, returning to her desk.

To his astonishment, there wasn't much he couldn't handle by himself: a few bills that Jenny would pay; some incoming checks to be deposited; a query from Acme Meats wondering if the club would like to try its product; and an indignant letter from a wife challenging the board's recent decision to allow the live-in girlfriends of divorcing male members the same club privileges as wives.

Gabe handed the letters from Acme Meats and

the wounded hausfrau back to Jenny, with instructions to turn the former over to the cook and the latter over to the board of directors.

With that Gabe stood up, stretched his arms, and announced that he was going up to the terrace to have a sandwich. "Call me, Jen, if the Wexlers arrive. I guess it's up to me to welcome them personally."

Four

The terrace, with its colorfully striped umbrella tables, was on the second level and adjacent to the main dining room. It overlooked the club's Number One Court, sometimes known as the Terrace Court, where most of the good matches were played. Below it, on tiered lower levels, were three more green-surfaced cement courts. The other three courts were on the opposite side of the clubhouse. Play on them couldn't be seen from the terrace, which was why the women and children and novice men players were expected to play there. Also, the club's teaching pro, Phil Neer, had permanent use of Court Number 6, except on Wednesday afternoons, when the place was overrun with doctors and dentists.

Because the sun was out bright and warm, all of the tables on the terrace were occupied by the time Gabe reached the top of the stairs. Even the small table in the corner, unofficially reserved for the manager, was taken.

"Pretty brisk business for a weekday," commented Gabe to Henri, the French-accented maitre d' who approached him with an armful of menus. "This must be apple pancake day."

"I think the attraction is Mike Flanagan, no?" Henri nodded in the direction of the Terrace Court, where an extremely tall and lanky snub-nosed man with tousled red hair and freckles, wearing tennis clothes and carrying a number of rackets under his arm, was preparing to play.

"That does explain it." Gabe was surprised that the world's number two player had been able to slip into the club without his noticing it. Usually Flanagan burst in with a noisy entourage consisting of his mother, trainer, and several 'go-fers,' and there was no mistaking the fact that he had arrived.

Another thing that surprised Gabe—and also pleased him—was how many of the members on the terrace were already aware that he was the new manager and apparently happy about it, judging by the many congratulations he received as he passed by their tables. A few even invited him to sit down with them.

Gabe finally decided to sit with Kim Randall, an independent movie producer who specialized in cheap exploitation films. Not that Gabe craved Kim's company or thought socializing with him might lead to a writing assignment but because Kim's table had the best view of the center court.

Kim was a dark-complexioned man in his late forties, lean and in good shape—he had once boasted to Gabe that he did fifty push ups before breakfast. He had a full head of nearly shoulder-length black hair and a handsome face that was tanned and unusually well preserved for a man of his age; there wasn't a visible line on it, and the skin was very taut around the corners of his mouth and under his eyes, which made Gabe believe he might have had a face-lift on one of his frequent trips to Europe.

As always, Kim was dressed as if he had just that moment stepped off a plane from the Cannes film festival—dark sunglasses, white Capezio slippers with no socks, white French jeans, and a blue-and-white-striped cotton shirt with the top three buttons unbuttoned, exposing a tan, somewhat hairy chest, and a Saint Christopher medal on a gold chain.

Kim may have dressed like a Georgio Armani model, but he was actually the son of a junk dealer from Boyle Heights. Gabe had known him since they were both in their teens and trying to make names for themselves in tennis tournaments. Kim never made the big time, either, though he did win a couple of local tournaments. But, to his credit, he had been able to use his tennis as a means to climb the social ladder and worm his way into the movie business. By playing with all the "right" people, who were anxious to be his doubles partner, he became first a script boy for a famous Hollywood director, then an agent at William Morris, where his great gift of gab, mellifluous voice and smooth manners enabled him to become friendly with top stars and anybody else who could help him, and finally a producer of low-budget pictures, usually filmed in Mexico or Yugoslavia with nonunion labor.

Lately, however, money had been tight around Hollywood, and Kim had been unable to get a film on the screen in over two years, despite running his ass off daily in the hot sun, trying to curry favor with the rich, famous, and influential. As a result, Kim had been forced to sell his house in Trusdale to get the cash to live on and maintain a front. Then he moved into a small bachelor pad across the street from the Racquet Club. That way, he could change into his tennis clothes and shower at home, saving the price of renting a locker. Also, he could run home at noon for a peanut butter sandwich if he didn't feel like springing for a meal at the club.

"Mazel tov on your new job," said Randall as Gabe dropped into an empty director's chair opposite him. "If I'd have known it was open, I'd have applied for it myself."

"Bad news certainly spreads fast," joked Gabe, picking up a menu and studying the daily special.

"I mean it, Gabe, managing this joint ought to be right up your alley."

"We'll see."

The waiter arrived just then, and the two turned their attention to ordering. Randall ordered a glass of ice water with a slice of lemon in it; Gabe chose a club sandwich and an ice tea, then settled back in his chair, and watched Flanagan stride to the baseline and begin his warm-up.

Gabe was not surprised to see that Flanagan's opponent in this practice match was Rick Reeves, the tow-headed nineteen-year-old son of Dr. Matthew Reeves, a longtime member and prominent Beverly Hills surgeon.

Flanagan and young Reeves had been tennis buddies since they were fourteen-year-olds and both had been highly ranked junior players in Southern California.

Flanagan had come from a poor family in Santa Monica and had taught himself to play on the public courts at Lincoln Park, where he'd made his first splash in tennis circles by winning a novice tournament at age twelve.

Rick Reeves, on the other hand, was a product of the Beverly-West Racquet Club. Dr. Reeves had introduced his son to the game when he was thirteen and for a time had encouraged his ambitions to become a world class player.

Flanagan and Rick had become friends while playing in the Southern California 16-and-under championships, which Rick had won, thrashing Flanagan in the finals. The two became friends despite their on-court rivalry and decided to pool their talents and form a doubles team. As a result, Rick started bringing Flanagan around the Racquet Club, where, because of the promise he showed, he was given an honorary membership; also free coaching by Phil Neer, the club's pro, who saw a spark of genius in Flanagan that he didn't see in the spoiled and wealthy son of Dr. Reeves, even though Rick had won more junior tournaments than his rival, including the National 16-and-under championship.

Flanagan's recent rise to world prominence proved Neer to be something of a genius when it came to assessing young tennis flesh.

Once the two of them graduated from the 16-and-under to the 18-and-under class, Flanagan started to pull rapidly ahead of Rick. After winning every local tournament in sight, he captured the U.S. and Wimbledon junior titles. Simultaneously, he became a player to reckon with in the senior events. He knocked off the number two ranking player in the world at the U.S. Open the following fall and immediately decided to turn professional. By the time he reached nineteen, he himself was number five in the world computer rankings, with an income of a half a million dollars his first year as a pro, which didn't include what he earned from endorsements.

His friend Rick, on the other hand, faded quickly after he started competing in the senior events. While Flanagan was heading for superstardom, Rick Reeves couldn't even qualify for entry in most major events.

The crowning blow came when pressure from the tournament heads and promoters forced Flanagan to drop Rick as a doubles partner and pair up with a bigger name. To save face, Rick announced his retirement from tournament tennis. He'd play in local tournaments, he said, but just for the fun of it.

"Great shot, Rick!" shouted someone at a neighboring table as the doctor's son hauled off after a long rally and socked a forehand winner past the surprised Flanagan.

As the crowd on the terrace burst into enthusiastic applause, Flanagan himself, in a gesture of appreciation for his former doubles partner's unbelievable shot, dropped his racket on the court and joined in the clapping.

"How about that?" somebody down the terrace exclaimed loudly. "The kid's still got it!"

"Aw," someone answered him, "Flanagan's just fooling around!"

As he watched the two young men continue to do battle on the Terrace Court below, both stroking the ball equally hard, Gabe realized more than ever that there really wasn't much difference, at least that the average person could notice, between a world class player like Flanagan and his buddy Rick. Both had excellent ground strokes, volleys, and serves. And both could run for hours without getting winded or tired. The difference, and it always came down to this, was that Flanagan had that indefinable spark that enabled him to win the "big" points while Rick usually blew them. It was something you were born with—but generally not in Beverly Hills.

Perhaps it had something to do with that worn-out word "hunger." Flanagan wanted it more than Rick.

The difference in their wills to win became more noticeable as they got deeper into the first set. With Rick serving at four-all and ad out, Flanagan ripped a backhand placement down the line that his opponent, on his way into the net, could only look at with admiration as it sailed by.

Leading 5-4, and serving for the set, Flanagan, with no noticeable effort, suddenly uncorked his world class game. He served a clear winner on the first point, outlasted Rick in a long rally to win the second point. During the third point, he appeared to be toying with Rick, running him unmercifully, some might say "sadistically," from side to side with his powerful two-handed backhand, then drop-shotting, then lobbing and sending him back to the baseline, and then ending it with a drop volley that Rick was just too winded to chase down.

When Flanagan won the first set with a tremendous hook serve that Rick couldn't get his racket on, the spectators on the terrace just shook their heads in amazement at Flanagan's racket genius.

"How would you like to be that age again and that good?" asked Kim, turning to Gabe.

"Is that question even necessary?" said Gabe dryly.

"Flanagan's really got the world on a string," declared Kim. "By the end of this year he'll probably be Numero Uno in the world, pulling down a million or so a year; he's young and handsome, and he's got his pick of every good-looking chick in the world. Where did we go wrong?"

"We were born thirty years too soon—that's where we went wrong," Gabe reminded him. "There wasn't all that big dough in tennis in our day."

Kim waited for the waiter to set Gabe's sandwich down in front of him before replying, "You can say that again. My biggest payday on the courts I got a silver-plated platter for winning the Motion Picture Tournament."

Gabe continued to watch the second set and munch lazily on his club sandwich until his concentration was broken by a Bronx-accented voice behind him. "Mind if I sit down? I'd like to watch my son."

Turning in his chair, Gabe found himself staring up at the square-jawed, bespectacled face of Dr. Reeves.

"Always room for one more," said Gabe politely, as Dr. Reeves pulled up an empty director's chair from the next table and stuffed his large derriere into it.

"How's Rick doing?" asked Reeves, indicating the court action.

"Pretty good," replied Gabe. "He only lost the first set by one service break, and he's down two-love in this one."

Dr. Reeves' attention didn't seem to be on Gabe's reply. His catlike gray eyes were riveted on the raw carrots and olives on Gabe's plate. "If you're not eating your garnish," he said, "do you mind if I finish it up for you? I hate to see all those vitamins go to waste."

"Be my guest," said Gabe, pushing his plate over to him.

"Thanks," said the doctor, selecting a carrot and taking a loud crunchy bite of it.

Amused, Gabe watched Dr. Reeves finish off

the raw carrots and the two ripe olives, then pick up a fork, and stab one of the tomato slices left on a plate at a neighboring table.

"I didn't feel like ordering a whole lunch today," he explained, as if Gabe and the rest of the members weren't onto the fact that Reeves, despite having one of the largest incomes in the medical fraternity, was known to be too cheap to pay for his own lunch, and preferred to table-hop every noon rummaging for unwanted garnish left on members' plates. He seemed to have no shame about it, and it disturbed him not one iota that the other members made jokes about it right to his face.

After Flanagan broke Rick's serve for the second time in the set and took a commanding 3-0 lead, Kim Randall lost interest, slung his shoulder-strap pouch-bag over his shoulder, and stood up. "See you," he said, drifting off to a table where a couple of good-looking wives were smiling at him.

Dr. Reeves watched the rest of his son's match, which was turning into a rout, with impatience bordering on anger. "Schmuck," he kept exclaiming as Rick made a string of unforced errors. "Stop trying to kill every ball!"

As if you could do any better, thought Gabe, suddenly feeling sorry for Rick.

Finally the match ended to scattered applause, and the two players walked off the court, Rick wearing the dejected expression of a loser.

"Pathetic," said Dr. Reeves, turning to Gabe with a shake of his head. "I wonder if you'd do me a favor."

"If I can."

"I want you to talk Rick into giving up the game and going back to pre-med school. There's no future in tennis for him. He just doesn't have it. I'm convinced. Look how he just wilted out there." His tone was a mixture of disdain and concern.

Gabe was surprised. "Why me? You're his father."

"You've been through it all," said Reeves, grabbing a carrot from a plate on another neighboring table that had just been vacated. "You reached a certain degree of proficiency when you were his age. But you didn't take your studies seriously enough to be great at anything else, and now look at you. You're forced to take a job managing this club. I want something better for my son."

"Thanks for the compliment," said Gabe, really annoyed. "I don't consider myself exactly a bum. I've made a lot of money in my business. I'm just going through a dry spell."

"Oh, I'm aware you've hacked out a pretty good living, but you never won an Oscar or an Emmy."

"Nor you the Nobel Prize," Gabe couldn't help firing back.

"Now don't get your back up. You know what I mean. You're not up there with the really big boys, either in sports or in Hollywood. Now admit it. Isn't that the truth?"

"Yeah," replied Gabe, a wave of depression suddenly sweeping over him. "I guess it is."

"So now that you're where you are," Reeves drove on relentlessly, "you're in a position to do my boy a favor. Tell him to quit before it's too late."

"I thought he had," said Gabe.

"I thought so, too." Dr. Reeves shook his head sadly. "But it's eating his fool heart out that his boyhood buddy is on his way to becoming a millionaire while he's making zip. You see, he has Rolls Royce taste and a Volkswagen pocketbook. He's now talking about joining the satellite tour, and that's no good. That's for has-beens and never-gonna-bees."

"Not necessarily," said Gabe. "He might still be able to make it."

"Bullshit. He's had it as a tennis player. And he won't listen to me. You know how kids are."

"I'll tell you what," Gabe finally answered. "I don't promise results, but if an opportunity arises, I'll give it a shot."

"Thanks. He's a good kid. I don't want to see his life ruined." Without bothering to ask, Dr. Reeves took a sip of Gabe's ice tea. As he caught a look of disapproval, he smiled guiltily and hastily set the glass down again. "I didn't think you wanted the rest of it," he apologized.

As Gabe stared at him in disbelief, Reeves glanced at his wristwatch, then pulled his large bottom out of his canvas chair, and stood up. "Well, I've got to get over to Cedars and yank out an appendix."

Wishing he hadn't committed himself, for Rick Reeves was a sulky kid, with an exaggerated opinion of himself, and a quick temper, Gabe remained at the table, sipping his ice tea, his forehead tilted toward the sun. Its warm rays felt good on his skin and made him feel like not wanting to return to his office. After a few moments, he was even able to forgive Dr. Reeves for the insults he had heaped on him. Like it or not, there was a lot of truth in some of the things he had said.

As he thought about the strange twists and turns one's life takes, Gabe watched Rick Reeves, wearing a cable stitch sweater and wiping his flushed, perspiring face off with a towel, climb the stairs to the terrace and sit down at a nearby table by himself.

As casually as he could, Gabe strolled over to Rick's table. "You alone?" he asked.

"Who'd want to sit with me the way I played?"

"Listen, it's no disgrace to lose to Flanagan," Gabe told him.

"Just making a joke," said Rick, picking up a menu. "I know I'm good, or I wouldn't have this." He fingered a little gold tennis ball that was on a chain around his neck. It was the trophy he'd been awarded for winning the National 16-and-under.

"That was a good win," said Gabe. "I never won it. Mind if I sit down, or are you expecting someone?"

"Maybe Flanagan, but I'm not counting on him."

"What happened to him?" asked Gabe, dropping into a chair.

"He's in the locker room, talking a big deal with his manager," he said, his voice fraught with envy. "Boy, the money that guy's making! He must have to take it to the bank in a wheelbarrow."

"Well, an athlete's life is pretty short. He has to make it when he can."

"Can you believe this?" exclaimed Rick. "Wilson's offering him four hundred thousand a year to play with their latest wide-bodied racket."

"Things *have* changed since I was a player," smiled Gabe, hoping to back into the subject dearest to Dr. Reeves' heart. "All I ever got for playing with a Wilson were free rackets and gut."

"It's un — bee — leeevable how they've

changed, Old-timer!" exclaimed Rick, setting the menu down as the waiter came over to take his order. "Un — bee — leevable!"

Old-timer, indeed! It wasn't bad enough he had to be insulted by his father. Now Rick was talking to him like he had one foot in Forest Lawn.

"I'll have the New York steak blood-rare and the asparagus hollandaise," Rick announced to the waiter. "And charge it to Dr. Reeves." With a laugh he turned back to Gabe. "You should hear my old man howl when he gets the tennis club bills at the end of the month. 'Do you have to order the most expensive thing on the menu?' he keeps telling me. Of course I wouldn't run up those bills if he couldn't afford it. But you should see what he charges for an operation. By noon he's usually performed three operations and made twelve thousand dollars."

Rick couldn't have given Gabe a more appropriate cue.

"Speaking of high fees," began Gabe, but he cut himself off with the arrival of Henri, who informed him that Jenny had just phoned to tell him that the Wexlers had arrived.

"Thanks, Henri." Turning to Rick, Gabe said, "Duty calls. We'll have to continue this some other time."

As he hurried down the steps to greet the Wexlers, Gabe was relieved that for the time being, at least, he'd been saved from having to talk with Rick about his future. It really wasn't any of Gabe's business, and Rick, with his mercurial disposition, was liable to resent it.

When Gabe found them, the Wexlers were standing in the club's cavernous living room, with their backs to him, admiring the gleaming silver trophies in the display case in the wall—trophies for various club championships.

It was a masculine-looking room, with the emphasis more on comfort and the sporting life than on style. Painted a warm terra cotta, the room featured a high wooden-beamed ceiling and a stone fireplace large enough to walk into. As a paean to the architecture, there were a few authentic country-Spanish antique wooden pieces scattered about, but most of the furnishings were traditional: two oversized worn leather couches, some club chairs, a refectory table littered with tennis magazines and other periodicals, a bridge table set up for those who couldn't stand the screaming in the regular cardroom.

Over the mantel was a large framed photograph of Bill Tilden in action in the Roaring Twenties, along with two crossed antique tennis rackets. On the other three walls hung more tennis memorabilia and sporting prints, including one of Center Court Wimbledon during the final between Don Budge and Gottfried Von Cramm.

From the rear, Mrs. Wexler lived up to all her advance publicity and was, by far, more interesting to look at than anything else in the room. She was a honey blond, with long shapely legs and a provocative behind, a tiny portion of which was peeking decorously out from beneath the hem of the underpanties of her short, white tennis skirt. Under one arm she was carrying a tennis racket in a Gucci cover and under the other a Vuitton purse.

Wexler, who looked a little like a hippopotamus from the rear, was in a dark business suit.

As always when he first met a couple, Gabe found himself instantly imagining how the two would look in bed. These two disparate figures didn't seem very compatible at all.

"Mr. and Mrs. Wexler, I believe," said Gabe, coming up behind them.

As the two spun around to greet him, and Gabe got a frontal view of Jan Wexler, he was pretty certain he knew why the all-male board of directors had given the two of them preference over other couples on the waiting list.

Jan Wexler had gorgeous white skin, delft-blue eyes, nearly perfect features, and a full bosom with firm nipples that were asserting themselves very provocatively under her white cotton tennis shirt. From their sculptured look, there was no question in Gabe's mind that Mrs. Wexler didn't believe in brassieres. The only question in Gabe's mind was what she saw in her husband.

Aaron Wexler was a chunkily built man of about forty, with horn-rimmed glasses, and long sideburns creeping out of what was obviously a toupee; Gabe could see the brown gauze pasted to his forehead under his widow's peak. With a wife like Jan, Wexler either had to be loaded or a hell of a lover, thought Gabe as he shook the new member's pudgy hand.

"You must be the nice man I spoke to on the phone this morning," said Jan Wexler, smiling cordially.

"Yes, I'm Gabe Steele, the new manager."

"You the same Gabriel Steele whose name is on those trophies?" asked Wexler, indicating them with a fat thumb.

Gabe nodded.

"You must be fantastic," said Jan. "I saw your name on the singles' cup five times."

"I was pretty good once," replied Gabe modestly.

"Maybe you could give my husband some pointers," said Jan. "He plays like a lox."

"Very funny," said Wexler.

"Well, you'd be better if you'd take off some of this," said Jan, gently patting Wexler's stomach, which was beginning to roll over his belt.

"Why do you think I joined this club?" he snapped back.

Hoping to head off a family fight before it developed into full-scale war, Gabe suddenly exclaimed, "I presume you two are here to play a little tennis, so let me show you around and get you a couple of lockers."

"Yeah, why don't you do that?" With a critical glance at his wife, Wexler picked up his matching Vuitton bag and racket carrying case from the floor at his feet and followed Gabe and Jan out of the room.

It didn't take long for Gabe to give the Wexlers a tour of the club's most salient features: the cardroom adjacent to the living room, the dining room, the dining terrace, the swimming pool and sunning area, the exercise porch with its exercising equipment, the hot pool and the tennis shop, where, Gabe informed them, they could buy anything from tennis balls and rackets to designer tennis clothes and shoes.

Phil Neer, the club's ancient and weather-beaten pro, was sitting at a table just inside the tennis shop door, munching on a sandwich and sipping a Coke. His tall, reed-thin body was attired in a powder-blue warm-up suit, and a white tennis cap was askew on his head, revealing a shock of wispy white hair.

As Gabe and the Wexlers stopped outside his door, Neer put his sandwich down and rose to greet them.

"Nice to know you," said Neer, tipping his

cap at Jan Wexler as he looked approvingly at her great figure.

"If you want lessons, Phil's your man," Gabe told the Wexlers.

"I love taking lessons!" exclaimed Jan. "How's tomorrow?"

"I think I can squeeze you in," said Neer, checking his appointment book. "Eleven okay?"

That was okay with Jan, so Gabe led them back to the clubhouse and over to the stairs to the locker rooms.

"You'll like taking from Phil," Gabe assured Jan as they walked. "I took from him when I was a kid."

"That must make him awfully old to still be teaching," stated Wexler.

"He's over seventy," said Gabe.

"Seventy!" Wexler whistled in surprise. "How come you have an old duffer like that here when there's so many big names out there on the circuit anxious to become associated with a high-class club like this one?"

"Well, in the first place, he's a hell of a fine teaching pro, even if he isn't a household name," said Gabe. "And he's especially good with kids, very patient, and he doesn't try to make it with the young wives. And in the second place, the club members feel they owe him something."

"Yeah? Why?" Wexler's tone was almost belligerent.

Gabe explained that Neer, winner of the U.S. Men's doubles title in 1946, was one of the founding fathers of the club; he and two men had started it back in the forties because the only other tennis club in town, the Los Angeles Tennis Club, did not accept Jews, and the Jewish residents of Beverly Hills, as well as picture business people, needed a place to play. His partners, both Jews, had put up the money to start the club, and Neer, because of his tennis experience, was given a one-third share in exchange for staying on and running the club. Years later, when Neer's wife Molly had become terminally ill with cancer, Neer had been forced to sell his share in the club in order to raise the money to pay for his wife's hospital bills.

The club kept him on as teaching pro, but he no longer had any say in its management; in fact, they could even fire him if they chose to.

"How sad!" exclaimed Jan. "To go from owner to just a paid employee."

"Dumb, I call it!" exclaimed Wexler. "If he needed money, he should have taken out a bank loan against his equity in the club and paid it off gradually."

"He's a tennis player, not a financier," explained Gabe. "He wasn't trained to think that way." By then the three of them had reached the landing at the top of the stairs.

To their right was the entrance to the men's

locker room and to the right of that the door to the women's locker room. Adjacent to the men's locker room door was the exercise porch. Several men were working out on the exercise equipment, and one lady, with very large boobs under a thin T-shirt, was dangling by her knees from the gravity bar.

"Well, it looks to me like you're all set to play," said Gabe, indicating Jan Wexler's cute tennis outfit. "But don't you want a locker anyway?"

"No, I prefer to dress at home," explained Jan. "It's more private."

"Well, I'll need a locker," said Wexler. "I like to shower after I play."

Advising Jan to wait for her husband on Court Number 2, which he had reserved for them, Gabe escorted Wexler into the men's locker room.

The locker room at the Racquet Club wasn't a whole lot different from most locker rooms, except that it was fully carpeted. There was a center aisle leading to the far end, with rows of lockers running perpendicular to it on either side. There were stall showers, a sauna, an outdoor porch off one end where Danny White, the locker-room attendant, hung out sweaty tennis clothes on a line to dry, and an alcove with a chair in it for Danny to shine shoes.

Decorating the walls were a number of small

printed signs bearing words of advice to the members:

DON'T LEAVE VALUABLES IN YOUR LOCKER WHEN YOU GO OUT TO PLAY.

DON'T USE THE SAUNA IF YOU HAVE HIGH BLOOD PRESSURE OR HEART TROUBLE.

DON'T HANG WET CLOTHES ON THE FRONT OF YOUR LOCKER: GIVE THEM TO THE ATTENDANT TO HANG ON THE DRYING PORCH.

DON'T STAY IN THE SHOWER TOO LONG. REMEMBER, THE WATER YOU ARE WASTING IS YOUR OWN. SING SHORTER SONGS!

When Gabe entered with Wexler, the locker room appeared empty, except for Danny White, who was in his alcove shining a pair of shoes and trying to read a Batman comic at the same time.

Danny, attired in a striped shoemaker's smock over white duck pants and a T-shirt, was about five foot five and barrel chested. He had a head that seemed overly large for his body, closely cropped mouse-brown hair, and a vacant expression in his eyes that gave him the appearance of a slightly punch-drunk fighter. Glancing up, he smiled vacuously at Gabe and Wexler, which added further to the pugilistic illusion.

"Hi, Danny," Gabe greeted him. "This is Mr. Wexler, a new member. He'll be needing a locker. Want to take care of him?"

"Sure thing, Gabe." Turning to Wexler, Danny

said, "Would you like me to get you a locker?"

As Wexler surveyed Danny curiously, Gabe said, "That's the idea, Danny. Do you have any empties?"

"I think so." He smiled the smile of a retarded boy at Wexler. "Do you want one near the showers or at the other end?"

"Is there a difference?" snapped Wexler.

"You don't have to walk as far to the showers if you have one close to them," explained Danny, suddenly letting out an explosive laugh that seemed to startle Wexler.

"That's obvious," said Wexler, annoyed. "Is there any other advantage?"

"Oh, sure. If you have a locker at the other end, you'll be in a draft when we open the door to the alley in the summer. Do you like drafts?"

"I can't say I'm dying to get undressed in one, no."

"Then you'd better take one near the showers." Danny picked up a clipboard with some papers on it and glanced down the list of locker assignments. "Oh, tough shit!" he exclaimed, glancing up finally. "I only have one empty locker, and that's near the door.

"Then why did you ask me?" asked Wexler.

"Because that's what they told me to ask."

Wexler glowered at Danny. "Whoever 'they' is, I think they meant if you had a choice."

"Yeah," snickered Danny. "I guess that's what they meant. HA!"

As Wexler gave Gabe a look of concern, Danny beckoned Wexler to follow him and led the way to the far end of the locker room.

Wexler hung back for a moment to speak privately to Gabe. "What's with him? He sounds a little slow."

"He's retarded," said Gabe quietly. "He's twenty-two, but he has the mentality of an eight-year-old."

"Why is he working here?" Wexler sounded alarmed.

"Because his father got him the job. His father's Ed White, the cinematographer. He's one of our oldest members, and he's got a lot of clout with the board."

Looking disturbed, Wexler snapped, "What the hell kind of a club is this that we have to put up with an idiot in the locker room? Retards can be dangerous."

"Not Danny," Gabe assured him. "He's been checked out by the best shrinks on Roxbury Drive. They say he's as harmless as a ladybug. Not only that, he shines a great pair of shoes."

"That I've got to see," grumbled Wexler, starting up the aisle after Danny with his tennis equipment.

Five

After getting the Wexlers started on Court Number 2, Gabe returned to the office, approved the lunch menu for the following day that the cook had dropped off, turned it over to Jenny for typing, and then sat back in his chair and thought about what a really pleasant day his first one as manager of the club had been. If this was what he was getting twenty-five grand a year for, plus room and board and a cut of the tennis ball profits, he wondered why he hadn't gotten into some kind of tennis-related work before.

Around two-thirty, with nothing further to attend to, Gabe strolled off in the direction of the locker room, hoping to find a tennis game for himself. Instead he found Aaron Wexler descending the stairs with an apoplectic look on his face.

"Mr. Steele," he shouted, "you're just the man I want to see."

In his haste to get out of the locker room, Wexler had not finished dressing; he had on his shoes, trousers, and shirt, which was unbuttoned down to his hairy navel, but he was carrying his tie and suit jacket over one arm.

"What's wrong?" asked Gabe.

"What's wrong? I'll tell you what's wrong." By now he had reached the bottom of the stairs and was breathing heavily. "I finished playing, I took a shower, I unlocked my locker, I went to get into my clothes, and then I discovered that someone had got into my locker and cleaned me out of five hundred dollars."

Oh, hell, thought Gabe. I counted my blessings too soon. "You sure you had all that money with you when you came to the club?" asked Gabe.

"Of course I'm sure. I always carry a lot of cash with me. I don't believe in credit cards."

"Didn't you see the signs in the locker room?" asked Gabe. "They're all over the place, warning you not to leave valuables in your locker."

"I suppose I saw them," admitted Wexler. "but I didn't think there was anything to worry about if my locker was locked and I had the key."

"Well, that's just the problem. We don't know who's doing it or how it's done."

"I don't see how a thing like this can happen in a club that costs forty grand to join. I mean, what member who's got that kind of dough to spend is going to steal?"

"Well, we're not sure whether it's a member or not."

"Maybe it's that idiot locker attendant."

"I doubt it," said Gabe. "Danny may be a little slow mentally, but we've found him to be very trustworthy."

"He has a passkey to all the lockers, hasn't he?" persisted Wexler.

"He has to have, in case a member leaves his own key at home."

"Well, what's this club going to do about my loss?" demanded Wexler. He sounded as if he expected Gabe to reimburse him out of his own pocket.

"You can write a letter to the board if you want, but I doubt if they'll accept responsibility since you ignored the posted signs."

"What a way to greet a new member!" exclaimed Wexler, slipping into his jacket and slinging his tie over his shoulder.

Jan suddenly emerged from the ladies' locker room and waltzed down the steps behind them, like a Las Vegas show girl.

"What's wrong, honey?" she asked.

"My locker was robbed," he barked, still looking as if he were going to explode. "I'm out about five hundred dollars."

"Oh, stop making such a big deal out of five

hundred dollars," exclaimed Jan. "You spend that in one night at Chasen's."

"Yeah, but that's deductible!" he snapped.

"Well, if I know you, Snookums, you'll find a way to deduct that, too." Smiling at Gabe, she said, "Don't pay any attention to Aaron. He's just in a bad mood because I beat him at tennis." She took Wexler by the hand, as if he were a small child, and led him towards the entrance. "See you tomorrow, Mr. Steele, and thanks for everything."

"Thanks for nothing!" grumbled Wexler.

"Oh, shut up, Aaron!" She pushed him out the door.

Annoyed that this had happened his first day on the job, Gabe climbed the stairs to the locker room three at a time, determined to get to the bottom of this mystery. As much as he resented being screamed at by Wexler, he had to admit that the new member had a point. Why should one of the most exclusive clubs in the world have a thief running loose in its midst? And how was it possible he never got caught? In Gabe's opinion, none of his predecessors had made a serious effort to catch the thief.

Danny was hanging some wet tennis clothes out to dry on the line on the drying porch when Gabe cornered him and brought up the matter of the latest mischief.

"You see anybody suspicious hanging around the locker room this afternoon?" asked Gabe.

"Uh-uh," said Danny.

"What about the door to the alley?" asked Gabe. "Has that been open at all?"

"Not that I know of."

"What about your passkeys?" asked Gabe. "Do you ever leave them lying around where somebody could borrow them for a few moments without you knowing they're gone?"

"Oh, no, Mr. Steele. I keep the passkeys on my belt." He jingled them for Gabe's benefit. "I guard them with my life."

"Strange," said Gabe. "You have the only key that we know of, and things still keep disappearing."

Danny suddenly looked frightened. "You don't think that I—?"

"No, no, Danny, nobody's accusing you. I just think it's strange, that's all."

"Gee, thanks a lot," said Danny gratefully. "Because I don't believe in stealing. It's against the Ten Commandments." He turned his pants pockets inside out to show Gabe that they were empty. They were, except for a package of bubble gum that fell to the floor.

"Well, from now on keep your eyes and ears open, will you?" suggested Gabe, returning to the main part of the locker room, with Danny at his heels. "And try to make your presence known in the locker room a little more. Don't just sit in the closet shining shoes and reading comic books all day. Patrol the aisles occasionally."

"You want me to play Dick Tracy for you?" He made a revolver out of his thumb and forefinger and pointed it at Gabe. "Bang, bang. Ha!"

"Yeah, play Dick Tracy."

"Oh, boy. I've always wanted to be a detective." Danny grinned and ducked back into his shoe-shining alcove as Gabe strolled up to the far end of the room where Aaron Wexler's locker was. Danny had already put his name on it, which showed that he was more with it than Wexler gave him credit for.

Wexler's locker was the one closest to the exit leading to the outside stairs going to the alley.

Gabe tried the door, which was the kind that could only be opened from the inside. There was no keyhole or knob on the outside.

Gabe sat for a few moments on the wooden bench in front of Wexler's locker, studying it solemnly, as if that would somehow give him a clue as to the thief's identity. Then he glanced at the other names in the same row of lockers: BEN BERNIE, president of the City National Bank; RALPH HUTCHISON, vice president of Smith-Barney's Beverly Hills office; CARTER BLACKMAN, TV executive; ALFREDO BANDINI, Italian film director; GREGSON BROOKS, a high-priced attorney who specialized in getting million dollar settlements for divorcing

Hollywood wives; DONALD YOUNG, industrialist turned environmentalist; MORRIS SCHULMAN, rabbi of Beth-Israel Temple; and MIKE FLANAGAN, millionaire tennis prodigy.

Certainly none of Wexler's neighbors ought to be having cash-flow problems, Gabe concluded, though it was conceivable that one of them might be a kleptomaniac. Beginning to suspect that it was far easier to write a TV whodunit than to have to solve a real-life crime, Gabe stood up again and was about to leave the area when he heard Kim Randall come down the aisle talking with Marvin Perlstein and go to their lockers on the opposite side of the row Gabe was standing in.

Perlstein, a portly man who had made a fortune in the clothing business, was one of a group of five o'clock hackers that Randall played tennis with regularly in the hopes of raising money for his theatrical ventures.

Kim was saying, "You're welcome to my pad anytime you want, Marvin."

"I really appreciate it, Kim. I hate like hell to take her to a motel. Most of them are so sleazy, and she's a real class broad."

"Just let me know far enough in advance," Kim advised him, "so you're not in conflict with any of my other customers."

"How about Thursday night? That enough notice?"

"I'll have to check my datebook," said Randall. "I'll get back to you."

Rather than reveal his presence and embarrass Perlstein, who always painted himself as the pillar of the garment business, Gabe exited quietly out the back door, feeling somewhat surprised at what he'd heard. Not that he wasn't aware from previously overheard conversations in the locker room that Perlstein cheated on his wife. But he was surprised at what Kim Randall was now stooping to in order to keep his money people happy. Gabe thought that things like loaning out your apartment for illicit sex only happened in stage and film farces.

Returning to the office, Gabe asked Jenny for a membership list. He thought possibly that by perusing the roster of names he might get some hint as to whom the thief might be. But after glancing down several pages of names, he realized there was about as much chance of getting a clue to the thief's identity from that as there was of finding a good pastrami sandwich in Pasadena. All of the members were prominent people, with allegedly healthy incomes. Unless he had access to their banking records of their psychiatrists' notes, their names revealed nothing. Of course, it was possible that somebody prominent or rich could be a kleptomaniac. But that theory didn't hold much water since no member was voted in without great character references. It would be difficult for a potential member to conceal a history of kleptomania.

After mulling the list over, Gabe finally concluded that the two best possibilities of apprehending the thief were: (1) to keep track of which members came to the club every day, together with their arrival and departure times; also which ones used the men's locker room, and at what hours. Unfortunately, the club wasn't like a ship; members didn't get logged in and out. Only guests had to sign in. So the burden of keeping track of arrival and departure times would fall heavily on Jenny (certainly he couldn't count on Danny to keep track of who was using the locker room).

And, (2) have the locks changed on the lockers. But that would cost money, and he'd have to first get approval from the board for that.

He spent what was left of the afternoon attending to routine managerial chores. And around three-thirty, he made a fourth in a doubles match with three doctors who were extremely upset that their regular fourth—also an M.D.—had been called away to perform an emergency operation—and on a Wednesday afternoon, yet.

The three doctors were real "C" players, but Gabe managed to play a customer's game with them and kept the match from being a rout for his side by occasionally dumping easy put-aways into the net.

After the tennis he didn't return to the locker room immediately. Instead he drifted over to the terrace, where he dropped into a chair, ordered a lime coke from one of the waiters, and sat for a while cooling off.

It was around five o'clock when Gabe put his empty glass down and walked into the locker room to change out of his wet clothes. The place appeared to be deserted, except for Danny, polishing shoes in his alcove.

As Gabe headed for his own locker at the far end, he was stopped in his tracks by an angry voice addressing him.

"Hey, Steele, I got a bone to pick with you."

Glancing in the direction of the voice, Gabe noticed Carter Blackman standing nude in front of his open locker, waving his Vuitton wallet and glaring at him.

Gabe didn't have to be a detective to sense trouble in those steely blue eyes of Blackman's.

Blackman, a bachelor, had been a member of the club for about five years, but Gabe had never been close to him. In fact, he didn't particularly like him, though he had no reason not to. He was successful, nice looking, the ladies liked him, and he played a good game of tennis for a man in his fifties. Perhaps he was just too smooth—like his teeth, which were so white and even they obviously had been capped.

Blackman worked for World Broadcasting, the "Fourth" network, but in what capacity Gabe had never been quite sure. All he really knew about the man was that he seemed to have plenty of money to spend, wore sharp-looking custom-tailored suits (even on his days off), lived in a million-dollar penthouse in a high rise on Wilshire Boulevard, carried a Vuitton attache case, and drove a 560 SL with not one but two cellular phones in it. Gabe knew that for a fact because one day Blackman had pulled his Mercedes up alongside Gabe's motorcycle at a stoplight, and Gabe saw him talking on both phones simultaneously. In Gabe's opinion, that said it all: the man was definitely top-drawer Hollywood asshole, in love with his own importance.

But sans clothes, with his cock dangling limply down in front of him, Blackman didn't look any more important than any other commoner in Tinseltown.

"What's wrong?" asked Gabe, as Blackman continued to glare at him.

"I'll tell you what's wrong, my wallet's empty. I had a thousand bucks in it when I went out to play, and now every penny of it is gone."

Just my luck, thought Gabe. Two locker-room thefts my first day on the job.

"You're sure you had it with you?" asked Gabe.

"Damn sure. I just withdrew the cash from the

bank before I came over here because I need it for the gin game. I don't like writing checks when I lose."

"I guess you shouldn't have left it in your locker," said Gabe weakly. "You've seen the signs on the wall about not leaving your valuables in here when you go out to play."

"Who pays attention to signs?" Blackman said with a scowl.

"Well, you should have. We didn't post them just so you'd have something to read."

"What a club!" exclaimed Blackman. "I've got a good mind to quit here and join Riviera."

Shooting Gabe another angry scowl, he threw his empty wallet in the bottom of his locker, slammed the steel door shut, locked it, and strode off in the direction of the showers, with his white buttocks in stark contrast to the rest of his sun-tanned body.

As Blackman disappeared into a shower stall, Danny wandered out of his alcove with a pair of shoes he had finished shining.

"Did you hear that?" Gabe asked him.

"No."

Gabe told him about Blackman's loss. "Who's been using the locker room in the last hour? You remember?"

"I've been shining shoes. I didn't see nothing, honest."

"I thought you were going to play Dick Tracy for me," said Gabe.

"Well, I got busy. You know how doctors are. They like their shoes shined."

"I know, they have to get the blood off them," said Gabe, slightly annoyed. "Well, do me a favor, Danny. Move your chair out into the aisle for the next few days and shine your shoes from here. That way you can keep a lookout. Think you can do that?"

"I'll try."

Disgusted that a new rash of thefts had to break out just when he had taken over, Gabe showered, and changed back into his street clothes.

Passing the cardroom on the way back to his office, Gabe had another thought: maybe the thief was one of the gin or bridge players. They were always playing for higher stakes than they could afford. There was no telling what a cardplayer, desperate for some quick cash to pay off a gambling debt, might do to obtain it.

About six o'clock, Gabe returned to the locker room and handed Danny, who had now moved his chair out into the doorway of his alcove, a pad and pencil.

"What's this for?" asked Danny.

"Starting right now, I want you to make a list of every member who comes into this room, whether it's to change his clothes or to use the john, and put down the time he arrives and the time he leaves. Think you can handle that?"

"I guess so." Danny sounded a little uncertain. Or was it unwilling?

Gabe handed him a ten dollar bill. "Starting right now," he said. "I'm going to give you an extra ten dollars a week if you'll do this."

As Danny grinned and stuffed the bill into his apron pocket, Gabe heard over the loudspeaker that he was wanted on the phone. Grabbing the receiver off the wall phone, Gabe growled "Hello" into it rather fiercely.

"My, you sound like you're in a great mood," teased Jenny.

Gabe laughed. "Sorry, Jenny. Two burglaries in one day have got me upset. What's up?"

She said that his landlord in the Pacific Palisades just called to tell him that there were a couple of envelopes in his mailbox that looked as if they contained residuals from the Guild. Did he want them forwarded, or would he pick them up?

"If they're checks, I'll pick them up right now," said Gabe. "There's nothing much doing around here. You'll close up for me, won't you, Jen, if I'm not back by seven?"

"Glad to. Have a nice night."

Despite heavy traffic, Gabe was at the Oceanview Manor by six-thirty and happy to note that there really were a few residuals among the junk mail and bills he picked up from the manager.

After that he stopped off in his own apartment to fill a small suitcase with some books and extra clothing and was just about to leave when the telephone jingled. Curious as to whom would be calling him here, he picked up the receiver. "Hello?"

"Mr. Steele, this is Dick Tracy," said Danny White, sounding breathless from excitement.

"You are a good detective, Danny. How'd you know I was here?"

"I heard you talking to Jenny in the locker room."

"What's going on that couldn't wait?"

"I did what you told me. I walked up the aisle when I heard somebody opening a locker who I didn't think had a locker there, and I saw who it was. Aren't I a good Dick Tracy?"

"Yeah, yeah," said Gabe impatiently. "Who was it?"

"You'll never guess." Danny laughed his silly laugh.

"I don't want to guess. Just tell me. And speak quietly, in case someone's listening."

"There's no one here," said Danny. "Oh, oh! I think I hear someone coming. I better call you back."

Gabe heard a sharp click on the other end as Danny evidently hung up.

With a shrug, Gabe sat down at his desk and started opening his mail, residuals first. He was pleased to see that among a few smaller residuals was one check for $850, for a "Kojak" rerun. Well, that would take care of a couple of months alimony payments, he thought, glancing impatiently at his watch and noting that fifteen minutes had passed since he'd talked with Danny.

Deciding that Danny, in his absentmindedness, might have forgotten about calling him back, Gabe picked up the receiver and dialed the club's switchboard. He let it ring fifteen times before realizing that it was after seven P.M. and that Jenny had undoubtedly closed the place and gone home by now. And since there was no direct line to the locker room, he had the choice of either waiting for Danny to call him back or to return to the club.

He gave Danny five more minutes then gathered up his mail, turned off the lights, and drove back to the club.

In his anxiety to get to the club in time to catch Danny and learn the identity of the thief before the kid went home, Gabe ran a couple of red lights. Fortunately, there were no cops around, and he made the trip from the Palisades to Beverly Hills in eighteen minutes. It must have been some kind of a record.

Gabe parked his bike in the white zone in front of the club, leaped out of the saddle, and took the front steps three at a time.

The clubhouse was deserted, and all the

rooms were dark. He flicked on the downstairs lights then raced through the living room and out to the locker room steps. He took them three at a time, too, and yanked open the locker room door.

"Danny!" he shouted. But the room was dark and nobody was around. With a disappointed feeling, he switched on the ceiling fluorescents and walked the length of the locker room just to make sure it was empty and that everything was in order. It was, except for some dirty towels on the floor. He picked them up and dropped them into a hamper, then peeked into Danny's alcove to see if there was anything amiss in there.

Seeing nothing of interest, Gabe made another quick inspection of the locker room. Everything seemed in order. The phone receiver was on its hook, the door to the alley was locked. The door to the utility closet, where Danny kept his broom, mops, and other cleaning equipment, was closed, and none of the showers had been left on to waste precious water.

Convinced that Danny had gone home, Gabe was about to leave the locker room when he thought he heard some movement in the white-tiled alcove where the johns and urinals were. Very cautiously he tiptoed over to the entrance and peeked into the alcove. No one was standing at the urinals, so he kneeled down and peeked through the openings under the john doors. No feet or legs were visible either.

With a shrug, he walked over to the three urinals. The one closest to the main part of the locker room hadn't been flushed. It was full of very yellow urine as if someone had just taken a leak, and it smelled awful.

Holding his nose with one hand, he pulled the chrome lever with the other and flushed the urinal clean. Then, dousing all the lights in the locker room, he hurried out and down the stairs to Jenny's office. There he looked up Danny's telephone number in the Rolodex, plugged into the switchboard, and dialed his apartment.

Nobody was home, so he phoned Danny's parents' house, figuring maybe he'd gone there for dinner. But all he got was one of those damn phone answering machines, saying that the Whites were out of town and wouldn't be returning until the following afternoon.

Next he tried Jenny at her home, thinking perhaps she'd seen Danny leave the club.

Mrs. Ho, Jenny's mother, picked up the phone first and then put her daughter on. But Jenny could shed no light on the mystery, either. She hadn't seen Danny leave, so she just presumed he'd gone out the alley entrance. "Sometimes he does that. Why are you so worried?"

Gabe quickly filled her in on the mysterious phone call he'd received from Danny and how it had ended so abruptly with Danny promising to phone him back and disclose the thief's name, which he never did.

"It probably just slipped his mind," said Jenny. "That can happen with someone who's retarded."

"And with someone who isn't, too," Gabe jokingly replied.

"So don't take your job so seriously," Jenny advised him. "Relax."

"I hate being kept in suspense," said Gabe.

"I'm sure what he has to tell you will keep until morning."

"You're right, Jenny. Actually I just wanted to hear your pretty voice. I thought maybe you'd let me take you out to dinner at a fancy restaurant. I just got a residual and I feel rich."

"Isn't there a bylaw prohibiting members from dating employees?" Though she had raised the issue, there was a slightly whimsical tone to her voice that belied the notion she was totally against the idea.

"I'm wearing two hats now," Gabe reminded her. "There's no bylaw saying the manager can't take his secretary out to dinner. So how about it? Where would you like to go?"

"To tell the truth, Gabe, mother and daddy are expecting me to eat dinner home. But if you like Sushi, I'm sure there's enough for you, too."

"What's your address?" asked Gabe. "I'll be right over."

Six

When Gabe awoke the following morning, it was with an entirely new and optimistic outlook on life.

The evening before, he recalled as he lay back against the soft pillows, had been a complete delight. Though Jenny was certainly old enough to have her own apartment, she still lived with her parents, who owned a fully paid-up white Bermuda bungalow in the Sawtelle section of Los Angeles, just west of the San Diego Freeway.

George Ho, a dark-skinned, full-blooded Hawaiian, who had the chest and shoulders of an ox, was, despite his huge size, a gentle, soft-spoken man. In his late forties, with a touch of grey in his hair, he earned a comfortable living growing flowers and tropical plants in his own nursery on Sawtelle Boulevard. Eileen Ho, Jenny's mother, was a moon-faced Japanese woman of the old school. She had a petite figure that was well hidden beneath the folds of the colorful Japanese kimono she was wearing and tiny feet in white slippers. No women's libber she, Eileen giggled a lot but was content to let the men do most of the talking while she served dinner and poured the tea, which she did with great ceremony. She seemed completely dedicated to making her husband happy and keeping her daughter from becoming deeply involved with a man until she knew what his intentions were.

Eileen's other strong point was Japanese flower arranging, at which she seemed to be a genius, judging from some of the samples around the house.

"Mother's been picked to exhibit her flower arrangements at the Japanese Cultural Exhibit at the Convention Center in July," Jenny told Gabe proudly. "Isn't she marvelous? I'm a complete dud at that sort of thing."

"She's great," answered Gabe. "I'd like her to do the flowers at my funeral."

Jenny laughed, and Mrs. Ho giggled, even though he suspected she didn't quite get his joke.

She did understand what young people wanted, however, and a short time after the dishes had been put away, she diplomatically announced that George had to get up early and that they were going to bed. Though her morality was of a less promiscuous era, Mrs. Ho didn't seem terribly worried about leaving her daughter alone on the living room sofa with Gabe. Evidently she knew her daughter well. Gabe wondered if his age bothered Jenny's parents—he was closer to their age than hers—but decided not to worry about that.

Though Gabe had heard that Oriental girls were supposed to be sexy, he had noticed that Jenny gave no indication during the evening that she wanted to engage in anything more erotic than sitting on the sofa and cuddling. Which was all right with him. He wasn't the kind who liked to sleep around for the thrill of scoring with a girl. He had to be in love in order for it to mean anything.

But Gabe had the feeling that even if she had been interested in sex on her first date, she wouldn't have dared try it under her parents' roof. They believed in cherry blossoms and wedding rings, and Jenny, being a caring daughter, obviously respected their principles. And Gabe respected her for respecting them and was perfectly content to spend just a comfortable evening being near her. He didn't even mind the smell of an incense candle burning on the hibachi table in front of the sofa.

As Gabe jumped out of bed, pulled open the blinds on another beautiful Southern California spring morning, and ducked into the bathroom to brush his teeth, he thought how lucky he was to be able to share an office with Jenny Ho. In fact, he found he could hardly wait for nine o'clock to roll around to see those large saucer-like brown eyes and the satiny finish of her Polynesian tan skin again. This sudden anxiety to be with her, he realized, was a bad sign for someone who had vowed never to get seriously involved with a woman again. But he couldn't help himself. It made him feel good simply being around Jenny.

In the meantime, with an hour still to kill before he'd have to open up for the Early Bird tennis crowd, Gabe decided to work out on the exercise porch. He felt a twinge in his lower back every now and then from serving too hard, but hanging from the gravity bar was supposed to help the condition. So he figured why not give it a try while he had the time?

Dressed in warm-up suit and tennis shoes, Gabe jogged through the club's empty living room and took the stairs to the exercise porch three at a time to test his wind. He found he was huffing a bit hard when he reached the landing and wondered if this was the day he ought to begin cutting down on his smoking, or perhaps quit altogether.

But the grisly sight that awaited him as he

stepped briskly onto the exercise porch sent such a shock through him that any concerns about his own health immediately evaporated.

Danny White's body, in the same clothes he was wearing the previous afternoon, was dangling from the gravity bar by a piece of clothesline that had been fashioned into a crude hangman's noose around his neck. His head was cocked to one side, his tongue, turned blue, was sticking out of his mouth, his eyes were bulging, and his complexion was grey-white.

Gabe broke out into a cold sweat as he stared at the body in disbelief. "Oh, God," he muttered. He shut his eyes briefly in the hopes that the nightmare would disappear, but it was no bad dream. When he opened them again, Danny's body was still dangling at the end of the rope.

Gabe shuddered as another cold chill raced up his spine. He couldn't get over how much the gravity bar, with Danny's body hanging between its two iron supporting posts, resembled a gallows.

Taking a cautious step forward, Gabe put a thumb and forefinger on Danny's wrist. He could feel no pulsebeat at all, and Danny's skin was as cold and clammy as a piece of raw meat.

Never having been in this position before, Gabe was ambivalent about what his next move should be: untie Danny from his self-made gallows and give him CPR? He'd learned the rudiments of CPR in a course the Writers Guild had sponsored for all its members. Maybe he could bring Danny back to life, for there was always a chance that even though Gabe couldn't feel a pulsebeat or hear him breathing that Danny was still alive. However, the realist in Gabe warned him not to tamper with the evidence. In the first place, Danny was obviously dead, for his arm, when Gabe let loose of his wrist, did not swing freely to his side. Rigor mortis had already begun to set in, which meant he'd been dead for five or six hours—maybe more. And in the second place, if his death were anything but suicide (and in his overly suspicious mind, Gabe couldn't help believing it might be homicide), it would be wrong to change the position of the body and risk destroying important evidence that he, as an amateur sleuth, was overlooking. No, he'd better leave the cutting down of Danny's body to the authorities, he thought as he backed up slowly and started to go for the phone. In his haste, he stumbled backwards over a stool that was tipped over on its side a couple of feet away from the gravity bar. "Jesus, what a klutz," he grumbled, scrambling to his feet. He was about to set the stool back on its legs when something told him the police wouldn't want him to touch that, either. Glancing over the dangling corpse, he realized that Danny must have used the stool to stand on while he was adjusting the noose around his neck. It was the only way he could have gotten the leverage to hang himself.

But had he hanged himself? Gabe speculated. Or was it just made to look like suicide by whomever it was who wanted to silence Danny—the locker room thief, perhaps.

As it occurred to Gabe that Danny was probably murdered because he'd been carrying out his instructions, he suddenly felt very apprehensive about being in the clubhouse alone. With a shudder, he bolted for the staircase, taking the steps two and three at a time, to get to the office and phone the police.

In his hurry to plug into the switchboard, he didn't bother turning on the office lights, though very little daylight was coming in this early through the two small windows. He just threw himself into Jenny's chair and began dialing. But his finger, wet from nervous perspiration, caused him to misdial twice before finally doing it correctly.

It seemed to take hours for the police to answer, but actually only about thirty seconds elapsed before a male voice at the other end of the line intoned, "Sgt. Mannie Manheim here."

"I don't know who I should be asking for," said Gabe, "but I'm Gabe Steele, the manager of the Beverly-West Racquet Club, over on Jacaranda Drive."

"Yeah, I know the place," said the sergeant in a bored voice. "What have you got—someone parked in your loading zone again?"

"I've got a dead body," blurted out Gabe. "Our locker room attendant, Danny White!"

"You sure this isn't a case for the paramedics?"

"Yes, I'm sure. He's either committed suicide or he's been murdered. I'm not sure which."

"Yeah?" Manheim sounded just like the fuzzy-headed cops that TV was always kidding. "What makes you so sure it's either?"

"Well, he's hanging by a rope around his neck, so it's certainly not a case of heart failure," snapped Gabe, finding it difficult to control his sarcasm.

"I see." Manheim clucked his tongue loudly. "Well, in that case maybe I'd better send a detective over."

"That would be a good idea," said Gabe. "The sooner the better. And while you're at it, you might put in a call for the county coroner, too."

"What are you, Mr. Steele, a wise guy—telling me how to run my business?"

"Well, isn't that the procedure?"

"Yeah, of course it is, but how did—?"

"I used to write 'Murder She Wrote,'" explained Gabe, hanging up.

At that moment some heavy pounding on the front door, followed by the sound of angry male voices demanding to be let in, propelled Gabe out of his chair in the direction of the club entrance.

"Oh, God, the Early Birds!" he exclaimed, noting by the wall clock in the entrance hall that it was already two minutes past eight

As Gabe unlocked the front door, Eddie Grant, the proprietor of Grant's, a chic men's clothing store on Rodeo Drive, pushed his stout figure into the foyer. He was followed by Harry Saltzman, a real estate tycoon in an Armani Jean outfit and sporting a Sassoon haircut, and Dr. Hamlisch, a plastic surgeon who'd made enough money altering the faces of prominent actors and actresses to own his own medical building on South Beverly Drive.

"What happened, Rip Van Winkle—you oversleep?" asked Eddie Grant, as he brushed by Gabe.

"Yeah, we've got a big doubles match to play," said Saltzman, "and we want Court Number One."

"*If* Ted Dawson shows," added Dr. Hamlisch, glumly. "If he doesn't, would you mind filling in for him, Gabe?"

Before Gabe could say yes or no, the three of them hurried off in the direction of the locker room stairs.

"I hate to spoil your morning's fun," said Gabe, catching up with them on the stairs, "but you probably won't want to play after you hear what happened. In fact," he squeezed by them and raced up to the landing, where he turned around facing them and blocked their march to the locker room, "You probably shouldn't come up here at all if you don't want to get the shock of your lives."

"What's got into you?" asked Grant. "You flipped or something?"

"Yeah, why shouldn't we play?" chimed in Hamlisch.

"Look, fellows," explained Gabe, "we have a real tragedy on our—"

"You mean, there's no hot water in the showers again?" Saltzman interrupted him.

"Worse than that," said Gabe grimly.

By now the three of them had reached the landing and were looking at Gabe for an explanation.

"I tried to spare you this," he said, "but now that you're here, you can see for yourself." He jerked his thumb in the direction of the gravity bar. "I just found him. I think he's dead."

"You sure?" asked Eddie Grant, glancing nervously in the direction of the dangling corpse.

"As far as I can tell," replied Gabe. "I'm no doctor."

"I'll see," said Dr. Hamlisch, approaching Danny's body cautiously and pinching the skin on the back of one of his hands to see if the flesh would spring back. When it didn't, he grimaced slightly and rejoined the others. "Yeah, I'm afraid Danny's had it."

The group stood in nervous contemplation of the body for a moment, shifting their feet uneasily, not knowing what else to say.

"Hey, wait for me, fellahs!" It was the voice of their fourth, Ted Dawson, arriving belatedly at the foot of the stairs, with a couple of rackets under one arm. "Sorry, I'm late, but I had to stop off at The Big Five and pick up my new rackets." As the portly-faced stockbroker reached the landing and saw Danny's body hanging from the gravity bar, he blanched and looked as if he were going to be sick. "Holy shit! Why doesn't someone cut him down?"

"Have to wait for the police to get here," answered Gabe.

"Why'd he do it?" asked Dawson.

Gabe shrugged. "Don't know for sure that he did. There's no note. My own hunch is, he might have been killed."

"Yeah?" Eddie Grant looked frightened. "Who'd want to kill such a shlemiel?"

Gabe gave them a quick thumbnail of the events starting with the previous evening's interrupted phone call.

The other three looked skeptical. "I think you have an overactive imagination," said Grant. "The job was probably too much for the kid."

"Yeah, he probably knew he didn't have much of a future hanging up jockstraps," theorized Saltzman.

"I doubt if he ever thought about his future," disagreed Gabe. "He was very happy in his simpleminded way."

"Well, it's too bad," said Dr. Hamlisch, "but there's nothing any of us can do. So let's get dressed, fellows."

"Get dressed?" exclaimed Gabe. "You still going to play? Don't you guys have any reverence for the dead?"

"Dead is dead," said Dr. Hamlisch, his hand already on the locker room doorknob.

"But maybe there's still a chance," insisted Gabe, afraid he was beginning to sound hysterical. "Maybe we should take him down, and you could try to resuscitate him while we're waiting for the police."

"Resuscitate him?! I'm just a plastic surgeon—not a magician. And besides, I'm sure the cops will want to see him the way you found him. I've learned to keep hands off police matters."

"Doc's right," said Dawson, glancing impatiently at his watch. "You're not supposed to touch a dead body, even if you're a doctor. You could get sued."

"So let's stop schmoozing and grab the good court," said Grant.

"Yeah. Let's not kill the whole morning," said

Saltzman, starting to loosen his tie. "I've got to see a man at ten o'clock who's interested in buying my building in Westwood."

"And I've got a ten o'clock, too," said Grant, starting to follow the other three into the locker room. "I'm sure you can handle whatever has to be handled when the cops get here, can't you, champ?"

"I guess I'll have to," grumbled Gabe as Grant disappeared behind the closing door.

Not crazy about keeping Danny's corpse company, Gabe returned to the foyer and stood by the open door to the street to wait for the police. To his relief, a squad car was just pulling to the curb in front of the building. Two people alighted—one, a tall young man in uniform, and the other, a short, dumpy looking lady of about thirty-five, in khaki slacks, khaki blouse, a navy blue cardigan sweater, and Adidas. She was hatless, had short brown hair, mannishly cut, and she rolled like a sailor as she walked.

She was evidently the "take charge" person of the investigation for she walked ahead of her uniformed sidekick and entered the clubhouse first. Seeing Gabe, she asked, "You the manager?"

"Yeah, I'm Gabe Steele. I'm the one who put in the call."

"Hi, ya?" She flipped open her wallet and showed him her detective's badge. "Judy

Trump, Homicide," she said brusquely. "I understand you've got a dead body you want me to see."

Gabe led the way to Danny's corpse on the exercise porch then backed off to allow Detective Trump the necessary space to make her investigation.

Although Gabe had written this scene many times, he'd never before been in on an actual police investigation of a death. He was surprised at how brief and perfunctory Detective Trump's examination turned out to be.

After circling the gravity bar and studying the body from all angles, she glanced around the exercise porch for further pieces of evidence. Spotting the overturned stool, she walked slowly over to it and studied it thoughtfully. Then she paced off the distance between the stool and Danny's body, following which she nodded sagely, as if verifying a privately reached conclusion. After a moment of cogitation, she moved closer to Gabe and said, "Looks to me like a plain-and-simple case of suicide. You got any reasons to believe different?"

"A couple," answered Gabe.

"Let's hear 'em," said Trump, pulling a small note pad from her hip pocket and poising a ball point pen over it.

Gabe gave her a swift history of the club's locker room thefts and ended with a detailed description of the happenings of the day before, including the phone call that Danny White never got to complete.

"I'm not a detective," concluded Gabe, "but it seems to me that whoever was breaking into the lockers heard Danny about to identify him and decided to get rid of the witness."

"Pretty circumstantial," said Judy Trump. "Especially since we don't know that Danny wasn't the thief. All things point to that from what you told me about his having a key."

"What's circumstantial about his phone call? Why would he bother if he was the thief?"

"Maybe he was going to confess to the crime himself but chickened out at the last minute. Guilty parties frequently do that. They want to come clean, but at the last minute, they change their minds."

"That doesn't account for his hanging up so suddenly and promising to call me back when the coast was clear."

"Maybe he was just trying to throw you off the track."

"Retarded people aren't that devious."

"Are you an expert on their behavior?"

"Okay, I'll give you that one," said Gabe. "But shouldn't you at least question our members?"

"What right do I have to do that? The club was closed when this thing happened, and no one was here, according to you, except you."

"Look, as a detective I think it's your duty to do some investigating before you close the case," said Gabe.

"Even a detective has to have something to go on," replied Trump. "If you can show me a shred of evidence to substantiate your theory, maybe I'll buy it. Until then—" she shrugged, "all I have to make a judgment on is a body with a rope around its neck."

"How about the fact that when I came back to the club twenty minutes later, Danny was nowhere around, and he hadn't finished cleaning up the locker room?" persisted Gabe. He was trying to conceal the irritation in his voice, but because of her unwillingness to view the death from any viewpoint but her own, he was frustrated and found he was nearly shouting.

"So he quit early?"

"Without cleaning up?"

"You said he was retarded, didn't you?"

"Yes, according to his folks, he had the mentality of an eight year old."

"Retarded people have short attention spans," she said. "He probably forgot in his hurry to go home."

"But he wasn't home when I phoned there, and he wasn't at his parents' place, either. And then he suddenly turned up here on the exercise porch this morning."

"That's no big deal," said Trump. "Either he

was in transit, or he just hid out here on the premises until you closed up, then sneaked out here and knocked himself off, for whatever reason the poor soul had. Though my guess is it was guilt."

"I have a different theory," said Gabe. "Someone strangled him then hid his body until I went to sleep. Then he took a piece of clothesline from our drying porch and strung him up to make it look like suicide."

"That's the way it is in the storybooks," said Trump, with an annoying smile, "but it's been my experience that most killers aren't that inventive. After committing their mayhem, they usually hightail it for the hills or the Mexican border."

"Are all killers alike?" demanded Gabe, really exasperated now. "Couldn't this one have his own methods?"

"Basically they're the same," she said in an impatient tone that made it clear she wished to dismiss the subject. "By the way, have you checked to see if the rope he used is the same one from the drying porch?"

"No, I haven't. I thought you were the detective."

Ignoring the dig, she said, "I gather you get to it through the men's locker room. Is it okay for me to go in there?"

"I'll see if the coast is clear." As Gabe started

to open the locker room door, Ted Dawson came out, still fully dressed in a business suit and tie. "Hey, Gabe, I have a problem. I left my locker key at home. You happen to know where Danny kept his passkey?"

"On his belt," said Gabe. "On a key ring."

"Well, will you get it for me?" asked Dawson. "I hate to go near dead bodies." He made a wry face as he glanced at Danny's corpse.

"You really have compassion," said Gabe. "The poor kid's dead, and you're worrying about getting into your locker."

"Hey, who do you think you are, talking to me like that?" said Dawson, sounding annoyed. "I'm a member in good standing. You're just a manager working for us now."

"I'm still a member of the human race," retorted Gabe, clenching both fists and looking Dawson straight in the eye. "Want to make something of it?"

"I—I—I just want to get into my locker," stammered Dawson, nervously. "The—the fellahs are waiting for me. See what you can do."

"The keys may be part of the investigation," said Gabe, glancing in Trump's direction. "You probably don't want to touch anything until the coroner arrives, do you?"

"You better believe it," she said, shooting Dawson a jaundiced look.

"Who's she?" asked Dawson, turning back to Gabe.

"She is Detective Trump," explained Gabe. "Detective Trump, Ted Dawson."

"A lady detective!" exclaimed Dawson. "What's happening to this world?"

"It's improving," said Trump dryly.

"Okay, I'll borrow some duds from one of the guys," said Dawson. With an uneasy smile, he ducked back into the locker room.

"I guess you get a lot of that sexist stuff," said Gabe, in an apologetic tone.

"I'm used to it," she said with a shrug.

"Well, I'm glad you don't let it bother you."

But her mind was on more important things. "By the way," she said, approaching the body and squinting at it from all angles. "I don't see any keys on poor Danny. Do you?"

She beckoned Gabe to come over and check the body himself.

"You're right," said Gabe, pointing to a belt loop on the front of Danny's duck pants. "That's where he always kept them."

"You sure about that?"

"Positive. If you ask me, that's another point in favor of my theory. The killer took the locker room keys with him."

Detective Trump turned to the uniformed policeman who had stood by silently all this time. "Sinclair," she said, "go downstairs and see if the coroner's here yet. If he is, show him up. And after that, take a look around the clubhouse for the missing keys." She wheeled on Gabe. "Now lead me to the drying porch."

As he led the way into the locker room, Gabe yelled to the Early Birds, who were in various stages of undress. "Cover yourselves, men. We have a lady detective coming through."

"Don't worry about me," grinned Judy, following Gabe through a section of the locker room that opened up on the drying porch. "I'm sure I've seen all their little goodies before."

She snickered, much amused by her own choice of words. Studying her, Gabe thought, she's not only seen them, she probably has them.

As Gabe suspected, the clothesline that had hung across the drying porch was missing, and the tennis shorts, shirts, and jockstraps that had been on it were scattered all over the floor.

"Yeah, it's gone," said Gabe, pointing to the hooks from which the line had hung.

"The old clothesline trick," said Trump, taking in the disarray at a glance. "Seems to me there'd be a lot fewer suicides if people would start using electric dryers." She shook her head in wonderment, then glanced down at the floor for additional clues, saw nothing of interest, and snapped, "Let's go."

When they returned to the exercise porch, Officer Sinclair was coming up the stairs with a heavy-set man in a light green polyester suit and Panama hat, who was carrying a doctor's satchel.

"Dr. Bob Gonzales, deputy coroner," he said, introducing himself to Trump and Gabe, in a Mexican accent.

Although Gabe guessed he was only about forty, Gonzales seemed like a relic left over from the days when Los Angeles was a Spanish settlement. He had an old-fashioned handlebar mustache, black hair almost down to his shoulders, and copper-toned skin.

Right behind him on the stairway appeared two white-coated attendants, carrying a portable gurney.

"There's the body," said Trump, jerking a thumb in Danny's direction.

As Detective Trump escorted Dr. Gonzales over to the body, she explained, "Ordinarily I would have taken him down and tried to revive him, but after I saw him, I didn't see any reason not to wait for that until you got here—there's no question he's dead—and I thought it might help you reach a verdict if you saw him in the same position the club manager found him this morning about an hour and a half ago."

"Good thinking," agreed Gonzales. "I hate cops who screw around with the evidence." He felt Danny's pulse area then tried to swing his arm. "Stage three, rigor mortis. I'd say he's been dead at least twelve hours."

While Gonzales snapped open his black bag

and went to work, Gabe took Detective Trump aside and said, "That twelve hour estimate doesn't quite fit your theory that Danny hid out in the locker room until I went to bed. If he did that, Danny couldn't have been dead that long."

Trump seemed annoyed. "What time did you go to bed?"

"About eleven-thirty."

"And did you come up these stairs to get to your quarters?" she asked with a slight sneer.

"No. The stairs to my room are in a different part of the clubhouse."

"Then he could have been swinging here since you went out to dinner, and you wouldn't have known the difference. That's twelve hours! Ergo, he still could have killed himself."

It made sense, but somehow Gabe didn't buy it.

By now, Will Jason, the fingerprint man, and a photographer named Hymie Fink, had arrived to do their things. Fink seemed the older of the two, bald, with a paunch, and wore a dark blue suit with flecks of dandruff on his shoulders. Jason was blond, thin, and dressed in jeans and a leather jacket. But both had evidently been through this same scene many times before, judging from the matter-of-fact way they went about their business.

While Jason was getting out his dusting powder and preparing to smear some of the steel uprights of the gravity bar, he glanced up at Danny and shook his head compassionately. "Poor kid."

"Yeah, makes you wonder why anyone wants to be young," said Hymie Fink, pointing his Nikon at Danny.

As the flash went off, he looked thoughtful for a moment, then prepared to shoot Danny from another angle.

"Better check the stool for prints, too," suggested Detective Trump, while Jason was still working on the gravity bar. "Not that I expect to find anything of any significance. Too many members have had their mitts all over this exercise equipment before."

"Yeah, I'm getting nothing on the gravity bar," admitted Jason. "It's pretty much a waste of time."

"Well, check the stool, anyway, to satisfy Mr. Steele here. He seems to think there's been foul play, and I don't want to upset him by overlooking a *clue*." There was a touch of sarcasm in the way she hit the word "clue."

After Jason and Fink had completed their work, Dr. Gonzales turned to the ambulance attendants and said, "Okay, men, put him on the gurney."

When they'd taken him down and laid him on the gurney, Dr. Gonzales carefully examined his neck and spinal column just below the cranium.

He found a large laceration mark on the skin between the Adam's apple and the chin, but no broken bones.

"I would say, 'death by strangulation,'" he announced to his audience.

"You mean *someone* strangled him?" asked Gabe, encouraged that the coroner seemed to be buying his theory.

"No, self-inflicted. There's a rope mark, but it didn't break the neck." He pointed to the rope mark then pulled the sheet over Danny's head.

"Oh." Gabe immediately felt deflated.

As Detective trump jotted the coroner's findings down in her pad, Gonzales continued. "I'll be able to make a more detailed examination at the autopsy, but I don't expect to find anything new. How about the boy's next of kin? Does he have any?"

"He has a mother and father in town here," answered Gabe. "They're members. They live in Westwood."

"Have they been notified?"

"Not yet."

"Why not?" snapped Gonzales. "Don't you think they'd like to know?"

"Their phone machine said they're out of town until this afternoon," Gabe informed him.

"Well, I'm going to need a relative to identify

the body before I can sign the death certificate," said Gonzales. "Keep after them, will you, Trump? They'll have to come down to the morgue to do it."

At that moment the four Early Birds burst out of the locker room, dressed in their tennis whites, and laughing and joking with one another about their games.

As they passed the exercise porch, they suddenly turned silent and solemn and remained that way until they reached the bottom of the stairs at which point Gabe heard Dawson say, "Let's play for lunch."

As Gonzales looked curiously at him, Gabe shrugged and said, "Life goes on."

"I'll take care of notifying the next of kin soon as I get back to the station," said Trump.

"Well, then I guess that's a wrap," said Gonzales, regressing into show business director's lingo. Snapping his bag shut, he turned to the attendants. "Take him away, boys."

While the attendants were strapping Danny's body to the gurney, Gonzales gazed down below at the panorama of courts, swimming pool, and shrub-covered grounds and exclaimed, "Nice place. Very hard to get into?"

"There's a long waiting list," said Gabe. "At least there was until today." With a grim smile, he led the solemn procession back to the ground floor.

* * *

Gabe stood on the sidewalk with Detective Trump while Danny was being loaded into the coroner's wagon. As the coroner drove off, Gabe asked Trump, "so what happens now? Are you going to look into my murder theory, or is this it?"

"All depends on the autopsy report," explained Trump. "If there's been foul play, Gonzales will find it. In that case, I may be back here asking a few questions of the members and yourself."

"But the chances are you won't?" persisted Gabe, sounding slightly impatient with her.

"Look, Mr. Steele," said Trump in an icy, almost threatening tone, "I wouldn't press this murder angle too strongly if I were you, because if the coroner's verdict is 'foul play,' you'd be our chief suspect!"

"Me?" Gabe was in complete shock.

"Yes, you, Mr. Steele." She stared him straight in the eye. "Except for the deceased, you're the only one we're sure was on the premises when all these shenanigans took place."

At that moment they were joined by Officer Sinclair, who reported to Trump that he hadn't been able to locate the missing keys.

"Doesn't that mean something?" asked Gabe. "If the keys were on Danny's body when he killed himself, wouldn't they still be there? They couldn't walk away."

"No, they couldn't," admitted Trump. She thought about it for a moment then said, "I guess that's one in your favor, Mr. Steele." She smiled thinly. "Well, I've got to get back to the station and make out my report. Have a good one."

And with a wave of her hand, she was off in the direction of the police car.

Seven

Watching the police car pull away from the curb, Gabe suddenly felt depressed and very much alone. Also, a little regretful that he'd taken on this job, which in a little more than a day, he'd already managed to screw up.

Aware of strong sunlight in his eyes, Gabe realized he didn't even know what time it was and glanced at his watch for the first time since he had got up. Only 8:55! It seemed incredible to him that only an hour and fifty-five minutes had elapsed since he had discovered Danny's body.

As the grim events of the preceding two hours flashed through his mind, Gabe shook his head, still not quite able to believe that Danny was on his way to the morgue because some two-bit thief chose to take a life rather than spend a few days (if that much) in jail.

With a feeling of helplessness, he started to go back up the walk to the clubhouse when he heard Jenny Ho's cheerful voice hailing him from the curb where she had just parked her Volkswagen Rabbit. Turning, he smiled, waved to her, and waited in front of the entrance for Jenny to catch up with him. As usual, her fresh, perky, slightly Oriental good looks intrigued him as she walked toward him swinging her hips and purse with careless abandon. Clad in a dress and leather thong sandals, with a long strand of jade beads around her lovely neck and a Gucci purse in one hand, she seemed the ideal blend of Polynesia and Rodeo Drive.

As she reached him, Gabe bent down and gave her a friendly kiss on the cheek. That she seemed in no hurry to back off, gave a much needed lift to his wilted spirits.

"Guess what!" exclaimed Jenny. "Mother and Daddy liked you a lot. You don't know how hard it is to satisfy those two creatures!"

Gabe couldn't help smiling at her directness. That's what he liked so much about Jenny: how terribly uncomplicated she was. No game playing. Right to the point.

"Maybe they wouldn't feel that way if they knew I was a murder suspect," said Gabe, feeling glum again.

"What are you talking about?"

Gabe told her what he was talking about on their way into the office.

"How awful!" exclaimed Jenny, studying him with concern. "I can't believe it."

"I'm just glad you weren't here," he said. "It was an unreal couple of hours. And the worst part of it is that this stupid detective refuses to believe my theory that Danny was murdered by one of the members, and that worries the hell out of me."

"You really think it's one of the members?" asked Jenny, following Gabe into his office where he sat down at his desk and reached for a pack of Marlboros.

"Well, it just occurred to me that only a member would know that Danny kept the stool he supposedly used to hang himself with locked up in the laundry sink closet. A stranger wouldn't have known where to get it."

"You're a pretty good detective," said Jenny, impressed.

"As Charlie Chan once told Number One Son, 'it doesn't take much talent to solve a crime. One needs just a little patience and the ability to put two and two together, and, of course, a lot of luck.'" He struck a match, touching the flame to the end of his cigarette, and sucked a mouthful of smoke down deep into his lungs. "And to think this was the day I was going to give up smoking." He looked penitent and waved the smoke cloud away from Jenny with his hand. "And I haven't even had breakfast yet."

"Would you like me to get you something?" offered Jenny. "I'll go tell the cook if you'll tell me what you'd like."

"I'd like my appetite back," said Gabe. "I've felt like throwing up ever since I saw Danny's body dangling at the end of that rope. I'm also getting a headache."

"Poor Gabe." Jenny moved behind his chair and, sliding her hands around his forehead, gently started to massage his temples, gradually working her dexterous fingers around to the back of his neck. "You're all knotted up here."

"I know. Keep it up."

Continuing to rub, she said, "This is the place where all the headaches start."

As he felt his neck beginning to relax, he said, "How'd you get so good at this? Not in secretarial school?"

She laughed. "My grandmother in Kyoto taught me."

She stopped rubbing and returned to her desk after two more Early Birds arrived in the lobby and called in their good mornings to her.

"You're right," said Gabe. "We've got a club to run, as much as I don't feel like it." Grinding his cigarette out in an ashtray, he called out to Jenny, "Want to see if you can get Jock Kornfeld on the phone for me? I think the president ought to know what's going on around here."

After a moment, Jenny called into him that Jock Kornfeld wasn't at home.

"How about his wife?"

"She's on the line," said Jenny.

"Okay. I'll talk to her." Gabe grabbed the receiver and said in an urgent tone, "Hi, Rita. We've got kind of an emergency down here at the club. It's important that I get hold of Jock. Danny White killed himself here last night or else he was murdered. The police aren't sure which."

"Jesus! That's awful."

"Yeah, it is awful. So will you tell Jock when you see him and have him call me?"

"I don't think I'll see him this morning. Why don't you try him at the office? He's been there all night."

"All night?"

"Yeah, there's been some kind of take-over talk, and there had to be an emergency meeting of the board of directors."

"Okay, I'll try him there," said Gabe, hanging up and glancing through the door at Jenny. He was about to tell her to try Jock Kornfeld at his office in Century City but held off when he realized that Jenny was on the phone with another call. "Certainly, Mr. Wexler," she was saying. "I'll be sure to give her that message." Unplugging Wexler's call, she glanced through the door at Gabe. "Our new member, calling from San Francisco," she explained.

"What's he want—his five hundred dollars back?"

"He didn't mention anything about that. He

just wants us to tell his wife to call him at the Fairmont when she comes in for her tennis lesson. He tried her at home, but she wasn't there."

"Well, don't forget to tell her," said Gabe, sounding more like a boss than he wanted. "We're in enough trouble with that guy."

"Aye, aye, sir." Jenny smiled, jotted Wexler's message down on a pink message form, and pinned it to the cork reminder board by the switchboard.

"Okay, Jenny, now try Kornfeld at his off—" Gabe interrupted himself as he saw Kornfeld, in a pinstriped blue suit, appear in the entrance hall on the other side of the glass. "Speaking of the devil . . ." He opened his door to the foyer. "Just the man I want to see, Jock. I've been trying to track you down."

Kornfeld seemed startled. "What's the matter—my wife been looking for me?"

"No, she just said you weren't home, you were at an all-night meeting."

"That's right. I was." He looked relieved that his wife believed his story. "It was a real ball buster. The meeting began yesterday at the cocktail hour and just broke up. Our firm might be taking over Estee Lauder. It's good news for the stockholders, but, man, I'm really beat."

"Well, I hope you're not too beat to talk to me," said Gabe, pulling Jock into his office. "I've got some ball-busting news, too. Danny White killed himself. Or so the police seem to think."

"Really? I'm shocked." But he didn't sound shocked, and the surprise his face registered seemed more manufactured than genuine. "When did it happen?"

"Sometime during the night. I found his body on the exercise porch this morning just after I got up. I called the police before I did anything else. They sent over a Detective Trump, and she—"

"A broad detective?"

"Yeah, a broad."

"How'd she look?"

"Like you'd expect a lady detective to look."

"Figures."

"Anyway, as I was saying," continued Gabe, "she brought in the coroner, who examined Danny, decided it was a suicide, and carted him off to the morgue."

"God! The poor disturbed kid!" Exclaimed Kornfeld, running his hand through his hair. "I wonder why he'd hang himself."

"I didn't tell you he hanged himself," said Gabe. "How'd you know that."

"Just assumed," said Jock, with a shrug. "There's not many methods of killing yourself on the exercise porch unless you have a heart attack from pumping too much iron." He smiled thinly. "What else should I know?"

Gabe filled Jock in on the rest of the gory

details, including his own hunch that Danny's death could have been murder.

"Well, I guess time can only be the judge of that," said Jock. "If the break-ins continue, we'll know it wasn't Danny. If they stop, the police theory is probably correct."

"Did I tell you," said Gabe, "that Danny's keys are missing? So, if he was killed by the thief, and the thief took them, the thief now has access to all the lockers, as well as the utility closet and the door to the locker room. There's going to be more thefts if we don't catch him."

"But you don't know that for sure. The keys could just be lost."

"Yes, but as a precaution, I suggest we call a locksmith and have all the locks changed."

"Yeah, I agree with that. We can't have any passkeys floating around. Why don't you run over to Beverly Lock and Key after we've eaten and talk to Max? He's done all our key work in the past. Maybe he can suggest some new kind of lock that's burglarproof. If not, maybe we ought to consider installing one of those TV monitoring systems in the locker rooms, like they have in banks and department stores."

"Not a bad thought, if we can find a locker room attendant who's alert enough to keep an eye on it. Should I call an employment agency?"

"I guess you'll have to."

"If you don't mind my sticking my nose in,"

interjected Jenny from her desk, "Tony has a nephew who just came over from the Philippines who needs work. Tony asked me just the other day if there was anything for him around here. He says he's smart and speaks good English and is a hard worker."

"Well, if Tony recommends him, that's good enough for me," said Gabe. "How about you, Jock?"

"Fine. Tell Tony to get him over here as soon as he can."

"Sure thing," grinned Jenny, turning on the PA system and announcing, "Tony Mendiola, Tony Mendiola, please report to the office on the double."

"Well, if that's everything," said Kornfeld, standing up, "I guess I'd better phone my old lady so she doesn't think I was out cheating on her."

After grabbing a quick bite of breakfast on the terrace, Gabe changed into street clothes and rode his Honda over to Crescent Drive where, very luckily, he found an empty parking space in front of the Beverly Lock and Key.

Entering the store, Gabe was surprised to see Kim Randall standing with his back to him at the glass counter, waiting for Max Weber, the proprietor, to finish cutting a key for him.

"Hi, Kim," said Gabe, stopping beside him at the counter. At the sound of Gabe's voice, Randall, in a white terry-cloth warm-up suit, jumped ever so slightly and looked at Gabe as if he'd been caught in the act of doing something dishonest.

"Oh, uh, hi ya," he said nervously. "What brings you here?"

"Just a little club business."

Randall smiled. "I'm surprised you could get out for anything this mundane."

"What's that mean?"

"I hear there's been some excitement over there this morning."

"How'd you know that?" asked Gabe, surprised that the news had traveled so fast.

"I just heard it on my car radio. You know, 'KFWB, all the news, all the time, twenty-four hours a day.'"

"I didn't know Danny's death rated radio news coverage," said Gabe.

"Well, don't forget, Ed White used to be one of our top cinematographers, back in the days before Arnold Schwarzenegger."

"Yeah well, what exactly did it say on the radio?"

"Not exactly, but approximate: It said the body of Danny White, the locker room attendant at the posh Beverly-West Racquet Club, and son of Oscar-winning cinematographer Ed White, was discovered early this morning by the club's manager, hanging from the gravity bar."

"Did it say anything else?"

"Only that there was no note, but it's presumed to be suicide. Why'd you think he did it?"

"I'm not sure that he did."

Kim whistled. "You think he was murdered?"

"I do. The police don't."

"Well, you have an overactive imagination—you write detective shows."

"I suppose," said Gabe as Weber finished making Kim's keys and dropped them on the counter.

After paying Weber and pocketing what looked like two Yale-lock door keys, Randall said, "Well, see you back at the *posh* Beverly-West Racquet Club." He grinned and walked out of the shop, as Weber put the money in the cash register and then came over to Gabe, smiling cordially.

Weber was a jolly-looking, middle-aged man, with a chubby figure, round red cheeks, and a barely noticeable Swiss accent.

"You know that gentleman?" asked Weber. He nodded in the direction of Randall's departing figure.

"Very well," said Gabe.

"Strange duck," commented Weber.

"In what way?"

"He's always losing the key to his apartment and coming in here for duplicates. I must have made eight in the past couple of months. He must have holes in his pockets."

"Or in his head," said Gabe.

Weber chuckled, and Gabe introduced himself as the new manager of the Beverly-West Racquet Club and explained what his problem was. "Do you know what would be the cheapest way to make our lockers burglarproof?"

"The cheapest, no; the best, yes." He chuckled again and added, "I come over to your club this afternoon and give you my honest opinion."

"I'll also need you to make us a key to our utility closet. The door's locked, and the key to that disappeared when our attendant died. Can you do that, or do you have to break down the door?"

"I see when I get there." He smiled and promised to be there after lunch.

Eight

When Gabe returned to the Racquet Club a little before noon, news of Danny's death had already circulated among the members who were there. And while a few of them expressed regret and shock, it didn't stop any of them from playing tennis. There were ladies' doubles on three of the courts; Phil Neer was giving a lesson to Jan Wexler on Court Number 6; and Rick Reeves was down on the Terrace Court getting ready to take his daily shellacking from Mike Flanagan, who had just made his entrance through the gate with an armful of rackets.

As he dropped into a chair on the terrace and watched Rick starting to warm up with Flanagan, Gabe was reminded that he still hadn't had that man-to-man talk with the boy. But with everything else that had been going on in the past twenty-four hours, Gabe decided he'd had a fairly legitimate excuse for procrastinating.

Since the warm sun felt good on his face, Gabe remained seated for a while, staring down at the tennis, not really paying attention, but just letting his mind wander freely in an effort to achieve some relaxation. He was just now beginning to feel a release from the tensions of the morning.

Watching Rick and Flanagan scrambling around so energetically on the court down below, Gabe tried to imagine himself back again in their time and space, when the only thing in life that really mattered was how well you could hit a tennis ball over the net. It's a wonderful feeling, he reflected, to have so little on your mind. But now that he thought about it, he didn't remember it being such a wonderful feeling then. There was pressure in those days, too. Just a different kind. Parent pressure. School pressure. Pressure to get laid and out of the virgin class. Pressure to win a tennis tournament. So when you get right down to the nitty-gritty—there is no time when you're completely free of worries, he decided, until you're dead. Dead like Danny.

That train of thought blasted his tranquility, and suddenly he was back in the present. Opening his eyes to the glare of the sun, he realized he'd dozed off for a minute or so. He blinked a couple of times to get his pupils adjusted to the light, remembered he still had a club to manage, and rose quickly out of his chair, heading for his office.

"The switchboard's really humming," said Jenny as Gabe stopped off in her office on the way to his own. "Everybody's calling about Danny. They want to know if there's going to be a funeral, and where."

"I'm surprised they're so interested," commented Gabe.

"I am, too."

"Tell them we won't know anything about a funeral until after the autopsy and the coroner makes his report. He won't release the body until then."

Gabe had just finished going through the mail and was lighting his twelfth cigarette of the day when Tony knocked on his door and came in without waiting for permission to enter. Having known Gabe since he was a child, the swarthy-looking little Filipino saw no reason why he should stand on ceremony with him now, just because he was the club's manager.

"I brought my nephew," said Tony, beckoning to someone outside the door. "Manuel, come meet Mr. Gabe."

"Yes, Uncle," said Manuel, entering rather diffidently.

Manuel, in a natty-looking navy-blue jacket

and white duck trousers, could have been Tony's twin, except he was much younger and was without the grey hair around his temples.

"That was fast." Gabe grinned at Tony. "What'd you do—knock Danny off so your nephew could get the job?"

Tony was shocked. "Oh, no, Mr. Gabe, you know better than that. Danny and I good friends."

"Just kidding, Tony." Turning to Manuel, Gabe looked him over, from his white-kid shoes to the top of his slicked-down black hair. "Well, Manuel, you think you can handle the job?"

"He handle it fine," Tony answered for him. "I show him the ropes."

"I'm not sure what your salary will be," said Gabe. "I'll have to check with the president."

"I already know," said Tony. "Seven hundred fifty bucks a month and free meals. That's what Danny got."

"If that's what Danny got, so shall your nephew."

"Plus tips," added Tony, grinning.

"Of course, plus tips," agreed Gabe. "Okay, take him upstairs and put him to work. I'm sure the guys are already complaining because there's no one upstairs to shine their shoes."

"Not everybody," said Tony, with an impish grin. "Just Dr. Reeves!"

As he had promised, Max Weber showed up

just after the lunch rush, carrying a tool case that contained his lock-jimmying equipment.

Gabe took him immediately up to the locker room, where Mike Flanagan, Rick Reeves, and several businessmen who played tennis during their lunch breaks were showering and getting back into their street clothes.

"This is the closet we can't get into," explained Gabe, pointing to the locked door by the telephone.

"No problem," said Weber.

He took a long, thin, pointed instrument that resembled a dentist's pick from his equipment case and inserted it into the key slot in the doorknob. After a couple of dexterous twists of its handle, he was able to turn the knob and yank the door open.

"*Voila!*" he exclaimed proudly to Gabe.

"That's all there is to it?" asked Gabe, impressed.

"If you know vot you are doing," replied Weber.

Gabe took a quick glance at the interior of the closet to ascertain if there was room in it for the killer to have waited there with Danny's body when Gabe returned to the locker room the previous evening. He decided that there was, because although the laundry sink took up most of the space, it didn't go all the way over to the wall on one side. There was an open area about twelve inches by two feet between the right-hand perimeter of the sink and the wall. A broom and a mop were occupying that space now, but a thin man could easily have squeezed in there and held the corpse feetfirst in the sink until the danger had passed. Then all he had to do was wait for Gabe to leave, take down the clothesline from the porch, and string Danny's body up on the gravity bar, using the small wooden stool from the sink closet to simulate a suicide.

While these thoughts were flashing through Gabe's mind, Mike Flanagan came running out of the shower area with Rick Reeves behind him playfully snapping a towel at his ankles.

As the two approached Gabe and Weber, they were laughing and kidding each other, the way good friends will and without a trace of the animosity that was so noticeable between them on the court.

Flanagan continued up the aisle to his locker, but Rick stopped next to where Gabe was standing with Weber and glanced in at the sink closet curiously.

"Hey, man, what's all this about?" he asked, looking from the closet back to Gabe and the locksmith.

"I suppose you heard about Danny, didn't you?" asked Gabe.

"Yeah, why'd he do such a stupid thing?"

"No one knows!"

"Why the locksmith?" asked Rick.

"Danny's keys were missing when we found his body, which makes me suspect it may have been foul play."

"Maybe he just took them home with him and left them in his apartment," suggested Rick.

"I don't think Danny ever got home," said Gabe.

"Oh?" Rick seemed thoughtful. "What makes you think that?"

"Just a hunch."

"Hunches are bullshit," he said. "He could have gone home and then come back."

"But without his keys, he couldn't have got back in," pointed out Gabe. "Ever think of that?"

"Just trying to help," said Rick snapping his towel at the new attendant as he walked by with an armful of wet tennis clothes. Startled, Manuel jumped and dropped the clothes.

"Cut it, Rick," said Gabe in a commanding tone. "The kid's new here. Don't heckle him!"

"Just having a little fun," said Rick, disappearing down the aisle to his locker.

"Kids!" exclaimed Weber, with a smile. "They think they own the world."

"Yeah. Now what about that door?" asked Gabe, pointing to the utility closet. "Can you make us some keys for this?"

"I suggest a whole new lock," said Weber. "It's easier than making a key for this, and safer since you don't know who wound up with the dead boy's keys."

"Fine. Anything you say," replied Gabe, taking Weber by the arm and leading him over to an empty locker. "Now this is what I really want to talk with you about. Someone's been breaking into the lockers even though the attendant had the only passkey on his person at all times."

"I see," said Weber nodding, as he examined the locking mechanism on the metal door. "These locks are the old type. They're as good as nothing. You don't even need a passkey, just a little pick like I opened the closet door with, and bingo! You got it open."

He demonstrated with the pick he'd just used. "You just need a little knowledge of how the tumblers work."

"Well, is there something better?"

"Yes. I could take these out and replace them with combination locks. With no keys, there is no passkey floating around. Each member knows his own combination, and don't keep a master list. Each member's responsible for his own."

"Sounds like a big job. How much will it cost?"

"Around ten bucks apiece, plus time and labor. How many lockers have you got here?"

"About a hundred and fifty," interjected Gabe. "Maybe a hundred and sixty, counting guest lockers."

Weber pulled a mini-computer from his pocket and began calculating. "You're looking at sixteen hundred dollars just for the locks . . . plus tax," he finally said. "I can't estimate the labor yet."

"Sounds fine," said Gabe, "but I'll have to get an okay from our president first. How long will it take to get the locks?"

"I don't carry that many in stock. I'll have to order them. It will take three days—maybe a week."

"Put a rush on it if you can. And I'll get back to you with the go-ahead later this afternoon."

Before leaving, Weber handed Gabe a bill for the new lock and two keys. Gabe pocketed one and handed the other to the new locker room attendant, explaining what the utility closet was used for and to keep it locked at all times.

When Jock Kornfeld returned to the club for his four o'clock doubles match with a city councilman and two stockbrokers, Gabe nailed him in the lobby and pulled him into his office. "I got the dope on the locks," he said, explaining what Weber had recommended and giving him an estimate of the cost.

"Sounds like something we can live with," said Kornfeld. He started to leave then turned back. "By the way, I spoke with Danny's parents. It's quite a blow to them, but they seem to be holding up."

"When you talk to them again," said Gabe,

"would you mind asking them to keep an eye out for Danny's keys when they go through his things at his apartment?"

"Why do you want to bother them with that?" asked Kornfeld.

"If the keys are there," explained Gabe, "it means he could have gone home or been on his way there when I came to the club to find him. In that case, he could have killed himself, if he could have got back into the club without his keys, which is doubtful. But if his keys aren't there, there's a good chance that the locker room thief took them after he killed him. That would explain why they're missing."

"Well, I don't think this is any time to bother the Whites with mystery solving," said Kornfeld. He frowned, started to leave, and turned back a second time. "Do me a favor, champ. Stick to what you know best—tennis. Stop playing detective!"

Nine

Thinking that perhaps Kim Randall was right, that he did have an overactive imagination, Gabe decided to take Jock's advice and forget about being a sleuth and have some fun. Maybe he could persuade Jenny to go out to dinner with him. But when he broached the subject around six o'clock, she disappointed him.

"Gosh, Gabe, I'd like to, but you'll have to give me a rain check," she replied, looking truly disappointed. "Tonight, we're having a family reunion—a lot of people from the Islands are in town—and I can't get out of it."

Since there was no one else Gabe cared to spend the evening with in his current state of frustration, he decided not to go at all. Instead, he grabbed a sandwich and a bottle of beer on the terrace before the kitchen closed and ate by himself while watching the last of the Four

O'Clock Hackers go through the motions of playing men's doubles on the Number One Court.

Between the beer and the hypnotic effect of watching the tiny white tennis ball flying back and forth across the net, Gabe felt himself becoming drowsy. He dozed off without intending to, but his eyes had only been closed a few seconds when he was snapped back into consciousness by the sound of loud shouts emanating from the men's cardroom at the foot of the stairs.

Arguments in the men's cardroom were not a rarity—in fact, they happened almost daily and usually weren't anything to get alarmed about. Just a few harmless invectives hurled back and forth across the green felt by short-tempered sore losers. But this argument sounded particularly virulent and seemed to call for some outside interference before blood was actually spilled.

Taking the stairs two at a time, Gabe arrived at the open door to the cardroom in a matter of seconds, but stopped short of actually going in.

The card game had evidently broken up, for the room was empty except for the two shouters, whom Gabe immediately recognized.

One was Herb Gross, the white-haired stockbroker who had the soul of a Las Vegas croupier, a reputation for grand larceny on the tennis court when it came to making close calls, and who hadn't missed an afternoon of gin in ten years except when he was having a prostate operation; the other belligerent was Marty Engels, the burly toy manufacturer whose firm was in Chapter Eleven, according to Jock Kornfeld, and whose totally bald head was concealed by a toupee so abundantly filled with wavy auburn hair that it immediately announced to the world that it was a product of Max Factor's.

As Gabe stood in the doorway unnoticed, Herb Gross was raising his voice another notch. "Look, Marty, I don't want any more of your fucking IOUs. If you can't settle up with cash at the end of the game, we don't want you to play anymore."

"For Christ's sake, Herb, don't you trust me?" Engels shouted back. "I'm good for it. I only owe the guys twelve hundred."

"Pay up, then we'll trust you," said Gross. "You god damned deadbeat."

"Fuck you, Herb!" Engels literally spat the words out. Simultaneously he took a swing at Gross, who was the smaller, more slightly built of the two, and landed a blow on his chin. This sent Gross reeling backwards against the card table, nearly knocking it over, but spilling a couple of drinks and ashtrays onto the floor.

As Engels started to hurl himself on top of Gross, Gabe rushed between them and pulled the two apart like a boxing referee. "Cut it out, you two. That's no way to act."

"You butt out!" Scowling, Engels put two hands on Gabe's chest and tried to push him away. As he did, his toupee was knocked askew and slid down over his eyes, temporarily blinding him. This gave Gross a chance to scramble to his feet. "Pig!" he shouted, rubbing his jaw.

"Well, next time don't call me a deadbeat," Engels muttered angrily as he straightened his toupee.

"There won't be a next time. This is a matter for the board. You can get your ass kicked out of the club for this."

"We'll see," said Engels, yanking his plaid jacket from the back of his chair and storming out with it under his arm. "We'll see."

"What a madman!" exclaimed Gabe. He watched him go, to make sure that he did, then turned back to Gross, who had a trickle of blood running down his chin from the corner of his mouth. "You all right, Herb?"

"Yeah, the momser didn't hurt me. He just caught me by surprise."

"You sure? You seem to have a little blood on your chin," Gabe informed him. "Better go wipe it off."

"I have?" Gross touched the bloodied spot with his forefinger, examined it, and headed for the men's room. "Chrissakes, now I know I'm going to get that bum kicked out."

While Gross was cleaning off his face, Gabe picked up the spilled glasses from the carpet and set them back on the card table, along with the deck of cards, the ashtrays, and the scorepads that had fallen during the fray. As he kicked up one of the scorepads, he noticed that Engels owed the others in the game about seven hundred dollars each from today's game only.

Not being a cardplayer, he never realized before just how much money was being won and lost in the club cardroom every afternoon. "If gambling's illegal in Beverly Hills, you'd never know it by the goings on here," he thought.

"Sorry about this," apologized Gross, as he returned from the men's room looking cleaner and more composed, and picked up his hat. "See you tomorrow."

After the foursome that he had been watching earlier had finished their match and had dressed and were on their way home, Gabe locked up the place and gratefully retired to his own apartment, where he hoped to spend a quiet night, reading and watching TV.

It turned out to be an extremely quiet night—quiet and creepy—with no one around to keep him company except possibly the ghost of Danny White.

Every time the cavernous old Spanish building creaked, Gabe jumped out of his chair and looked nervously around in back of him, thinking it might be someone up to no good.

Before turning in, he switched on the television news to check for something about Danny. He figured that if the coroner's verdict was murder, Danny's demise would probably make the headlines, but if it was simple suicide, there'd be nothing.

There was no mention of it, so Gabe turned off the set and went to bed. It had been a long day.

He slept fitfully, impatient for the morning sunlight to arrive. When he did sleep, it was not very restful, for he had to suffer through reruns of the bad dreams he usually had when he was worried and over stimulated: either he was in a pit full of rattlesnakes, or the jet liner he was on was crashing into the Brazilian jungle.

When finally the sun did peek in through the blinds, it was only six o'clock. For obvious reasons, he decided to skip the exercise porch this morning and go out and buy a newspaper instead at Carl's Market around the corner from the club.

Standing at the newspaper dispenser in the empty parking lot at Carl's, Gabe scanned the Metro Section of the *L.A. Times* for any news of Danny's suicide. There was no news story, but he did get a mention in the vital statistics section. "Funeral arrangements pending."

With a shrug, Gabe stashed the newspaper in his saddlebag, then went inside the market and bought some doughnuts and a container of coffee, which he brought back to the club and ate on the terrace while reading the *Times*. He read everything twice, including the business section, before it was time to open the club for the Early Birds.

While he was unlocking the front door at eight o'clock sharp, he heard the phone ringing. Sprinting wildly into the office, and partially maiming his thigh on a sharp corner of Jenny's desk in the process, he dropped into her chair and grabbed the receiver. It was Detective Trump.

"Just thought you'd like to know that the coroner determined there was no foul play," she informed him in a cheerful voice. "There were no extraordinary marks on the body—especially in the neck area—that would lead him to any other conclusion."

"And what about your investigation?" asked Gabe. "You willing to accept the coroner's report?"

"There doesn't seem to be any reason for us to pursue the matter," she said. "Our print man turned up nothing. The uprights on the gravity bar—and the bar itself—were just a melange of overlapping indistinguishable prints. And he could identify no prints but Danny's on the stool he jumped off. So that just about says it all."

"Seems to," said Gabe, weary of fighting city hall any longer.

"But don't let this discourage your own efforts," said Trump. "If you happen to come up with anything suspicious, give us a buzz. We'll be happy to give it a look-listen."

"Yeah, I'll do that." Gabe banged down the receiver angrily. "You stupid assholes!" he muttered, suddenly picking up a pencil and hurling it across the office. "How'd you ever manage to get the jails so overcrowded? Must have been luck."

Around noon, Jock Kornfeld called to say that the funeral services were set for Saturday at one P.M. at Pierce Brothers, which was a few blocks away from the club on Maple Drive, and that Gabe should post a notice on the bulletin board, informing the membership. "And if you have time after that, champ, I'd like you to give me another lesson on my backhand."

At the funeral service, which was simple and brief, and delivered by Rabbi Schulman, a member in good standing of the Four O'Clock Hackers. Gabe, in a dark blue suit, and Jenny, wearing a black sheath dress, sat next to each other in the last row of pews.

The coffin was closed and bedecked with an expensive blanket of flowers sent and paid for by the combined membership of the Racquet

Club (the pro-rata share would appear on each member's bill at the end of the month). It was a nice send-off for a boy who had never received that much attention when he was alive.

As he was accustomed to doing at funerals, Gabe paid little heed to the meaning of the words flowing from the podium. As the rabbi droned on, he purposely allowed his mind to wander as far away from death as it could possibly get.

There was a healthy turnout of Racquet Club members, plus a number of Danny's grieving relatives. The Whites, a handsome, silver-haired couple, sat in a separate alcove near the podium, their tear-stained eyes hidden behind dark glasses.

To keep the tears from running down his own cheeks when the organ started to play Danny's favorite song, "Danny Boy," Gabe tried reading the faces of the other Racquet Club members for possible signs of guilt. But he learned nothing from them. Some were socializing with the person next to them; some were sniffling into handkerchiefs; and the rest just sat there impassively, a study in controlled emotions, waiting for the service to end.

After the service, everyone filed past the casket and out a side door into the sunlit parking lot. Gabe, with Jenny on his arm, stood off to the side, looking solemn and feeling glum. He was waiting to pay his respects to the Whites, who were the last to emerge from the chapel.

Since a large crowd had already gathered around the Whites, Gabe and Jenny hung back to wait for the gathering to thin out. As they stood there, Gabe heard a slight toot of a car horn behind him. Turning, he realized the back of his legs were being nudged by the bumper of a fire-engine red Ferrari. Rick Reeves was at the wheel, grinning, and beside him was Donna McCleary, a spaced-out looking blond, with formidable breasts, who was his current girlfriend, and who most of the older male members of the club would have risked AIDS for the thrill of laying.

As Gabe and Jenny jumped out of the way to allow the Ferrari to pass, Rick unrolled the window on his side and exclaimed loudly, "What do you think of this baby?"

"I think Flanagan's a pretty nice friend to let you use it," commented Gabe, not trying to make a joke.

Rick looked indignant. "Hey, man, this isn't Flanagan's. I'm thinking of buying this. The dealer's letting me try it out this week."

"Isn't it super?" exclaimed Donna. "I just love it."

"Ba—ah—yyyeee!" yelled Rick, throwing the Ferrari in gear and stepping on the accelerator hard. With a roar that was obscenely loud for a funeral, the car shot out of the parking lot, just missing a couple of mourners.

Aware that the cluster of sympathizers around the Whites had thinned out by now, Gabe took Jenny by the elbow and said, "Come on, doll, let's get this over with."

Paying a condolence call on the bereaved was something Gabe didn't look forward to with any relish, for he never seemed able to come up with anything but the standard cliches. However, he didn't expect to be attacked for starting to say, "I'm sorry, Elizabeth, Ed. If there's anything I ca—"

"Yes, there is, you third-rate hack!" screamed Ed, his normally placid and friendly face contorted and red with anger. "You can get the hell out of my sight!"

Elizabeth White flared up just as explosively. "You killed our son, and now you're saying you're sorry." She spat out the words. "Hypocrite!"

Unprepared for this onslaught, Gabe stood paralyzed and speechless as the Whites turned their backs on him.

"Now wait a minute," Gabe said, walking around in front of the Whites to face them again. "I know you're upset . . . you have every right to be . . . but certainly you can't blame Danny's death on me." He knew he probably sounded more belligerent than he should have, but he was determined to defend himself.

As his words tumbled out, Elizabeth White screamed, "Leave us alone!" She turned her back on him again and started to weep into a handkerchief.

"You heard her," said White, shaking a clenched fist under Gabe's nose. "Now get out of our sight before I let you have this."

His fist was practically touching Gabe's chin.

Pushing it away, Gabe took a step backward and said, in a controlled voice, "I'm not going away, Ed, until we get this misunderstanding straightened out."

"There's no misunderstanding, you son of a bitch. You drove him to suicide. You accused him of stealing, and he couldn't deal with it."

"I did no such thing," insisted Gabe. "Who told you that?"

"Danny did."

"When'd you talk to him if he didn't come home?"

"We talked to him over the phone around six-thirty, when he was still at the club. We wanted to tell him we were going out of town for a day. And that's when he told us."

"I don't believe he told you I accused him. What exactly did he say?"

"Well, he didn't put it in so many words. But we could tell he was worried that you were really suspicious of him."

"That's ridiculous. He must have just misinterpreted something I said because of his—" he was hesitant to use the word "retarded" "—well, you know what I mean, condition."

"You mean, retarded. That what you're trying to say?"

"Well, yes, I guess I am."

"It's not bad enough that you killed him. Now you're insulting the memory of our son!" said Mrs. White in a quavering voice.

"I was trying to get his help," said Gabe. "I even offered him an extra ten bucks a week out of my own pocket if he'd keep an eye out for the thief."

"Bullshit!" yelled White, doubling his fists again. "That was just a trick to get him to trust you. But underneath it all, you felt he was really the thief and that he'd crack under the guilt of it and confess. Well, he cracked all right. But not the way you wanted. He took his own life."

"I don't believe that he did that, either," said Gabe.

"You're going to dispute the police and coroner's reports?"

"There's a lot about the case they've overlooked, in my opinion."

"Your opinion isn't worth shit," he yelled.

"If you'd just listen a minute and stop twisting everything I say—"

"I'll stop after I get you fired and not before.

As soon as there's another board meeting, I'm going to go before it and see that they boot you out on your ass. Why, you no more deserve to be running this club than Klaus Barbie. Now get out of my sight."

"I'm going to stand here until you listen to me."

"You momser!" White suddenly leaped for Gabe's throat with both hands. Caught completely by surprise, Gabe fell over backwards with his assailant on top of him.

As the two rolled around together on the blacktop, with White trying to establish his hands more firmly on Gabe's throat, two of the mortuary ushers came running frantically over.

"Hey, what's going on here?" demanded the first one.

"Yes, for heaven's sakes!" said the other, in an effeminate voice.

Together they managed to pull White off Gabe's chest and to his feet. Meanwhile, Gabe struggled to his own feet, his face red with embarrassment.

"We're sorry about this, sir," the first usher apologized to White, brushing him off briskly with his hand.

"Hey, listen," said Gabe, "he started this. I was just—"

"Heathen!" yelled the second usher. "Don't you know this man just lost a loved one?"

As Gabe looked at them in disbelief, the two ushers managed to coax the Whites away from the scene of battle and into one of the black limousines waiting to take them to the cemetery.

"Creeps!" exclaimed Jenny. She turned back to Gabe and started to brush off the back of his suit. "Are you all right?"

"I'll survive." He took her hand, and the two of them started across the parking lot to her car. "I'm just a little disappointed in the human race."

"You think he meant that about trying to get you fired?" asked Jenny, her expression one of deep concern.

"I wouldn't doubt it," said Gabe.

"You think he can?"

Gabe shrugged. "I guess that depends on how good a job I've done so far. And so far, in less than a week, I've presided over two burglaries and one death."

"But you just said you didn't think it's suicide. And neither do I."

"But Danny's dead, nevertheless. And if I hadn't told him to snitch on the thief, the thief wouldn't have had a reason to silence him."

"But that's not your fault. You were trying to do your job."

"Let's hope the board agrees with you, Jen. In the meantime, I'm going to try to save my job myself—by catching the murderer. Maybe the board will give me points for that," he said as they reached Jenny's car, and he opened the front door for her.

Ten

"Hey, Jenny, you didn't happen to see Jed Horner at the funeral, did you?" asked Gabe.

They were back in their offices now, and he was calling to her through the connecting open door.

"No, I didn't. But I could have missed him in that crowd."

"Then try him at his office. I'd like to speak to him."

Jenny looked at him, surprised. "Don't tell me this job is driving you into analysis?"

"I couldn't afford it. I just have to get the doctor's professional opinion about something."

"Something to do with Danny?"

Gabe nodded.

"Gotcha," she said, plugging into the switchboard.

She was back to him in a couple of minutes with word that Dr. Horner had just finished with his last patient of the day and was on his way to the Racquet Club.

"That's even better," said Gabe. "Keep an eye out for him, will you?"

"Sure thing, Gabriel."

"Hey, what's with this Gabriel nonsense?"

"I like the sound of it better than Gabe. It's more dignified."

"Dignified!" exclaimed Gabe, kiddingly. "I was hoping our relationship was growing more intimate, not more formal."

She laughed. "I can be intimate with a man named Gabriel. Just you wait and see."

"How long do I have to wait?"

He was disappointed that she never got to answer.

"Is the man busy?" he heard Phil Neer asking Jenny through the opening in the glass. "I need to have a word with him."

"Can I tell him what it's about?"

"It's okay, Jenny," Gabe called to her through the door. "Send him in. He doesn't have to stand on ceremony with me."

Having just returned from Danny's funeral himself, the club pro was not in his usual warm-up clothes and Adidas. Instead, he was attired in a dark grey business suit that seemed several years out of style.

It was probably something he only dragged out of his closet for funerals, thought Gabe, unable to remember the last time he'd seen the tennis pro in street clothes.

Looking very conspiratorial, Neer closed the connecting door to Jenny's office before sitting down.

"Glad I caught you in," he said. "You've got to help me, son."

"If I can. What's the problem?"

Leaning closer to Gabe so that he could keep his voice low and confidential, Neer said, "I don't know if you're aware of this or not, but there's a group here at the club that's trying to give me the old heave-ho."

"Really?" Gabe was surprised that anyone would want to get rid of the man responsible for starting the club. "Why? You're still up to the job, aren't you?"

"Of course I am. I've got more energy than ever. You should see all the vitamins I take every morning. And without getting personal, I have to tell you that this old codger's still pretty good in the sack, too." He winked at Gabe, then turned serious again. "But there's a guy they want to bring in. He used to be the pro at La Casa . . . Hugh Seward. He got to be friends with a lot of our group when they used to go down there on weekends. But he got booted out when La Casa hired Pancho Miranda. So now Hugh is playing on their sympathies and telling them what a much better teacher he is than I am, and that I'm too old for the job. He's even told them I stopped having our weekly Tennis Burgers because I'm lazy. Which you know isn't the reason at all. I stopped because none of the guys want to play in a mixed-doubles tournament with their wives."

"I'm surprised they'd buy that bullshit," said Gabe. "It's absolutely self-serving. Who exactly is in this group that wants you out?"

"Your president, the almighty Jock Kornfeld," he said with a note of derision. He glanced nervously around the room as if he half expected to see Kornfeld spying on him from behind a filing cabinet. "He's the ringleader. The s.o.b. I could wring his neck!"

"Why does he care who's pro?" asked Gabe. "He doesn't take lessons. He comes to me for free advice. And his wife doesn't play at all. She's half-bombed most of the time."

"Well, I hope I'm not telling secrets out of school," said Neer, "but I think it's that Wexler dame who's got his ear—among other parts of his anatomy." He chuckled quietly, enjoying his role of club gossipmonger, which, Gabe was tempted to tell him, could be another reason they wanted him out. He always was spreading rumors about someone.

"You mean, the new member?" asked Gabe.

"Yep. There's a little hanky-panky going on between them. I know because the other day I caught her on the phone with him down on my court after I'd come back from going to the john. Sometimes I have to take a piss now, right in the middle of a lesson. I've got a prostate problem, I think."

"Sorry to hear it."

"It's life. It'll happen to you someday."

"Sorry to hear that, too."

"Anyway," shrugged Neer, "it sounded to me like they were planning an afternoon quickie."

"What's this got to do with your being pro or not?" asked Gabe, annoyed that Phil couldn't stick to the point.

"Well, she took lessons from Hugh when she used to go down to La Casa with her husband. She might have a thing with him too. She's a vixen, that one. Wouldn't mind giving her a boff myself. But she's treacherous as hell. She tells me how much I've improved her game and then sneaks behind my back to get her boyfriend to boot me out."

"What would you like me to do?" asked Gabe.

"I want you to go before the board and tell them how good I am for the club."

"I don't know if I'm in any better position around here now than you are."

"What are you talking about, kid? You're doing a great job."

"Danny White's father doesn't think so. He's

saying I'm responsible for Danny's suicide. He's going to the board to try to get me out."

"No kidding?"

Gabe nodded. "He just told me that at the funeral."

"So that's what that donnybrook was all about."

Gabe nodded glumly.

"I'm sure he didn't mean it. He was just letting off steam. Between you and I, he should be glad to get rid of that kid."

"Oh, come on," said Gabe, "he was a sweet boy. You shouldn't say that."

"We don't have to bull each other. Any shrink'll tell you Danny was going to give his old man plenty of trouble before he was through."

"Tell that to a distraught father."

"Don't worry," said Neer. "If you can prevent them from giving me the old heave-ho, I'll stick up for you."

"That's like one horse thief being a character witness for another."

Neer smiled without conviction. "You can kid about it," he said. "You're still in your forties. But if I lose this pro job, no other club is going to hire an old duck like me. If that happens, I may as well get a rope and go join Danny."

"I wouldn't panic if I were you," said Gabe. "You've got a lot of friends here who I'm sure are loyal to you."

"Friends!" Neer contorted his features into a contemptuous expression. "You know what you can do with them, don't you? You can shove them. And the first one on my shit list is Kornfeld. Why, when I owned this club, I helped him get in."

"Now just calm yourself," Gabe urged him.

"No I won't," said Neer, raising his voice despite himself. "That hypocritical bastard. If he dumps on me, I've got a good mind to go to his father-in-law and tell him what Jock's doing to his daughter. Jock would be out of Giverny Cosmetics quicker than a hen lays eggs."

"I'll try to help you," promised Gabe.

"I'm counting on it." Neer stood up and shook Gabe's hand. "Thanks, old buddy. And one last favor. Keep everything I told you about Jan Wexler under your hat. I wouldn't want it to get around that I'm a gossipmonger."

"Of course not." Gabe grinned at him as he left through his private exit.

As soon as Neer was gone, Gabe jumped up and opened the connecting door to Jenny's office. "How'd I get so lucky as to land this job?" he grumbled. "There's more intrigue here than there is in the movie business."

"What's his problem?" asked Jenny.

Gabe told her.

"Poor thing," sympathized Jenny. "He sounds positively desperate."

"He is. I think he'd kill in order to keep this job."

"By the way," said Jenny, "Dr. Horner came in when you were locked up in there. I didn't want to interrupt so I just told him you wanted to see him. I think he's upstairs right now changing clothes."

"Good. Maybe I can catch him before he goes out on the court."

On his way to the locker room, Gabe tried to look the other way when he passed the exercise porch, or the "hanging porch," as it was getting to be known since the tragedy.

"Oh, Gabe. I'm over here." It was Dr. Horner's cheerful voice coming from the exercise porch. Glancing in that direction, Gabe noticed Horner hanging upside down by his knees from the gravity bar.

Approaching that spot reluctantly, Gabe said, "Could I get a professional opinion from you without it costing an arm and a leg?"

"If it doesn't take too long." He continued to dangle by his knees with his shiny bald head nearly touching the green Astro-turf that covered the floor of the porch.

Horner was in his seventies, with sallow, liver-spotted skin, a white handlebar mustache that matched the fringe of white hair around his scalp, and a muscular but spindly body that, in the very skimpy swim trunks he was wearing, resembled the late Mahatma Gandhi's.

"Excuse the position," he apologized, his face getting redder by the minute, "but I find this is good therapy for my sacroiliac."

"I guess you know about Danny White," said Gabe.

"Oh, yes, I attended the funeral. I even heard that ruckus between you and Ed White."

"What did you think of that?"

"Unexpected shock does strange things to people's minds."

"Aside from that?" asked Gabe.

"Are you talking about whether I believe he committed suicide?"

"Yes. You see, I don't believe he did."

"What makes you say that?" He suddenly grabbed the two uprights and pulled himself to a sitting position on the bar.

As quickly as possible, Gabe filled him in on the entire story from his own biased point of view.

Horner shrugged. "I'm no policeman," he said, "but it seems to me that's going to be a tough thing to prove. Especially if you haven't the faintest idea who the killer could be."

"Well, it would help," said Gabe, "if you could tell me whether you think a boy with a retarded mentality like Danny's is likely to commit suicide. From what I remember in college psychology, retarded mentalities are among those least likely to knock themselves off."

"You're quite right," agreed Horner. "Retarded mentalities can be driven to kill someone else under certain circumstances. But a low IQ mentality generally isn't high strung enough to feel the guilt necessary to commit suicide. And that's particularly true in a case like this where he'd have to misconstrue your words to a point where he believed you were actually accusing him."

"I'm relieved to hear you say that."

"In fact," Horner went on, "when I first heard about it, I said to my wife that I didn't think Danny was the suicide type. And now that I know what you just told me, I'm convinced of it."

"Does that mean I have an ally?" asked Gabe.

"An ally but no clues." Horner smiled sympathetically. "Until you have something more than conjecture to go on, no one's going to believe *me* or you."

"I'm just surprised the police can't see these obvious things," said Gabe. "A good detective ought to have a knowledge of elementary psychology."

"Pure laziness," declared Horner. "Without a prime suspect, the easiest thing is to blame every unnatural death on suicide. You've seen it all the time in Hollywood's long list of mysterious deaths—Monroe, Natalie Wood. At least that's been my experience whenever I've been called in to give expert testimony."

"But if I decide I want your help, will you repeat what you just told me to the police?"

"On one condition."

"What?"

"If you'll help me with my serve." He grinned. "I'm serving too many double faults lately."

"You've got it," said Gabe. "Just tell me when."

By closing time Saturday night, Gabe was ready to get away from the club for a few hours. After the week he'd just been through, he needed a couple of strong drinks, a rare steak, and a girl with a sympathetic ear to listen to his complaints.

Fortunately, Jenny was available and willing to cooperate. She even supplied the car for the ride to the Moonshadows, a popular not-too-expensive steak and lobster place just south of the Malibu Colony on Pacific Coast Highway.

"I hope you're not mad that I didn't want to ride to the beach on the back of your motorcycle," apologized Jenny as the two of them were driving out Sunset Boulevard with Gabe behind the wheel. "I just didn't feel like getting my hair blown to bits."

"Why should I mind?" asked Gabe. "Your car's comfortable, and you're paying for the gas."

Jenny laughed. "Oh, some men are so macho about their motorcycles. They're in love with them. They think it turns a girl on to have to hug them tight around the waist while they're zipping through traffic at sixty miles an hour and scaring them to death."

"Not me," said Gabe. "My motorcycle's just something to get around on until my finances are in better shape. Ex-wives don't get bought off cheap, even in this era of women's independence."

At the Moonshadows, where Gabe had had the foresight to make a reservation, for it was Saturday night and very crowded, they were shown to a booth for two, with a commanding view of the moonlit ocean breaking on the rocks below.

"I feel better now that I talked to Horner," said Gabe, after they were seated and were sipping their Mai Tais. "At least I know I'm not a complete fool for thinking Danny didn't commit suicide."

"But as Dr. Horner said, how's that going to help?" asked Jenny.

"Well, at least I can be on the alert. If the killer

is also the thief, he might strike again. Isn't a criminal supposed to return to the scene of the crime?"

"So they say," sighed Jenny. "But this one's probably too cagey. He'll probably wait awhile before he starts going into lockers again."

"You're right. He can't be a run-of-the-mill klepto if he's a member of the Beverly-West Racquet Club. He has to be a brain and an outstanding citizen to get accepted." He laughed quietly. "He'll probably keep a low profile until the clues get cold."

"What clues are there?"

"I made a list while I was waiting for you to get dressed." Gabe pulled a piece of crumpled notepaper from his pocket. "One: the phone call to tell me who the thief was. Two: the missing keys. Three: what Jed Horner told me. Four: the time discrepancy."

"What's that?" asked Jenny.

"According to the coroner he'd been dead about twelve hours when I discovered him. And he certainly wasn't hanging on the exercise porch when I left the club that night to go to your house to dinner. So where was he then?" He referred to the list again. "Five: why would he choose the club as a place to kill himself? Why wouldn't he do it at home, so he wouldn't have to hide out and wait for me to leave? And six—"

"I hate to throw a monkey wrench in your theory," Jenny interrupted him, "but why would a killer choose a public place like the Racquet Club to do his dirty work, either?"

"I don't think he *chose* it," Gabe pointed out. "He just happened to have been around when it became necessary to quiet Danny forever."

"Yes, that makes sense."

"And it goes with Clue Number Six," added Gabe. "The utility closet. I looked at it the day the locksmith opened it up. It's the perfect place to stash a body, if you're suddenly caught with it in the locker room. Provided you had a key. And Danny had that right on his belt." He put the paper back in his pocket and looked in Jenny's eyes. "Anything I've forgotten?"

"No, but—"

"But we still have nothing tangible and a maniac who is probably a member in good standing of the Beverly-West Racquet Club's still running around loose," added Gabe dryly.

"That's the other thing that frightens me," said Jenny. "You having to sleep there."

"So far he doesn't have a motive for killing me," Gabe reassured her.

"How can you be sure? Suppose he hears that you're not accepting the suicide verdict, and you're pressing for an investigation. Wouldn't he want to get rid of you, too?"

"Perhaps. But I don't think it's in the cards

right at the moment." Putting his hand on hers, he glanced out the window at the silver path of moonlight on the Pacific. "Now let's enjoy the view and stop thinking about death for awhile."

Eleven

"How was your day off?" Gabe asked as he strode into the office after breakfast Monday morning and found Jenny already at her desk, looking bright and perky.

"Quiet. I just hung around the house and helped mother with her flower arrangements."

"It was quiet here, too," Gabe told her. "No deaths, no robberies, just tennis. And not very good tennis at that. The husbands were playing mixed with their wives. Sunday, you know. It's either mixed doubles or 'Hit and Giggle.'"

"Hit and Giggle?" Jenny looked puzzled. "I don't believe I know that term."

"Women's doubles," explained Gabe. "The woman hits the ball, misses the shot, and giggles."

"Chauvinist," grinned Jenny.

"I know, but that's how it looks to the top men players."

"What a world!" exclaimed Jenny. "Once a week the husbands decide to give their wives a thrill by playing tennis with them. The rest of the week they hardly know they're alive. Is that what marriage is all about?" She laughed.

"It is at the Racquet Club," said Gabe. "Nevertheless, I must confess I missed seeing your pretty face."

"I could say the same, except I was asleep. I guess the excitement of the week finally caught up with me." She sighed. "But I did have a nice time with you Saturday night. Did I thank you for it? Even if I did put on three pounds from all those Mai Tais and two helpings of cheesecake."

"On you, cheesecake looks good." He gave her an affectionate hug and asked, "Anything important come in the mail?"

"It just got here. I haven't had a chance to look through it. Want to do it for me?" She handed him a small bundle of envelopes, which he carried to his own desk and riffled through. Most of it was junk mail and utility bills for the club, along with some of his own bills and Guild literature that the post office was now forwarding to his new address.

But there was one plain white envelope—the kind you buy at the post office already stamped—which was addressed to Gabe "personally" at the Racquet Club that he was curious about. It was typewritten, with no return address. That it came directly to the club interested Gabe since he hadn't yet bothered telling any of his friends that he had moved—and didn't plan to until he knew for sure if his job was secure.

Opening the envelope, he pulled out the piece of four-by-six notepaper and unfolded it. The typed message leaped out at him.

DON'T LET THE POLICE INTIMIDATE YOU.
DANNY WHITE DID NOT KILL HIMSELF.

SOMEONE WHO KNOWS

After reading it, Gabe let the paper drop to the desk. He didn't want to cover it with his own fingerprints and take the chance of obliterating whomever else's prints might be on the paper.

"Hey, Jen," he called to her excitedly. "Come in here. I think we've got our first real clue."

As Jenny studied the note, Gabe asked her what she made of it.

"It's creepy and I'm scared. Who do you think could have sent it?"

He shrugged. "If we knew that, we'd know a lot of things. But the possibilities are endless." Too nervous to sit, he jumped from his chair and started pacing the room. "The logical thing is, it was written by someone who witnessed the murder and for some strange reason is afraid to come forward and be identified. That in itself poses a number of interesting questions. Is he or she an accomplice to the killer or did he just *happen* to see it? If he was an accomplice, he's afraid of getting charged along with the actual killer, and if he just happened to witness it without having a hand in it, he could have other reasons for not wanting to be identified. The obvious one being that he's afraid of retribution by the killer." He stopped pacing and just stood in the center of the office for a moment, lost in thought. "Or if it's none of them, the sender could even be the killer deliberately calling attention to himself."

"Why would he want to do that?" asked Jenny.

"A psychiatrist would probably say because he feels guilty and wants to get caught. He craves publicity and wants to be in the spotlight and get all the attention, even as a murder suspect."

"You sound like an expert on anonymous notes," said Jenny.

"When you've written as many detective shows as I have, you'll discover that anonymous notes are one of the staples of mystery writing."

"Which one do you think it is?"

"I don't know. But I know who it isn't. It isn't the accomplice, for I doubt if the locker room thief worked with anybody else."

"How do you know that?"

"Just a wild guess. When he started out, he probably fell into his wicked ways fairly accidentally, in my opinion. Someone left the locker next to his open, with his wallet in it. The thief, noticing this and feeling pressed for cash, decided to help himself to what was in his neighbor's wallet while the man was either on the court or in the shower. Finding the wallet to be an unexpected gold mine, and not getting apprehended, he tried it a second time on someone else, and then a third. Pretty soon it was a habit, and he began to wait for people to forget to lock their lockers. Quite possibly he'd even borrowed Danny's passkey once when he was taking a shower and made an impression of it on a piece of soap."

"Sounds like you're an expert on locker room thieves, too," said Jenny.

"No, that I figured out last night when I was lying awake here wondering if the creaking noises I kept hearing outside my door were being made by mice, small earthquakes, or someone out to get me."

"I thought you weren't afraid for yourself," said Jenny.

"I wasn't until you convinced me I ought to be," said Gabe, not sure himself if he was kidding.

Jenny shrugged. "This *is* beginning to scare me. Why don't you take the note over to Judy Trump and dump it in her lap."

"I've been considering it, but I'm a little reluctant. She hasn't been much help in this case so far."

"Don't forget she didn't have anything tangible to go on before. But now you have a real piece of evidence that she can actually see and touch. I don't see why you want to withhold it."

"Simple," grinned Gabe. "Fear of rejection."

"Well, you'll just have to chance it," Jenny chided him. "You can't learn anything from this note. You don't have the setup. It'll take a fingerprint expert and someone to analyze the type. You have to turn it over to her. Otherwise you just have a slip of paper confirming what you already know, but which the police and the coroner refuse to take seriously."

"As usual you're right," admitted Gabe. "Get Trump on the phone and ask her if she wants to make it her place or mine."

Detective Judy Trump was in a remarkably receptive mood when Gabe met with her in her spartanlike office in the basement of the Beverly Hills City Hall an hour and a half later.

The anonymous note, which Gabe had been careful to preserve the integrity of by placing it in a manila folder with a pair of Jenny's eyebrow tweezers, lay between them on Trump's blond flattop desk, which reminded Gabe of a school teacher's desk—functional and ugly.

"Well, what do you think?" asked Gabe as Trump, her brow now deeply furrowed, studied the note with a practiced eye for nearly a minute before saying a word.

"Very interesting," she finally replied, nodding her head several times. "Very interesting."

"Then you agree with me that Danny White was murdered?"

She smiled at Gabe as if he were an idiot. "Not necessarily. It could have been written by a prankster or a crank. We get dozens of these notes whenever a sensational case hits the headlines. Usually they turn out to be nothing."

"But you do check them out?" persisted Gabe.

"Of course. And we'll check this little baby out, too. The wheels of justice never stop grinding here in the city of Beverly Hills. I'll send this right up to the fingerprint shop and see if they can get any decent prints off it. After that I'll turn it over to our typewriter expert."

"Just suppose you do find some fingerprints on it other than my own, what would you do then?" inquired Gabe.

"We'd check our files and see if they match anything we have here or on the 'wanted' lists."

"The chances are they wouldn't match anything you have here," pointed out Gabe. "Especially if it was sent by one of our members. We don't have any members with criminal records."

"How do you know one of the members sent

it?" she said, jumping on Gabe's statement as though he had let something out of the bag that might have incriminated himself.

Gabe shrugged. "If there hasn't been much publicity about it, who else would know?"

"Maybe someone in one of the neighboring apartments. Maybe they saw something peculiar the night of the murder."

"Ah ha, you do think it's murder," exclaimed Gabe jubilantly.

"I didn't say that," she said, with a deprecating smile. "I'm just not closing any avenues."

"I'm glad to hear that," said Gabe. "But speaking strictly as an amateur, I don't think it could be a neighbor. Where our exercise porch is situated on the clubhouse, together with all the shrubbery and trees around the club's perimeter, it's pretty secluded. The guy who did our landscaping did his planting with privacy in mind. I doubt if anybody can see the exercise porch from a neighboring building."

"I'm aware of that," said Trump. "I took a drive around the outside perimeter the other morning after I left you."

"Why'd you bother with that if you were so certain it was suicide?" asked Gabe.

"I never leave a stone unturned," said Trump, again exhibiting her genius for coining a fresh phrase. "A woman detective can't afford to make mistakes. If I do, they'll boot my tush right out of this job." With a cynical laugh, she flipped a lever down on the intercom before her and barked into it, "Oh, Heywood, you want to trot in here a minute? I got a job for you."

Heywood, a callow-looking blond, with cold blue eyes, wearing a policeman's uniform, appeared almost instantly.

Closing the manila envelope on the note, she handed the whole package to Heywood, with instructions to take it up to the lab and have it analyzed for prints and the kind of typewriter used. "And tell them to get back to me as soon as they can."

As Heywood departed, Trump stood up and shook Gabe's hand. "Thanks for thinking of us, Mr. Steele. If anything turns up, I'll get back to you."

"Does that mean if nothing turns up, we're at a dead end again?"

Her expression wasn't too encouraging. "Well, there aren't many ways you can find an anonymous note sender. If there aren't any prints, or if there are prints, there's nothing to check them against. And if the typewriter isn't an unusual one—and chances are it isn't—our hands are tied."

"But aren't there psychological implications?" asked Gabe. "Can't we put together a composite picture of the kind of person most likely to send an anonymous note and try to figure out why he wants to stay anonymous? Wouldn't that help you zero in on the person who might have sent it?"

"I can give you that in a nutshell," offered Trump. "If the sender isn't a crank or a joker, there's only two basic reasons why he wants to remain anonymous. A, he's afraid of the killer, or B, he was doing something wrong himself at the time of the crime. Ergo, if he were to testify, he'd have to admit a wrongdoing of his own, and obviously he doesn't want to do that."

"At the same time he's a good enough human being not to want a killer to go unapprehended," pointed out Gabe.

"Yeah, we'll give him a merit badge for that," said Trump dryly, "but we'll have to give him a couple of demerits for his lack of courage." She smiled and, walking him to the door, opened it. "Have a good afternoon," she added, "and don't serve too many double faults."

As he drove back to the club on his Honda, Gabe was a little uncertain as to what exactly he had accomplished by taking the note to Judy Trump. There was, of course, the slim chance that an expert would pick up an important clue from the note that so far wasn't obvious to him or Detective Trump. But in all probability, nothing would come of it; the note would wind up in a folder in the police department's files under the heading: "Cases, closed." After all, didn't the revolver that figured so importantly in catching Charlie Manson languish for a whole year in the L.A. Police Department's files after it was turned in before anyone recognized its importance?

Gabe's pessimism seemed to be justified by lunchtime, when he was called to the dining room phone by the maitre d' halfway through his corned beef sandwich.

"Steele, this is Detective Trump. Just thought you'd like to know we checked out the note and the results are negative. It's clean of prints and the typewriter used was your standard IBM Correcting Selectric III with ten-point 'Courier' type. The type ball is too new to have any blemishes on it that would distinguish its printing from any other of the same model. You're going to find this machine in every office in L.A. It's needle-in-a-haystack time, if you ask me."

"So what's the next move—nothing?" asked Gabe in a slightly sarcastic tone.

"You got it, Mr. Steele. We'll put this in the file and wait for something else to turn up. But I wouldn't want to hang that long," she concluded with a chuckle.

Meanwhile, poor Danny's rotting in his grave and his unhappy folks think I'm to blame, reflected Gabe glumly as he sat down at his table, where he found he had now so little appetite that he handed the rest of his sandwich to Dr.

Reeves, who was passing by in his daily quest for unwanted garnish.

"By the way, have you had that talk with my son yet?" asked Dr. Reeves, sitting down at Gabe's table without a word of thanks for the half of the sandwich he had just lucked into.

"No, I haven't," said Gabe. "I've been a mite too busy with all the excitement around here."

"Oh, Danny! Yeah, kind of a shocker," replied Reeves in a flat unemotional tone that belied his words. Then, changing gears, he quickly slid into a subject closer to his heart. "Well, now that all that's behind you, I'd appreciate it if you'd get around to my son pretty soon. The damn kid's wasting the best years of his life being a tennis bum."

Annoyed that Rick Reeves had suddenly become his responsibility, Gabe excused himself and wandered down the terrace steps to a grassy area between the clubhouse and the Number One Court. As he stood there, relieved to be away from the company of Dr. Reeves, he suddenly remembered he wanted to tell the new locker room attendant that he was doing a good job and to keep it up. Nothing like a little encouragement to get the best out of people, thought Gabe, trotting up the steps to the locker room.

He was about to go inside when some ineffable force caused him to change his mind and stroll out onto the exercise porch instead. Perhaps it was a hunch, or perhaps it was the ghost of Danny. But something drew him to the gravity bar and made him turn around and study the panorama of apartment buildings and condos circling the three sides of the club grounds visible to him.

Most of the buildings were either obscured by tall Jacaranda trees and shrubbery or the high canvas-covered fences of the tennis courts. But through an opening in a clump of trees at the south end of the club grounds, Gabe could see the outside balcony of an apartment that could conceivably belong to Kim Randall. He knew it was Randall's building, but through the small opening in the foliage, he couldn't tell what floor the balcony was on, nor did he know Randall's apartment number.

As he stood there, he wondered if Kim Randall was the one who had seen the skullduggery on the exercise porch and sent the note. Should it not be Kim's place, it could be the person who did live there. But that wouldn't explain his or her reluctance to come forth. More likely, it was one of the married men from the club Kim let use his apartment for extramarital screwing. Yes, that made more sense than the first two possibilities. These husbands had something to cover up. Kim didn't, as far as Gabe knew. In either case, it was worth checking out.

Inspired by the thought, Gabe bounded down the stairs to the ground floor and through the living room to Jenny's office.

"What's Kim Randall's apartment number?" asked Gabe. "I may be onto something."

"Really? What?" she asked, pulling out the club roster containing the names and addresses of the members.

"I'll let you know after I check it out."

Glancing up from the roster, she said, "501 Jacaranda Drive, apartment 410."

"Thanks, doll." he kissed her on the forehead, flew out the club entrance, and ran up the block towards Fourth Street.

The Racquet Club took up all of the western half of the four hundred block on Jacaranda Drive. Fourth Street bounded the club on the southern end and directly across the street, on the corner of Jacaranda and Fourth stood Randall's building—a contemporary, boxlike structure about six stories high, with some Mondo grass and a small fountain in front that never had any water in it because the manager was saving money.

From the sidewalk down below, it was impossible for Gabe to tell which floor the balcony in question was on. He thought it was Randall's, but he couldn't be certain until he stepped out on it and looked through the trees towards the clubhouse. Preferably at night, for he'd never know if he could see the exercise porch in the dark unless he personally tried it. Unfortunately, he didn't know how receptive Kim Randall would be about admitting him for the purpose he had in mind. If he knew one thing about Randall, he knew he was the complete sycophant; he'd do anything to protect the people he was trying to wangle money out of, even cover up murder. So there was no use playing on his sense of duty and telling him the real reason he wanted to gain entrance to his apartment. No, if he wanted to see the place without divulging his motive, he'd need as good a reason as Randall's regular customers.

He'd also need a girl to make the charade look legitimate.

The girl turned out to be no problem. "Now you understand," he told Jenny before she left for home early that evening, "I'm just going to tell Kim I want to use his apartment to bring a girl to. But we're not actually going to do anything when we get there, which he'll never know. It's just a charade to get in."

"I get it," said Jenny, with an understanding smile, "I'm no dummy."

"I know that, but I just want to emphasize that point so you don't think I'm going to try to take advantage of you when we get there. I mean, this is no office harassment bit."

"Believe me, I'm not worried," said Jenny. "I wouldn't expect you to pull anything. You're a gentleman." He wasn't sure if that was disappointment he heard in her tone or not. "But tell me one thing, Gabriel. What reason are you giving Kim for needing his place? We're two grown people. We're single. And if we want to have sex, we don't have to hide it."

She looked into his eyes searchingly.

"I've got that all figured out," said Gabe. "Just tell me what night's good for you in case he says yes."

"It just so happens I'm free every night this week, including tonight," she grinned.

"I doubt if I can arrange it that quickly," he said. "Maybe tomorrow night. But I'm glad you're so anxious, anyway."

Twelve

Gabe knew he could count on Randall to show up at the club the next morning between ten and eleven. Not to play tennis—his customer games were later—but to read the *Wall Street Journal* and the Hollywood "trades," which the club subscribed to as a service to its members who were in the entertainment business. Kim was too cheap to subscribe to the newspapers himself, and since he lived right across the street, found it no problem to drop into the club after breakfast and catch up on the latest lies being promulgated through Tinseltown by *Daily Variety* and *The Hollywood Reporter*.

Often, if Kim thought no one was watching him, he'd sneak the trades out of the club in his large leather pouch purse he always had slung over his shoulder and take them back to read in the comfort of his own apartment.

Today being the first of those bone-chilling,

foggy, Southern California mornings that turned up as regularly as the Capistrano swallows for about six depressing weeks every spring, Kim Randall had decided to do his reading in the sauna in the men's locker room.

When Gabe caught up with him, Kim was standing in front of the sauna, completely naked, with both trade papers and the *Wall Street Journal* grasped in both hands.

"Looks like a good idea. I think I'll join you," said Gabe, starting to pull off his own clothes.

The sauna at this time of day was the perfect place to have a quiet talk away from curious ears, for rarely did any of the male members use it before noon. The ones who played before going to their offices had no time afterwards for lounging around in their own sweat. As a result, it was empty at the moment.

"So what's new with you?" asked Kim as Gabe opened the door and sat down beside him on the second tier of redwood benches, where the air was much hotter. "Still like managing this little palace?"

It was the perfect lead-in to what Gabe wanted to discuss.

"It's not a bad life," he said, "but it's a little confining."

"In what way?"

"I'd like to bang that Jenny Ho," explained Gabe, "and I think she'll cooperate. She's coming on to me pretty strong. But I don't want to chance it in my place here. It might get her in trouble, if anyone finds out. And we can't go to her place because she lives at home with her folks."

Kim smiled deprecatingly. "One of those, huh?"

"Unfortunately," replied Gabe. "And I hate like hell to spend the money on a motel."

An idea seemed to be forming in Kim's head as he scratched his balls. "If I loaned you my place for a couple of hours," he began slowly and a bit ponderously, "would you be willing to do something for me in exchange?"

"Your place?" Gabe tried his best to sound surprised.

"Yeah, I supply this service to some of my real close friends at the club. And I certainly include you in that category. As I said, I expect something in return. I guess you'd call it sort of a *quiff pro quo* deal." He laughed at his play on words.

"You talking about money?" asked Gabe.

"In a sense, yes." He sounded a little sheepish now. "I've got a slight cash-flow problem the last couple of months. I don't know if you're aware of it, but I haven't paid my club bill since February—I think I owe something in the neighborhood of fourteen hundred dollars—and—"

"And you're afraid we'll invoke the three-month rule on you?" Gabe cut in.

"Exactly, champ."

"What would you like me to do—pay your bill?"

"Course not. Just speak to the board and see if you can get 'em to be a little understanding with me until I can get this property I have an option on off the ground. I think it's pretty bankable if I can get Dustin Hoffman or Arnold Schwarzenegger to play the lead."

"I'd say so," replied Gabe, amused that Kim considered those two actors interchangeable.

"Well, what do you think?"

Gabe shrugged. "They've been pretty firm about not making any exceptions to the three-month rule. You know the old saw, if we let one get away with it, everyone'll expect the same treatment."

"But I'm like you. I'm no Johnny-come-lately to the good old B.W.R.C. I've done a lot of good for this place. They can't just toss me out on my *gadarum.*"

"I can't promise you anything," said Gabe, "but I think I can get them to give you a little breathing space." He wasn't sure he could do even that, but he figured that by the time he got a decision from the board, he'd have already been in the apartment and seen what he wanted to see.

"Fine." He seemed enormously grateful. "What night do you want the place?"

"Would tonight be too soon?"

"Boy, you must have a real hard-on for that broad." He grinned. "Sounds okay. Tuesday's a slow night. But I'll have to check my datebook to make sure when I go back to the apartment."

At noon Jenny had to run into Beverly Hills to take care of some personal errands, so Gabe volunteered to handle the switchboard and front desk for her.

While Gabe was sitting there waiting to handle his first incoming call, Jock Kornfeld strode in and sat down in the visitor's chair. "Got a minute, champ?" he asked, putting his gold Dunhill to the tip of his cigarette and lighting it.

"As long as the switchboard doesn't start jumping. Right now it's pretty quiet."

Jock took a deep, cancer-inducing drag on his cigarette. "I suppose you heard about the donnybrook in the cardroom the other afternoon."

"I not only heard about it, I broke it up."

"So I was told. Any ideas what we should do to Marty?"

"Well, he's certainly no asset to the club. And I doubt if he'd be missed. But what do the bylaws say?"

"That he should be kicked out."

"After one offense? Shouldn't he be given a second chance?"

"This *was* his second chance. Also his third, fourth, and fifth."

"In that case, he probably ought to get the maximum." Gabe ran his finger across his throat. "Off with his head."

"That's what the other members I've talked to think."

"Then why are you asking me?"

"I just want you to be aware of what's going on. Engel thinks I'm the one who's behind the movement to boot him out. I figure he'll probably come to you to get you to change your story at tomorrow's board meeting because you're the only witness."

"I thought the board meeting's not till the end of the month?"

"This is an emergency meeting," said Jock, "because the sooner we can get rid of Engel, the sooner we can take in a new member. One who'll pay his bills. In these recessionary times, that's important."

"I'm just going to tell the board what I saw," Gabe assured him. "No more, no less."

"Good boy," said Kornfeld, mashing out his cigarette and jumping onto his feet. "That's what I wanted to hear. I've got the best-looking dish you've ever seen and her hubby all primed to become members as soon as there's a vacancy."

He laughed and headed for the locker room.

Jenny was still out doing errands when Kim Randall dropped by the office around two and handed Gabe the key to his apartment. "It's a green light for tonight," he said. "Just drop the key in my mailbox when you leave. I'll be gone from seven till one A.M. That should give you ample time to fuck yourself into an early grave."

"I'll try to quit while I can still walk," Gabe assured him, with an uneasy smile.

"I hope so, because you still have to take care of my bill problem," said Randall, slipping quietly out the office door.

Jenny returned just in time to see Randall leaving.

"Well, that was easy," said Gabe, holding up the key. "We've got his den of iniquity for six hours tonight. I'll pick you up at your house, we'll have a fabulous dinner somewhere, and then we'll go to Kim's apartment." His face fell and Jenny, sensitive to his moods, picked up the change immediately.

"Something wrong, honey?"

"I suddenly realized that I don't have to put you through all this. Now that I have the key, I can go to Kim's apartment alone. He'll never know the difference."

"No, but I will," replied Jenny with a mischievous grin. "I've been looking forward to being alone with you in Kim's apartment ever since you first mentioned it. And I expect you to keep your word!" With a laugh she jumped up and kissed him squarely on the lips. "Pick me up at seven-thirty."

Thirteen

As they reached the door to Kim Randall's apartment and Gabe started fumbling for the key in his jacket pocket, he didn't know why he felt so nervous. Was it because he was on the verge of finding out if one of the pieces to the jigsaw puzzle fit into the place where he thought it belonged? Or was it because Jenny looked and smelled especially seductive and was carrying a little overnight bag that he presumed contained a nightie and other intimate objects a girl about to get laid required. As he glanced at her pretty face again, he decided it was probably a little bit of both, but with the emphasis on the latter.

"Oh, this is darling!" exclaimed Jenny, as Gabe opened the door and turned on the lights.

Knowing Kim's taste in clothes, Gabe wasn't surprised to find himself and Jenny entering a typical bachelor pad, expensively done and kind of garish.

The decor was contemporary, and the color scheme black and white. There was thick white shag carpeting; a black-lacquered low coffee table shaped like a heart; a white linen sofa loaded with a number of oversized black-and-white checkered throw pillows; a small get-behind bar, lacquered black; and one of those rear projection television sets with an enormous screen. On the wall over the sofa was a large oil painting of a reclining nude girl on a chaise that seemed to be a flagrant imitation of the naked Maja. On the other two walls were a number of smaller works of art, including a few expensive examples of *Icart* watercolors and etchings of partially clad females. On the side of the room overlooking the Racquet Club was a large sliding glass door to the outdoor balcony, where a number of potted palms, artistically lighted, could be seen. A video tape player was on a black lacquered table near the TV set, along with Kim's library of video tapes—everything from *Gone With the Wind* to *Last Tango in Paris* to some hard porn flicks with titles like *Between Lovers, Daisy Chain*, and *Carlotta Whips Up an Orgy*.

"Well, Jen, you think you can be happy here?" asked Gabe after the two had taken it all in.

"I'd like it better if we could get rid of that ugly painting." She nodded to the direction of the reclining nude. "It looks like it belongs in a bar in San Pedro."

"Yeah, it is pretty raunchy," agreed Gabe, "but—" his eyes were suddenly riveted on the view of the club through the sliding glass door.

"But you didn't come here to be an art critic," Jenny chided him.

"Right," he said, going straight to the glass door and sliding it open. "I came here to be a detective." He stepped out into the damp Southern California night and, going straight to the balcony railing, peered at the club through the small opening in the trees. He could see the exercise porch, the gravity bar, and all the other equipment, plus the door to the men's locker room, even though there was just a single seventy-five-watt bulb burning in the fixture over the door. But he didn't believe he'd be able to recognize faces from that distance.

Nevertheless, it meant the killer could have been seen carrying a body onto the exercise porch and stringing it up by the neck.

"Well, Jen, it looks as if I was right," exclaimed Gabe. "Whoever was here, could have seen Danny's body being carried out. He probably couldn't recognize the face of the person doing the carrying, which is why he didn't put the name of the killer in the note."

"That's probably it," said Jenny. "My eyes are twenty-twenty and I couldn't make out a face from here."

"Now all we have to do is find out who did

the seeing and what exactly he saw," said Gabe, staring at the exercise porch in the distance.

Returning to the living room, Jenny flopped down on the sofa and kicked off her shoes while Gabe walked over to the bar. "How about a brandy?" he asked.

"I'd rather have a glass of white wine. Brandy makes me sleepy, and I'm not going to waste tonight sleeping."

"I'll see what he has," grinned Gabe, pleased that she seemed so horny.

He opened the small bar refrigerator and then held up a bottle of Mumm's. "I don't see any white wine on ice, doll. How about champagne?"

"I'll force myself." She laughed and fell back into a small mountain of soft pillows. "I'll say one thing about Kim. He has real down in his pillows."

"His customers are used to the best." Chuckling, Gabe uncorked the champagne and carried the bottle and two glasses over to the coffee table. As he filled the two glasses and handed one to Jenny, he said, "Maybe this'll inspire us to solve the rest of the mystery. Or more specifically, to discover who the philanderer was who was using this den of iniquity the night Danny was killed."

"I don't see how you're ever going to find that out," said Jenny, looking thoughtful behind her champagne glass, "unless Kim reveals his customer list. And even if you do learn that, what makes you think the mystery man's going to be any more willing to come forward now than when it first happened?"

"As my ex-wife's shrink used to say, 'One crisis at a time, my dear.'"

Emptying his glass and refilling it, Gabe sank back into the pillows next to Jenny. "I know who one of his customers is, Marvin Perlstein, but if my memory serves me correctly, he used this place Thursday night, or maybe it was Friday."

"How do you know that?"

"I overheard him booking a reservation for this joint with Kim in the locker room the day Wexler was robbed. I happened to be in their section, because it was near Wexler's locker, and I was trying to see who his neighbors were." He sat for a moment, thoughtfully sipping his champagne and letting his mind hark back to the events of that particular day. "Hey, I just happened to think." He sat up straight again on the edge of the couch. "Kim keeps talking about having to check his datebook. He mentioned it that day, and he even mentioned it this morning in the sauna. If we could just find where he keeps that—"

"What are we waiting for?" exclaimed Jenny excitedly jumping to her feet. "The sooner we can find it, the sooner we can—"

"The sooner we can what?" asked Gabe, looking at her with amusement.

"The sooner we can solve the mystery." She looked at him with a pixyish expression and started down the hall. "You take the living room, I'll take the bedroom."

Gabe searched in all the obvious places: the telephone table, under a stack of *Playboy*s and *Penthouse*s on the coffee table, in the bookshelves, behind the bookshelves, under the sofa and chair cushions, in the chandelier, under the zebra rug in the dining room, in the liquor cabinet, in the freezer compartment of the refrigerator, in the vegetable bin, in Kim's desk drawers, under the pile of film scripts on top of the desk, in the linen and silverware drawers, in the washer and dryer, in the broom closet, and in all the pockets of the coats and jackets hanging up in the guest closet in the entrance hall. But he couldn't find the datebook anywhere.

"How are you doing in here?" Gabe asked, walking up the hall to the bedroom.

"So far not a sign of it," said Jenny. "See for yourself."

Kim Randall's bedroom, done in New Orleans bordello-red, seemed made for sex, if not lovers. The king-sized mattress was firm, with just the right amount of resilience to it; the lights were on a rheostat and could be adjusted to suit your particular lighting hang-ups while engaging in intercourse; and the walls and ceiling were covered with mirrors.

Behind the bed hung another garish painting of a nude woman, and on the wall opposite was a French bridal armoire, painted white, with carved trim along the top depicting love birds and baskets of flowers.

Gabe gave the room a perfunctory examination then sat down on the bed. "He probably has it with him, but at least the evening hasn't been a total loss. We know the workout porch can be seen from his apartment."

"So why waste any more of the evening?" said Jenny, starting to get undressed. "Let's go to bed."

"You know something," said Gabe, "you're my kind of assistant." With a grin he drew her into his arms.

Afterwards, as the two lay entwined in each others arms, enjoying those first wonderful moments of postorgasmic release, Gabe had to marvel at how all this came about. A TV season in which all his script assignments had dried up. A retarded boy dead of unknown causes. And a sexy Girl Friday who didn't seem in the least offended by going to bed with her boss.

"What are you so busy thinking about?" asked Jenny, suddenly coming alive.

"Oh, just how different you are from my ex-wife."

"In what way?"

"She was so inhibited about sex, it took all the joy out of it. She'd use any excuse to avoid it—even that old cliche that she'd just had her hair done and didn't want to muss it."

"Maybe you didn't satisfy her. That can turn a girl off quicker than anything."

"What makes you say that?"

She hesitated before answering. "Promise you won't get mad if I tell you?"

"I'll try not to," he replied cautiously. "What?"

"Well, you didn't quite satisfy me. I barely got my engine started before it was all over."

"That's because I haven't had a girl in quite awhile," he explained. "Next time will be better."

"Next time I'm not taking any chances. We're going to go about it differently."

"How differently?"

"This differently," she said, taking his penis into her mouth and working it over with her lips and tongue until it was hard and throbbing with anticipation. While he was wondering if she wanted him to come in her mouth, she answered his question by suddenly yanking her head off him and flopping back on the pillow. "Now me," she whispered demandingly.

As she spread her legs, he inserted his tongue in her vagina until it was touching her clitoris.

Then he took her clitoris all the way into his mouth and rolled it around on his tongue and sucked on it until it became firm.

"That's the way," she gasped, starting to roll her hips around in response to his oral stimulation. "Oh, that's soo----oooo------ooo good, honey! Keep it up."

As he sucked with more vigor, her hip movements became so frenzied it was difficult to hang onto her clitoris with his mouth. At the same time, she kept his cock in her hand to make sure it didn't lose its erection. Then with a loud scream, she pushed his head away with her free hand. "Okay, Gabe—now I want all of you."

Scrambling quickly to his knees between her welcoming thighs, he plunged deep inside her warm moist pleasure zone. Simultaneously, she wrapped her legs around his back and started a wonderful rolling up and down motion with her hips in response to his own thrusts. It felt so good he hoped it would never stop. Wishful thinking! But to keep from disappointing Jenny again, he suddenly slowed the frequency of his movement.

"Don't stop now, baby," she screamed. "Don't STOP YET!"

Summoning up all his willpower, Gabe was able to stay with her until he could tell by her frequent sighs and heavy breathing, and felt her body beginning to tremble like a leaf in a tropical storm, that she was on the verge of her own orgasm.

"NOW!" she yelled.

As he gratefully spilled his seed into her, she gave one mighty upward heave of her buttocks, then relaxed backward onto the pillow panting heavily.

"Oh, Gabe, that was heavenly," she whispered. Then, with a grin, she added, "I'll bet you never did it that way with your wife, or she never would have hated sex."

"She never would do it anyway but the norm. She thought oral sex was dirty."

"Thank God, you don't."

"Nor you."

As he lapsed into silence, she raised herself up on one elbow and gazed into his eyes. "I'll bet I know what you're thinking," she said.

"All right. What?"

"You're wondering where I learned all that."

"Well—"

"And how many lovers I've had before you?"

"Well, it crossed my mind."

"I thought so," she grinned down at him impishly. "Well, I'm not going to tell."

"That many?" he teased.

She laughed, "Okay, more than one but less than five. But nobody I could really get excited about, except maybe Number Three. I lived with him a while when I was attending the University of Hawaii. But when I found out he didn't ever want to get married, I decided I wanted more than just a fucking relationship. I wanted kids and a father who'd give them his name and stick around permanently."

"You didn't have to explain all that."

"I know I didn't."

"But I'm glad you did. But just remember one thing. As much as I believe I love you right now, I'm not promising marriage, either—at least not right away."

"That's all right. I'm in no hurry. Except to have you make love to me some more." She took his penis into her mouth again, but this time it didn't respond.

"You may have to give me a little more time," he apologized.

"That's right. You are getting on in years," she teased.

"Oh, shut your big mouth." He gave her buttocks a playful slap.

"Just trying to get a rise out of you." She laughed, then sank back into the soft pillow and put her hand on his inert cock, hoping to arouse it with a gentle massage. Then suddenly she sat bolt upright. "Gabriel," she murmured, pointing over his shoulder to a section of the ceiling mirror directly over the armoire. "I believe I've found the hiding place for Kim's datebook."

With a twist of her nimble body, she slid off

the bed, pulled a chair up to the front of the armoire and climbed on the seat.

"It's up here, I think." Getting on her toes, with her pear-shaped backside stretched to the fullest, she reached over the carved ornamentation on top of the armoire with her right hand, pulled out a black-covered datebook, and waved it triumphantly at Gabe.

"*Voila!*" she shouted as she leaped off the chair and ran over to Gabe.

Handing the datebook to Gabe, she put an arm around his neck and sat down on his naked lap to examine it with him.

Gabe quickly riffled through the pages, stopping at:

WEDNESDAY, MAY 9

The page was divided into three sections: MORNING, AFTERNOON, and EVENING. Under the "evening" heading were just two initials printed in pencil in Kim's hand.

J.K.

The initials leaped out at Gabe like a cobra from a basket.

"It's all beginning to fit," said Gabe, pointing to the page. "J.K. Jock Kornfeld. Remember last

Thursday morning when I talked to his wife, and—"

"And she hadn't seen him all night," added Jenny, her face lighting up with excitement.

"And then when he showed up at the club for breakfast, he made such a point of announcing that he'd been at an all-night business meeting about a company take-over."

"That's *right*!" exclaimed Jenny.

"And when I told him about Danny, I thought how peculiar it was that he didn't seem more surprised, just nervous. He pretended he was, but it wasn't very convincing—as though he already knew what I was telling him. It all makes sense now. He must have seen someone carry Danny out to the exercise porch and string him up."

"And the reason he was so nervous," said Jenny helpfully, "was that he knew he was concealing a crime but didn't know how to say he'd witnessed it without admitting he was having an affair with someone who wasn't his wife."

"Exactly," said Gabe.

"And you know who that could have been?" said Jenny. As Gabe looked at her for the answer, she said, "That Mrs. Wexler. She hadn't been home all night, either."

"How do you know that?"

"Well, I don't for sure. I'm just deducing that

from what her husband told me when he phoned the club from San Francisco. He said he'd tried her at their home that morning and hadn't been able to find her there. Now I know she wasn't out grocery shopping."

"Sure," said Gabe, thoughtfully. "That explains Jock's reluctance to come forth. Not only was *he* cheating on Rita, but he was banging his tax lawyer's wife. If he was called on to testify, he might have to admit all that. And if it got too messy, his father-in-law might fire him."

Too stimulated for any more sex, he gave Jenny a playful slap on her bare bottom and stood up suddenly, sliding her to a standing position on the floor.

"Of course he could have made up another reason for having been in Randall's apartment," conjectured Gabe as he started to get into his undershorts, "but since he'd already lied to his wife about the all-night board meeting, there was no reason why she'd ever buy his second lie. Which explains the anonymous note. His silence was beginning to trouble him, which proves he has some conscience, but not enough to risk his name and reputation and his position in his father-in-law's firm."

"What an excuse for a man!" exclaimed Jenny.

"Please—you're talking about our president." As he reached for his shirt, he noticed Jenny standing naked by the bed, looking rather forlorn.

"That's it for tonight?" she asked, sounding disappointed.

He walked over to her and gave her a affectionate pinch on her cheek. "Sorry, honey, but I don't think I'd be much good in the sack with all this other on my mind."

"Okay, Gabriel, I'll take a rain check." She smiled agreeably and reached for her bra.

After he'd finished dressing and was waiting for Jenny to put on her lipstick and comb out her hair, Gabe went through Kim's calendar book, this time paying attention to other dates. He was surprised at how many members of the Racquet Club were customers of Kim's. At least a dozen were regulars in addition to Kornfeld, and that included Rabbi Schulman and Dr. Sullivan, a psychologist who'd written a best-selling book called, *Is ExtraMarital Sex Really Worth It?*

Before they checked out of Kim's place for the night, Gabe got up on the chair and put the datebook in its original hiding place atop the armoire.

"I hate to leave it here with all that good evidence in it," he said, sliding the chair back to where it belonged. "It might come in handy if I can put the rest of this puzzle together."

"You could take it and have it Xeroxed," suggested Jenny.

"Don't think I haven't thought of that. But unfortunately, nothing's open tonight. And how would I ever slip it back in here again tomorrow? Kim will be coming back right after we leave. He might miss it. Probably refers to it everyday."

"Well, as long as you know the book exists, you can always have it subpoenaed," said Jenny.

"Hey, how'd you know that?" he asked, opening the front door for her.

"I worked for a lawyer once. For about ten minutes." She made a wry face. "I hated it, so I quit and took this low-paying job at the club."

"Are you sorry?"

"Not anymore," she said, giving his hand a squeeze.

During his motorcycle ride back to the club from Jenny's house, Gabe wondered what the best way would be to persuade Kornfeld to talk. Surely, if I handle him right, I can get to his conscience, thought Gabe. He must have one. He's a respected member of the community; he gives twenty grand a year to UJA; and he once won the B'nai B'rith Humanitarian Award.

A man like that certainly wouldn't want a murderer on the loose, when he knows that with just a few well-chosen words he could put him behind bars forever.

If he and Kornfeld put both their heads together, they could certainly come up with a foolproof way for Kornfeld to identify the murderer without revealing he was having an affair with another man's wife that night.

Gabe's mind was a windmill of practical and impractical ideas on the subject as he parked his Honda in the manager's space in the alley behind the club, chained it to a post, and let himself in the back entrance. But he knew one thing: he'd stay up all night if necessary to dream up the right story that Kornfeld could tell the police without compromising himself and Jan Wexler.

It would just take some heavy thinking, he reflected, but he'd come up with it, and he'd take it to Kornfeld first thing in the morning.

Striding briskly along the brick path to the clubhouse in the dark, Gabe had a sudden premonition that something was wrong. He couldn't explain it; he just felt uneasy as he let himself into the clubhouse and turned on the floodlights that illuminated the club grounds, something he'd got into the habit of doing every night before turning in.

An overturned canvas chair on the pool decking caught his eye first, then an object floating in the swimming pool. For a moment he thought it was just a rubber mattress that the pool attendant had forgotten to put away for the night. But as he studied it, he realized it wasn't wide enough to be a rubber mattress. It looked more like the body of a man.

Gabe reached over to the pool edge and kneeled down.

There was no mistaking now what the object was. It *was* the body of a man, floating face down. "What in damn hell!" he muttered to himself.

With the icy fingers of fright playing a glissando up and down his spine, Gabe grabbed the long metal pole to the leaf skimmer and attempted to fish the body out with the net. It was too heavy, but he did manage to nudge the body closer to the side where he could get his hands on the man's coat lapels. As he struggled to pull the body onto the pool decking, the man's head bobbed to one side, his glazed eyes staring up at Gabe as if pleading for help.

But Jock Kornfeld was beyond help.

His water-bloated, lifeless features told the whole story.

Fourteen

Within the hour, Judy Trump and her company of men were swarming all over the grounds and clubhouse hunting for clues, and Dr. Gonzales of the L.A. Coroner's office was doing a preliminary examination of the body, which was lying on a gurney by the swimming pool, waiting to be identified by Rita Kornfeld, who was on her way over in a police car.

All the lights both inside and outside the clubhouse had been turned on, including the ones on the tennis courts, lending a touch of unreality to the macabre scene—as if it were about to be the site of one of the club's gala parties and the corpse was just part of the decorations.

As Gabe and Judy Trump looked on from a short distance, Dr. Gonzales removed the stethoscope from his ears, pulled the sheet up over

Kornfeld's blue-white face, and turned around to his audience.

"Well, what's the verdict, Doc?" asked Detective Trump, as Gonzales folded his stethoscope and slid it into the inside pocket of his plaid jacket.

"I do not know for sure until after the autopsy," he explained in his Mexican flavored sing-songy voice. "But off the top of my head, I will tell you he did not kill himself or accidentally drown."

"How do you know that?" asked Gabe, not at all surprised by his conclusion.

"No water in his lungs, which would indicate he was dead before he hit the water. It looks to me like death at the hands of an unknown party or parties."

"By what method?" asked Trump.

Gonzales shrugged. "That is difficult to say until we have the complete autopsy. There are no bullet holes in him or his clothing or any other signs of violence on his skin. And no bumps or abrasions on his head that would indicate a blow by a blunt instrument."

"Which leaves?" interjected Trump.

"Strangulation," declared Dr. Gonzales. "Something cut off his wind before he landed in the pool, otherwise he would have swallowed a lungful of water. Obviously there was a struggle, of some sort, judging by the overturned chair."

"Well, well, it looks like we have a murder case on our hands," Judy exclaimed to Gabe, almost as if she relished it. "What do you make of that, Mr. Steele?"

"It's what I've been trying to tell you ever since Danny's death," said Gabe. "They were both murdered—and by the same person."

"How'd you reach that opinion?"

"Simple," said Gabe. "Whoever killed Danny killed Kornfeld, because Kornfeld knew he did."

"And how did Kornfeld know he did?" asked Trump.

"I don't know—I just feel it," said Gabe, immediately clamming up. At the risk of losing his own credibility, he didn't care to expose the sleazy goings-on at Randall's apartment or reveal the existence of a datebook that would place Kornfeld there with a girl the night Danny died. Not that he gave a damn about protecting Randall, and it certainly wouldn't matter to Kornfeld any longer. But if Gabe told the whole truth and the full story broke in the newspapers, it would not only be embarrassing to the grieving widow, who was going to have enough problems just coping with the death of a husband, but the publicity would be ruinous to the club. He could see the headlines now:

POSH BEVERLY-WEST RACQUET CLUB
ACTUALLY SEX CLUB

PRODUCER HELPS HUSBANDS RENDEZVOUS
WITH GIRLS IN EXCHANGE FOR
FINANCIAL BACKING

It could be a worse scandal than the Woody Allen-Mia Farrow affair. For the club's sake, he'd like to keep a lid on that Pandora's box for the time being anyway.

"If you ask me, it's a pretty wild guess," said Trump, when it became apparent that Gabe wasn't going to enlarge on the subject. "Even if I buy the fact that Danny might have been killed by other hands, and that Kornfeld somehow witnessed it, how in heck did the killer know that Kornfeld knew it?"

"That's been a puzzlement to me, too," said Gabe. "But if I knew the answer to that one, I could probably solve your whole mystery for you."

Trump shrugged. "Your theory sounds like the kind of baloney you hear from one of those TV detectives."

"Why don't you ask Mrs. Kornfeld?" suggested Gabe. "Maybe she could tell you who might have wanted to kill her husband."

"Oh, I'll have a talk with her," stated Trump, "but I doubt if she's going to be in shape for any serious questioning until after the funeral and the shock of this wears off."

She was right about that. When Rita Kornfeld,

clad in a pink quilted robe over her nightie and furry pump slippers, arrived just moments later hanging onto the arms of two uniformed policemen for support, she looked as broken as a survivor of the Holocaust. Her bleached blond hair, with some dark showing around the roots, was uncombed, as if she'd just gotten up out of a sound sleep, which she had; her face was unmade; and eyes were bloodshot from crying. Or was it booze?

Gabe could hardly bear to see her in this condition. He could remember when Rita Kornfeld was one of the prettiest, most stylish women at the club. But tonight, though she was barely fifty, she looked older than the La Brea Tar Pits.

She lost a slipper as she was led in and over to her husband's body, and one of the policemen had to pick it up for her and put it back on her red-toenailed foot.

"Just like Cinderella," she said with a tearful smile.

"I am sorry to have to get you over here," apologized Detective Trump, "but this'll only take a minute."

Rita nodded numbly, almost unseeingly, as Judy Trump pulled the sheet off Jock Kornfeld's face.

As she stared at his bloated features, Rita Kornfeld let out a shriek that sent a shiver up Gabe's spine, and hurled herself on Jock's body.

"Oh, my darling," she cried out. "Oh, my darling!"

Then she kissed him on the lips, almost passionately, as if that would bring him to life again. A futile gesture, in Gabe's opinion. If Jock hadn't responded to her lips when he was alive, she certainly wasn't going to reach him now.

Wearing an expression of genuine sympathy, Detective Trump firmly but gently pulled Rita off Kornfeld's inert figure and nodded to Gonzales to cover him up again.

As she watched Jock being wheeled out of the club on the gurney, Rita collapsed in a faint on the pool decking.

"Mama Mia!" exclaimed Gonzales, hastily producing a bottle of smelling salts and waving it under her nose.

She came to after a few seconds, and smiling apologetically, allowed Trump and Gonzales to help her to her feet. But she was still terribly wobbly and had to be half-carried to the police car that was waiting out front to drive her back to her home.

After Rita and the policemen had left the pool area, Gonzales said to Trump, "I don't think she should be left alone. See that her family doctor is called. And whoever is her closest relative should be notified, too."

"She has a father here in L.A.," said Gabe. "And a daughter who's married and lives in

New York City. I believe her married name is Jane Elliot."

"You wouldn't by any chance know who her doctor is?" asked Trump.

"Yes, I do. He belongs to the club. Dr. Bartlett."

"Why don't you go along with her, Steele, and take care of these things for her?" suggested Trump. "I suppose you're a friend of the family?"

"I guess you could say I am. But I don't know if I can leave the club open like this, with all these strangers running around here." Gabe nodded in the direction of some policemen who were combing the dark corners of the grounds with flashlights. "I'm more or less the caretaker here."

"You can trust my men," said Trump. "And we'll be here for at least a couple of hours. You should be back by then."

When Gabe caught up with her in the back seat of the police car, Rita had regained some of her composure. She was sniffling into a handkerchief, but otherwise seemed in control of her emotions, and fairly alert.

"I thought you might like some company," said Gabe, almost apologizing for the intrusion, as the car pulled away from the curb with the two policemen in the front seat.

"Thanks, Gabe." She sniffled and squeezed his hand, then lapsed into silence for a few blocks. Gabe remained silent, too, not wanting to intrude on her thoughts, even though there were some questions he was dying to know the answers to.

Then, almost as if she had read Gabe's mind, Rita suddenly exclaimed, "I don't know who could have wanted to kill Jock. He had so many friends."

"Yes, he did." Gabe didn't want to go into his theory of both murders at this moment, so he became silent again. But she wanted to talk about it.

"Do you, Gabe?" she persisted.

"No, I don't." It wasn't exactly a lie because he didn't know *who* killed Jock; only the reason why. And that was just a guess, so why upset her further by going into that right now? There would be time for her to know the truth when she was better able to take it.

However, as long as she insisted on talking, there were a few questions he had to ask.

"Do you mind talking about it?" asked Gabe as they drove up Loma Vista to the Kornfeld house, which was in the Trusdale Estates.

"No, I want to," she replied, sniffling into her hankie.

"Then could you tell me about tonight? What was Jock doing at the Racquet Club?"

"I really don't know," said Rita haltingly. "We got a call when we were having dinner—a call from the someone who ki - ki - killed him, I guess. It seemed like this person wanted to talk to him about something terribly important. But I don't know what."

"Do you have any idea who it could have been?" persisted Gabe.

"No. Not really."

"Well, has he had any problems with anybody at the club since he's been president?"

"Not that I know of. I mean, nothing worth getting killed over."

"Tell me about it."

"Last week he got pissed off at Danny White's father."

"Over what?"

"Over you, I'm pretty sure. Ed wanted you fired. He blames you for Danny's suicide."

"I know."

"But Jock told him to go fuck himself. He told Ed that you were the best manager the club's ever had."

"Then could it have been White who called?"

Rita shrugged. "I can't say. I didn't answer the phone."

"Who did?"

"Our housekeeper, Masie."

"Do you remember what she said when she called him to the phone? I mean, whether it was a man or a woman calling?"

"I don't remember what she said exactly. I'd had quite a bit to drink." She sniffled some more. "When Jock first started talking, I thought it could have been a girl on the other end . . . from the guarded way he was talking in front of me. But after he made a date to meet this person at the Racquet Club, I figured it probably wasn't. Although . . . although—" she seemed to be debating with herself about whether to be honest with him or not "—the Racquet Club might have been a code name for the place he usually met his cunts." As she realized what she'd let slip, she looked Gabe straight in the eye and said, "Oh, what's the use of kidding you, Gabe? I knew about Jock's girlfriends, although I don't think he knew I knew." She started to sob, suddenly losing all composure again, and as this happened, she threw herself into Gabe's arms.

"Okay, okay," he said, trying to think of something comforting to say as he held her in his arms. "Let it all out. Have a good cry. That's what friends are for."

She was still hanging onto him as the police car pulled into the circular driveway in front of her contemporary one-story house, which was on the very summit of the hill.

One of the officers opened the car door for them and escorted them up the walk to the entrance.

Having rushed out of the house without her purse or key, Rita had to ring the doorbell. After a full minute went by, the door was opened by Masie, a fat, Aunt-Jemima-type black woman in a bathrobe.

"Sorry to wake you, Masie," apologized Rita, "but I forgot my key."

"Company at this hour?" exclaimed Masie. Then noticing the uniformed men beside her mistress, and the black-and-white police car in the driveway, her annoyed expression changed to one of alarm. "Something happen, ma'am?"

"I'll explain later," Gabe said as he followed Rita into the entrance hall, which was starkly modern, with white walls, a terrazzo floor, a Calder mobile hanging from the ceiling, a real Jackson Pollack on the wall, and a view of the sparkling lights of nighttime L.A. through the living room beyond. "Right now, let's get Mrs. Kornfeld to bed. And bring me her private telephone book. I have to make a couple of calls for her."

Masie, who'd been with the Kornfelds for most of their marriage, stood her ground, waiting to take her instructions from the mistress of the house, and nobody else.

"I don't think I want to go to bed right now," announced Rita. "I could use a drink instead."

Turning on the living room lights, she walked over to a sunken bar and reached for the Scotch, which was in a cut-glass crystal decanter. As she popped some ice cubes into an old-fashioned glass and poured a stiff shot of Scotch over them, she said to Gabe, "How about you?"

"Yeah, I could use a drink," he answered.

While Rita was pouring, Gabe walked back to the front door and dismissed the policemen. "No point in you guys hanging around," he said. "Go home and get some sleep. I'll get a cab back to the club when I finish up here."

When he returned to the bar, Rita had a drink in one hand and a Princess phone in the other. She already had her father on the line and was saying, "I've got some horrible news, Pops. Jock was killed tonight." There was a long pause while her father evidently reacted. "Nobody knows what happened yet." Rita went on, beginning to sniffle loudly again. "The club manager found him in the swimming pool."

"Lordy, Lordy!" exclaimed Masie.

"I agree with you," said Gabe, quietly sipping his drink. He wasn't a Scotch drinker, but right now, after what he'd been through in the past couple of hours, this hit the spot.

"No, I haven't told Jane yet, Pops. I just haven't had the heart to . . . Would you phone her for me? . . . Thanks, Pops . . . Well, if you're up to it, of course I'd love you to come over now." Putting the phone down, Rita exclaimed, "Poor Pops. Just lost my mom last year."

She finished off her drink without coming up for air then poured herself another stiff shot and flopped down on the sofa with it, spilling half the drink in her lap. As Masie rushed over with a bar towel to dry her mistress off, Gabe asked, "You wouldn't by any chance know Dr. Bartlett's phone number, would you, Masie?"

"Sure do. Got it right at the tip of my tongue: 273-4040."

"Thanks, Masie." Gabe dialed the number, and after fifteen rings, Dr. Bartlett's exchange answered. When Gabe told them it was an emergency, they put him right through to Dr. Bartlett, who answered in a sleepy voice. After Gabe told him the news, Bartlett said, "I'll be right over."

"Why do we need him?" asked Rita, as Gabe hung up the receiver. Her voice was growing drunkenly thick now. "He'll just send me a bill."

"I just think it's a good idea," he said. "You might need something to make you sleep."

She shrugged, and taking another large swallow of her drink, leaned back against the pillows, and closed her eyes.

"Don't look like it," commented Masie, casting a glance at her sleeping mistress. After a moment, she walked over to the bar and picked up the Scotch decanter. "I could use a little of this myself."

While Rita dozed, and Masie sat on a barstool

enjoying the Kornfeld's fifteen-year-old Scotch, Gabe took advantage of the moment by doing a little detective work.

"You have any idea who might have wanted to kill Mr. Kornfeld?" asked Gabe, sitting down next to Masie on a barstool.

Masie shrugged.

"That mean you do or you don't?"

"I don't."

"You have any idea who phoned Mr. Kornfeld at dinner tonight?"

"No, suh. Just that it was a man."

"It wasn't any of his friends?" Gabe couldn't help thinking that if he was persistent enough, she'd come up with some useful information. After all, a maid who'd been in the household as long as Masie had been usually was familiar with the family intrigues.

"Nope. It wasn't any of his friends."

"You sure about that? I mean, absolutely sure."

"No. Not absolutely. Mr. Kornfeld had lots of friends. Too many to keep track of."

"Could it have been Mr. Wexler?"

"I couldn't say for sure. Mr. Wexler calls the house a lot on business. I think I know his voice." She shrugged. "But it could have been."

"What *did* the person sound like?" persisted Gabe. "Was it an old voice or a young voice or . . ."

"I wouldn't wager on it, but it sounded more young than old."

"Anything else you can remember?"

"Only that he sounded sneaky."

"What makes you say that?"

"He wouldn't give me his name when I asked him."

The doorbell rang before Gabe could think of any more questions. "That's probably the doctor," said Gabe. "I'll let him in."

Dr. Sy Bartlett was around sixty, with a red jowly face, crew-cut grey hair, and steel-rimmed spectacles. It was apparent that he, too, had been routed out of bed by the emergency call, for in addition to the look of harassment on his face, he was wearing peppermint-striped pajamas under his camel's hair topcoat.

Upon seeing Gabe, he shook his hand limply and exclaimed, "What a day this has been. First the market drops seventy points, and now this!"

The ringing of the doorbell had evidently awakened Rita from her catnap, for by the time Dr. Bartlett and Gabe reached her, she was back at the bar, pouring herself another drink.

"My dear poor Rita," said Bartlett in an unctuous voice, as he clasped her to his chest in a bearhug. "I just can't tell you how sorry I am."

While he was comforting her, the doorbell rang a second time. Gabe went to the door again, this time admitting Tom Harrington, Rita's father. Harrington was a handsome silver-haired man of eighty, with an alert face and a body that stood as straight as a West Point cadet's, even at his age and at this ungodly hour. He was fully dressed, in gabardine slacks and a grey tweed sports jacket, and smelled of Giverny cologne. Being the founder of one of the most successful cosmetic firms in America, Harrington wasn't the type to leave his house in his pajamas, even in an emergency.

He and Gabe knew each other from some of the social events at the club, so there was no need for introductions. They exchanged sympathetic nods, and then Harrington asked gruffly, "Where's my daughter?"

With his glass of Scotch, Gabe gestured in the direction of the living room.

"Thanks." Harrington went in, taking long, purposeful strides.

Going straight to Rita, Harrington swept her up in his strong arms and kissed her on the cheek. Then, noticing the bottle of Scotch in her hand, said in a loud voice, "By George, I could use some of that."

Gabe hung back near the archway to the entrance hall, letting father and daughter enjoy their grief in private. But when Dr. Bartlett accepted their invitation to have a drink, too, and the scene, after two rounds of "doubles," began to take on the aspect of an Irish wake,

Gabe excused himself, called a cab, and waited out front in the driveway to be picked up.

It was four A.M. when the cab dropped Gabe off in front of the Racquet Club. Noting the time by his wristwatch, Gabe suddenly felt terribly bushed. It had been a full day and night. Everything from intrigue to sex to murder. It seemed incredible that it had only been eighteen hours since he had sat in the sauna with Kim Randall making plans to use his apartment. It felt more like a couple of years.

Opening the clubhouse door, Gabe was relieved to see that Detective Trump and her men were preparing to leave. Trump, in fact, was lying on the love seat in the foyer, waiting for Gabe to arrive. Seeing him, she smiled and jumped briskly to her feet.

"How'd it go up there? Everything taken care of?"

"She's asleep, and her father's staying with her."

"Good! Then I guess that wraps everything up for the night."

"Find anything interesting?" asked Gabe.

"Just this." She held up an alligator-skin wallet that appeared to be soggy with water. "Kornfeld's. We fished it out of the bottom of the pool."

"Does that mean anything to you?" asked Gabe.

"You betcha! It wipes out one of my theories—that the motive could have been robbery. The bugger didn't even take his watch. It was still on his wrist when the coroner examined him." She held up Kornfeld's diamond-and-gold Rolex. "This tells me a lot. And it pretty much knocks your theory in a cocked hat that the locker room thief and the murderer are one and the same."

"What makes you say that?" asked Gabe, weary from playing Q and A all night but still interested in her professional opinion.

"Well, this wallet contains a thousand bucks, and this gold Rolex is worth at least six thousand smackeroos." She looked admiringly at the Rolex. "No locker room thief is going to let an opportunity like that pass by."

"Maybe he didn't have his scuba-diving equipment with him," said Gabe grimly.

"You are a funny fellow," said Trump, with a deprecating smile. Before putting the Rolex back in her pocket, she looked at again and shook her head in amazement. "You know, there was only one thing this little baby didn't tell us. And that's what time the death occurred. In Sherlock Holmes' day, it was a piece of cake to tell what time somebody drowned, because their watch generally stopped around the same time they hit the water. But now they're making watches too good. The owner may kick off, but the watch goes right on ticking." With a philosophical shrug, Judy slipped the Rolex back into her pocket. "Well, that's progress for you," she said with a frown as she headed for the front door.

Fifteen

It was nearly five in the morning when Gabe finished locking up the club and was finally and wearily climbing the circular stairs to his quarters, where he hoped to catch a few winks of sleep before having to get up to let in the Early Birds.

But after he had put on his pajamas and crawled into bed, he realized he was much too stimulated to sleep. It would take either another strong shot of booze or a sleeping pill to send him to dreamland, and he had neither in his apartment.

The wheels of his mind were spinning like a windmill as he lay tossing and turning in the depressing grey light of dawn. He didn't know what to let his mind dwell on first. His affair with Jenny Ho, which should have been the high-light of the night, if not his life. Or Jock's murder and all its scary implications.

As he let his mind drift, he fell into an uneasy sleep and had a dream in which he and Jenny were being stalked by an unknown killer. It woke him immediately, for it reminded him that he could be in jeopardy living alone here at the club, with a maniac on the loose who apparently had a way of gaining access to the grounds.

Aside from his own and Jenny's safety, what concerned Gabe the most was the setback the solution to Danny's murder had been given by the demise of Jock Kornfeld. Now it was back to Square One again. There was just no way ever to prove that Kornfeld had seen the killer string Danny up on the exercise porch. Even if Gabe went to Judy Trump with Kim Randall's datebook and showed her that Kornfeld had been there the night of Danny's death, it still wouldn't mean a thing to that stubborn excuse for a homicide detective without the additional support of Kornfeld's testimony. There was just one glimmer of hope: the anonymous note. If it had actually emanated from a typewriter in the executive suite of Giverny Cosmetics, there ought to be a way to find out.

The thought of this excited Gabe and made further sleep impossible. So he got up, went through the usual morning ablutions, changed into slacks and a clean sport shirt, and drove over to Jack's Diner, an open-all-night coffee shop on Pico and Robertson, to have a bite of breakfast and see if there was any mention of Jock's murder in the newspapers.

There wasn't a word about it in either the *L.A. Times* or *USA Today*, he discovered as he sat in a corner booth in the empty restaurant and scoured the pages of both newspapers while he munched on a breakfast of poached eggs, bacon, and a couple of cups of inklike coffee.

Obviously, Jock's death had been too late to make the final editions. Which presented another problem: nobody at the club would know that their president was dead. Should he or should he not open the door for play that day? There was no precedent to go by; as far as Gabe knew, no president or any other member of the club had ever been murdered before. On the other hand, lots of members had died in the thirty years Gabe had been playing there, and as far as he could recall that had never been a reason to close the club. The Beverly-West, in fact, had never closed its doors, not even during the Cuban Missile Crisis. Gabe remembered sitting in the club living room in 1962 with a half a dozen other concerned members watching Chet Huntley on national television give a running account of the suspenseful negotiations between Kennedy and Khrushchev. The fate of the world, as well as the club's, hung on the result. But, Gabe recalled, the card-room at the time was jam-packed with gin and bridge players bickering and cheating each other as if it were any other day, and there wasn't a vacant tennis court on the grounds.

By the time Gabe had arrived back at the club, he had changed his mind about opening the place on his own. He decided to seek permission from a higher authority—Bob Gilmore, who, as vice-president, was next in line of succession. Sitting down at the switchboard, Gabe put in a call to the new president at his home.

Gilmore was a lawyer of about Gabe's age who had become filthy rich in what was a relatively new line of endeavor in the world: masterminding the careers of superstar professional athletes.

Gilmore's wife Betsy answered the phone sleepily and informed Gabe, in Barbra Streisand Brooklynese, that her husband was in Vero Beach, Florida, at the Dodger spring training camp, trying to sign a promising rookie pitching star to a management contract.

"Do you have a number on him?" asked Gabe. "I have to get in touch with Bob."

"What for?" asked Betsy suspiciously.

"Jock Kornfeld was murdered at the club last night."

"Jesus, that's terrible," exclaimed Betsy. "Who'd want to do such a thing?"

"I wish I knew," said Gabe. "Anyway, I've got to tell Bob. He's the president now."

"Sure, doll. Just hang on."

She was back in a moment with the number of the Tropicana Motel in Vero Beach. "And if you should be so lucky as to reach him," said Betsy, "tell the dirty bum I miss him and wish he'd come home."

After getting the operator at the Tropicana, Gabe was put right through to Gilmore's room.

A girl answered "hello" in a sexy voice.

"I guess I must have the wrong room," apologized Gabe. "I want Bob Gilmore."

"Oh, he's here." After a long pause, she explained, "I'm his secretary," she giggled. "Who should I say is calling?"

"Tell him Gabe Steele, the manager of the Beverly-West Racquet Club."

Gabe heard her relay his message to Gilmore. After a moment the man himself picked up the receiver.

"Hi, Gabe. What's on your mind?"

Gabe told him the bad news.

"Wow!" exclaimed Gilmore. "That's a bummer!"

"Yeah, it is," agreed Gabe.

"But what is it you want from me?" asked Gilmore, sounding anxious to get back to his "dictation."

"Since you're the president now, I want to know if I should close the club today under the circumstances."

There was a brief pause before he shot back with the answer. "Hell, no. We need the revenue. There are too many fucking holidays as it is with no money coming into the club."

"I see what you mean," said Gabe. "I was just wondering. You know, out of respect to Jock."

"He doesn't need any respect," declared Gilmore. "Knowing him as well as I do, I can tell you, he'd have wanted it this way. That's the kind of guy Jock was."

"That's what they always say about the dead," retorted Gabe irritably, "but do you really know he would have wanted it this way?"

"Look, I've got no time for philosophy," said Gilmore. "I have to get back to these contracts. Just let me know when the funeral's going to be. Maybe I'll jet in for it if I can get this Chicano pitcher to put his X on the dotted line."

"Well, good luck." Gabe was about to hang up when he remembered that Jock had called a board meeting for that night to discuss the Marty Engels situation. With the president dead, and the vice-president in Florida, Gabe decided it would be a waste of time to go through with the meeting, and he asked Gilmore for permission to postpone it. "There won't be a quorum without you two."

"Don't postpone it!" Gilmore snapped. "Cancel it! Who can worry about such trivia now? If the cardplayers want to kill each other let them."

"Really?"

"Sure, in a few days the whole incident will be forgotten, and they'll be back playing gin with the sucker again. You know how cardplayers are."

"I don't know. I've never been one."

"Take it from me," said Gilmore. "Just give Marty a warning, and let it go at that."

As he put down the phone, Gabe was suddenly struck with a bizarre thought. It was a far-out theory, but not beyond the realm of plausibility.

Could Marty Engels have killed Jock?

Maybe he had enticed Jock to the club to persuade him not to kick him out. An argument ensued, in the course of which Engels lost his temper and strangled Jock.

Of course, just to remain a member in the club didn't seem to Gabe to be a strong enough motive to kill over. But stranger things than that had caused people to murder in the past.

Then, too, there could have been another motive, entirely apart from the club ejecting him.

What if Engels were the locker room thief, as Jock had once suggested? Maybe Danny had caught Engels in the act of pilfering a locker. Engels heard Danny talking to Gabe on the phone, killed Danny in order to silence him, and made it look like suicide, unaware that Jock was witnessing the whole thing from Randall's apartment.

If somehow Engels knew that Kornfeld knew, he'd have had a double motive to kill the president. But how did Engels find out that Kornfeld knew? Ay, there was the rub, to coin a phrase from Shakespeare.

Unfortunately, both theories were pure speculation, without one shred of evidence to back them up. And so far Judy Trump wasn't buying circumstantial evidence.

On that depressing note, Gabe picked up the phone and called the remaining members of the board to advise them that the meeting that night was canceled, and the reason why. Then he sat down at Jenny's IBM and composed a short announcement to the membership, which he tacked up on the bulletin board just inside the entrance.

ATTENTION: B.W.R.C. MEMBERS

THE MANAGEMENT REGRETFULLY ANNOUNCES THE DEATH LAST NIGHT OF OUR BELOVED PRESIDENT, JOCK KORNFELD.

BECAUSE YOU'LL UNDOUBTEDLY BE HEARING ALL KINDS OF RUMORS, FALSE AND OTHERWISE, ABOUT HIS DEATH, I FEEL I MIGHT AS WELL TELL YOU THE WHOLE TRUTH. MR. KORNFELD WAS FOUND FLOATING IN THE SWIMMING POOL, AND ACCORDING TO THE L.A. CORONER'S OFFICE, HE WAS THE VICTIM OF FOUL PLAY.

IF ANYONE OF YOU HAS ANY INFORMATION THAT COULD LEAD TO THE ARREST OF MR. KORNFELD'S KILLER, PLEASE GET IN TOUCH WITH THE MANAGEMENT.

SADLY YOURS,

GABE STEELE

All the members who showed up at the club that day were, of course, shocked by the news. Not just because they had lost a very fine president but because they didn't like the idea that there might be a killer among them.

As a result, the courts were emptier than Gabe had ever seen them on a Wednesday, Wednesday being the day most of the doctors usually abandoned their patients to sharpen their tennis games.

Jenny Ho was as upset over Jock's murder as anybody because she felt Gabe's life might be in danger, too.

"Why mine?" asked Gabe.

"Well, you're the one who didn't accept Danny's death as suicide right from the start. And you haven't been especially bashful about saying so."

"I'll be careful."

"If you're going to go on sleeping here, maybe you should get a gun for protection."

"What good's a gun?" asked Gabe. "If someone's out to get me, he'll surprise me. He's not going to give me time to pull a gun out of a drawer."

"Well, it's something," said Jenny. "Lots of people keep guns by their beds."

"Look, honey," he said, pulling her into his arms. "I give money to Mrs. Brady's antihandgun campaign. How would it look if I suddenly junked my principles and joined the NRA?"

"This is no time to worry about principles," insisted Jenny. "Your life's in danger. I want you to get a gun."

"I'll think about it." Glancing away from Jenny in order to get her off the subject, Gabe was startled to see Judy Trump standing in the doorway.

"Top of the morning," she greeted him cheerfully.

Gabe didn't know why but just seeing her there gave him a jolt. Jenny nodded a greeting at the detective and left.

"Morning, Judy," he said, trying to cover his nervousness. "What can I do for you?"

"Oh, just dropped in to gab a little. We didn't get much chance last night, what with all that murder and mayhem I had to take care of." From the arch smile on her hard, thin lips, Gabe had the distinct impression that he was her prime suspect. He'd have to watch his words around her.

"Sure. What would you like to gab about?" To

keep his anxiety from showing, he opened a fresh pack of cigarettes, offered one to Trump, and upon being turned down, lit one for himself.

"Well, for starters, I'd like you to run over your activities last night up until the time you found Mr. Kornfeld's body."

"I told you all that last night."

"You did, but I thought I'd like to hear it again and take a few notes." She pulled a pad from her trouser pocket and a pencil from behind one of her ears and prepared to take notes.

"Well," began Gabe, choosing his words very carefully so as not to say anything that would make her any more suspicious than she evidently was, "I locked the club up around seven, picked up my girlfriend at her house around seven-thirty, and—"

"Does this girlfriend have a name?"

"I'd just as soon not give it to you."

"Why is that? Is there some reason why you shouldn't be seeing each other?"

"Not really. But I'd rather keep her out of all this if I can help it. Her parents might get upset."

"Why? Is she a minor?"

"No, she's a grown lady."

Trump cleared her throat. "All right, you picked up this unnamed grown lady at her house." She smiled. She seemed bent on giving Gabe trouble. "Then what did you do?"

"We had dinner at Roberto's."

"Roberto's?" She looked at Gabe questioningly. "Oh, you mean that overpriced steak joint across the street from Cedars-Sinai on Beverly Boulevard."

"Yeah, that's Roberto's, all right."

"Anyone see you there who would swear to it?"

"Roberto's wife, Teresa. She's the cook—also the owner now that Roberto died. And the bartender would remember me. And probably our waitress, Cindy. I've been going there for years. It's a real mom-and-pop operation. I'm sure any one of those people will tell you I was there."

"What time did you finish dinner?"

"I'd say about nine-thirty."

"Then what did you do?"

"I paid the check and we went over to a friend's apartment."

"What did you do there?"

"Talked, mostly."

"And how long did you do that?"

"We left the apartment about midnight, and then I drove my girl home."

"Can anyone verify that you were there during those hours?"

"Just the girl I was with."

"What about your friend whose apartment it was?"

"He wasn't there. He cleared out because he

knew we wanted to be alone. But he knew we'd be there till midnight."

"Does this friend have a name?"

"Yes, but I'd just as soon not reveal that either. He might not appreciate the publicity. And neither would his landlord."

"I don't think you're going to appreciate the publicity either, if you get charged with Kornfeld's murder," declared Trump, her beady eyes focused on Gabe in a most unsettling way.

"You think *I* did it?" asked Gabe incredulously.

"Well, right now you're the nearest thing we have to a suspect. You could probably take some of the heat off yourself if you'd tell me the names of your girlfriend and your friend, the apartment loaner. But since you insist on being so secretive, I must assume you have something to hide."

Tempting as it was to blurt out the entire story and clear himself, no matter who it smeared or got into trouble, Gabe kept his lips tightly sealed.

Trump shrugged and took a piece of paper from her pocket and looked at it. "I got the results of the autopsy a little while ago," she said. "Kornfeld was definitely killed by strangulation, according to the coroner. There was no water in his lungs or any other indication of drowning." She carefully folded the paper and put it back in her pocket. "As nearly as Gonzales can pinpoint it, death occurred sometime between nine o'clock and midnight. Those are the hours you're so vague about." A slow smile spread across her leathery face. "He was a rather large man, that Kornfeld. He'd have to have been strangled by someone with very strong hands." She glanced pointedly across the desk at Gabe's large hands that were folded across his lap.

"You didn't need a coroner's report to inform you of that," said Gabe, a little testiness in his voice. "I told you last night I thought he was strangled, and by the same person who killed Danny. As you know, I never believed Danny killed himself."

"I'm beginning to get that notion," said Trump dryly. "But let's get back to Kornfeld. How'd he know that?"

"You remember what we were discussing the other day?" Gabe reminded her. "That possibly someone in one of the surrounding apartments saw what occurred on the exercise porch that night, and then feeling guilt-ridden about hiding a killer, sent the anonymous note. Anonymous because he didn't want to reveal what he'd been doing that wasn't so kosher himself the night of Danny's death."

"You seem to know an awful lot about Kornfeld that you're not saying." Trump twisted her mouth in a slight smile.

"I don't *know* anything," said Gabe, irritated

that he had to undergo this polite third-degreeing. "I'm just playing my hunches. And my hunch is Kornfeld sent that note."

"Pretty far fetched."

"Well, you could check the typewriter in Kornfeld's office. What have you got to lose?"

"Typewriter!" exclaimed Trump in a scoffing tone. "That's a huge company, that Giverny Cosmetics. Must be a hundred typewriters there."

"Well, it'll give your typewriter analyst something to do for his money. After all, how many murder cases are there in Beverly Hills for you people to practice on in any given week?" It was a smart-alecky thing to say, and he knew it would only antagonize her, but he couldn't help himself, for he was getting annoyed at her constant skepticism.

She looked at him askance but didn't bother to reply.

"You might also want to ask Mrs. Kornfeld if her husband was home the night of Danny's death," suggested Gabe. "I know he wasn't."

"I've got that on my list," said Trump. "Right now she's under pretty heavy sedation. I just checked with her doctor before I came over here."

"It'll keep, I suppose," said Gabe, "unless you want to railroad me into the gas chamber in the next couple of days."

"Mr. Steele, I'm just trying to get some facts," said Trump, her voice abruptly turning soft and plaintive. "I'm not trying to railroad anybody."

"I told you my theory of the murder, and you don't seem to want to buy it."

She sighed wearily. "All right, Mr. Steele, if what you say is true, that Kornfeld was killed by Danny's killer, what were the two of them doing at the club after closing? How'd they get into the grounds? Don't you secure the place before you leave, say you did leave?"

"Jock had a key, I believe. All our presidents do. And if we go on the assumption that his killer is the same one who killed Danny, and Danny's set of club keys are still missing, then he too had the means to get into the club."

"And what was the purpose of their being there?"

Gabe sighed wearily, then plunged on. "According to what Mrs. Kornfeld told me last night, Jock got a call during dinner from some mysterious person who claimed he had something urgent to see him about. Whatever the subject matter, it was important enough to kill over.

"Why would the killer choose the Racquet Club?" asked Trump. "Unless you're bananas, you don't choose a public place like a club to knock someone off."

"I don't think the killer intended to murder

Kornfeld when he asked for this meeting," replied Gabe. "But a fight must have broken out over what they were talking about."

"But why come to the club to talk over something private?"

"Because they figured they could be alone here. The club, after closing, is a pretty private place."

"With you living on the premises?" She raised her thin eyebrows skeptically.

"Obviously they knew I was out."

"How'd they know that?"

"My apartment was dark. My motorcycle was not in its space."

"But if they'd planned this ahead of time, they'd have to know ahead of time that you were going out."

"He didn't have to know ahead of time. He just had to know when he made the call to Jock at dinnertime."

"But how'd he know you wouldn't be coming right back? That you didn't just run into Beverly Hills for a corned beef sandwich?"

"Maybe what they had to discuss wasn't going to take very long."

"If it was that important, they'd still want to know your schedule," pointed out Trump. "How long you'd be gone and when you'd be back. If it was just going to take a few seconds, they could have met on the street corner. Or in a dark alley or in a phone booth."

"That's true," admitted Gabe. He wondered himself how Jock knew he'd be gone. But as he thought about it, it occurred to him that Kim Randall might have told Jock. Possibly Jock had asked him for the use of the apartment that night, and Randall had had to inform him that it was already booked and by whom.

"Did you mention to anyone that you were going out?" asked Trump. "Or said where you were going?"

"Nope. The only people in on it were my girlfriend and the person I borrowed the apartment from."

"If you're not going to tell me their names, how am I going to know you're not just making this all up?" asked Trump. "Why should I believe your story that you found him here? Why shouldn't I believe that you killed Kornfeld, that you were the one who called him during dinner? You're the only one I know for sure was on the premises after closing, aside from Kornfeld, that is. Maybe you two had an argument, and you lost your temper and strangled him and threw him in the pool."

"Every crime has to have a motive," said Gabe challengingly. "What's mine?" Gabe was sure that Trump would have difficulty coming up with a motive for him to have killed Jock.

"You want to know the motive?" asked Trump, with a note of triumph. "Kornfeld came here to tell you that you were fired, and you wouldn't accept it?"

"Fired?!" exclaimed Gabe.

"Yes, fired. Booted out of this cushy job you have here."

Gabe laughed. "Why would he fire me? He just hired me."

"That was before Danny's suicide. But after that there was pressure on him to boot you out."

"How'd you know that?" asked Gabe, astonished and a little shocked at Trump's knowledge of the club's politics.

"I was at Danny's funeral," said Trump with a sly grin. "I saw the fight between you and old man White."

"What in hell were you doing there?" asked Gabe, fidgeting nervously in his seat.

"Oh, just poking around incognito among the mourners to see if my antennas—" she touched one of her pointed ears "—could pick up anything that might suggest Danny's death was something other than what it seemed."

Gabe was forced to admire her thoroughness, even though he didn't agree with her conclusions.

She went on, "I always go to the victims' funerals in this kind of case. You'd be surprised at the things you learn that you can't get just from questioning somebody formally. Like this brouhaha between you and White. I talked to

White the day after they buried the kid. He told me he'd already recommended to Kornfeld that the board dismiss you at the next meeting."

"If you ask me, that's a pretty weak motive," declared Gabe, breaking out into a cold sweat. "I don't generally kill somebody just because I get fired. If I did, there'd be a lot of dead producers and story editors in this town."

"It'll do until a stronger motive comes along," asserted Trump, buffing her fingernails on the palm of her other hand. "Or a better suspect."

"That's ridiculous," insisted Gabe. "Kornfeld never mentioned anything to me about firing me."

"Then you did have a discussion with him?"

"Not about that. I haven't had any discussion with him since the morning I found Danny, when I told him about it. If you believe it was me, then you have to believe it was me who made that call at dinnertime. And I was at Roberto's between seven-thirty and nine-thirty, and that can be easily verified. Just pick up the phone and talk to Teresa. As a matter of fact, I'll get her on the line for you." Jumping out of his chair he opened the door between his office and Jenny's.

"Hey, Jen. Get Roberto's on the phone for me, will you, dear, and ask to speak to Teresa."

He took advantage of the break in her questioning to light another cigarette. As he inhaled the first drag, Jenny called in and announced she had Teresa on the line. "Thanks, Jen." Gabe exhaled some smoke and picked up the receiver. "Hello, Teresa, this is Gabe Steele. There's a detective in my office who wants to speak to you. Judy, meet Teresa." He handed Judy the receiver and sat back, trying to relax but finding it difficult.

"Hello, Teresa. Judy Trump of the Beverly Hills Police Department, Homicide Division. I'd like to check something out with you, if you have a minute. Was Gabe Steele at your place for dinner last night between seven-thirty and nine-thirty? . . . I see . . . And was he with anyone? . . . What'd she look like? . . . Very pretty and slightly Oriental looking . . . I see." She glanced in the other office at Jenny, and grinned. "All right. Thank you very much."

"Happy now?" said Gabe, taking the receiver from Trump.

"Not so fast," said Trump, "if they have a phone at Roberto's, who's to say you couldn't have called Kornfeld from there?"

"And what did I do with my girl while I was murdering Kornfeld?" asked Gabe sarcastically.

"You could have dropped her off at her home before you met Kornfeld."

"I could have done a lot of things, but what I'm telling you is the truth. If you don't believe me, give me a lie detector test."

"I might have to." She was silent for a moment, then she shrugged and got to her feet. "Well, I guess that about does it for today, Mr. Steele. If I want to talk to you again, you'll be around, won't you?"

"Yes, I'll be doing business at the same old tennis ball stand," said Gabe. "Unless I'm fired."

"Good. I wouldn't want you to leave for parts unknown until all this is settled. See you at the funeral."

"You going to this one, too?" asked Gabe, walking her to the door.

"You betcha."

"Well, get your tickets early. This is liable to be a big affair."

After Judy Trump departed, Gabe meandered into Jenny's office and sat down on the edge of her desk. "Do me a favor, will you, Jen? See if you can find out if Ed White was home last night around the time Jock was killed. I'd do it myself, but the Whites aren't talking to me."

"You think Ed White did it?"

"I don't know, but it's worth checking out. Last night Rita told me that Jock and White had a violent argument about me. White wanted Jock to fire me, and Jock said absolutely not. It's possible that White had another meeting with him at the club here, that White lost his temper and strangled Jock—you know, the way he tried to strangle me at the funeral." He studied Jenny's face for some kind of reaction, but she was expressionless. "Doesn't that make sense to you?"

"I don't think he'd have killed his own son."

"No, but the two deaths don't necessarily have to have been committed by the same person. It's even possible that Danny did kill himself, if you buy that White killed Kornfeld."

Judy raised her eyebrows contemplatively. "Did you mention any of this to Judy?"

"Hell, no. I figured no use giving her anything more to substantiate her theory."

"Which is?"

"That I did it. I don't know if she's purely on a fishing expedition or not, but from her line of questioning just now I kind of got the idea that I'm her prime suspect."

"That's ridiculous," exclaimed Jenny. "You have a foolproof alibi. You were with me. I can testify to that."

"I left your unsullied name out of my story," said Gabe. "Also where we were and what we were doing."

"But why? I'm not ashamed of what we did."

"Well, in the first place, I don't know how it will set with the members here that you and I are having an affair, since it's against the club's bylaws."

"Who cares?" Jenny cried out. "I'll work somewhere else if it's a question of you not taking the blame for a murder you didn't do."

"It isn't just you I'm protecting," said Gabe. "You have any idea how ridiculous this club will look if Kim Randall's operation is made public?"

"Again, who cares?"

Gabe shrugged. "What about us using Kim's apartment?"

"We had a reason," said Jenny. "We were trying to solve a case. And what about the datebook? Wouldn't that prove something? You've got to tell Detective Trump about it."

"It'll only prove something if she'd believe my theory of the murder. But for some reason, Trump's unwilling to buy that story. Besides, how am I going to get it out of Randall's apartment? He wouldn't give it to me if I told him why I wanted it. It would expose his operation, and he'd look like a first-rate asshole in this town. Not only that, the members' wives would insist he be booted out of the club. But say I could get it, it would still prove nothing to Trump. You need Kornfeld alive and the datebook, to give any credibility to that theory. Unless we're fortunate enough to have some other clues drop into our laps."

"Well I'm not going to stand by and let you be accused of Kornfeld's murder. I don't care how it makes the club or anyone else look. I can at least prove you were with me."

"In the meantime," suggested Gabe, "you can help by finding out if the Whites were home last night."

"And just how am I supposed to find that out? It's not exactly any of the club's business."

Gabe gave it some thought. "Make up a story," he finally suggested. "Tell them you're a ratings taker from one of the networks, and you want to know if they watched *The Thin Man* Tuesday night. If they said they did, they're lying, because it's not on Tuesday night. And if they say they were out and didn't watch anything, chances are Ed White didn't kill Jock?"

"How do you know that?"

"Because if he had, he wouldn't admit to being out."

Jenny smiled. "That's pretty cool thinking. I'll get on it right away."

"Before you do—" he pulled her into his arms and kissed her as ardently as he had the night before.

While the two of them were enjoying a close embrace, Rick Reeves entered the foyer from the street and smirked at them through the glass. "Naughty, naughty," he said, with a laugh.

Startled at being caught in each other's arms, Gabe and Jenny abruptly broke apart and stood there trying to look innocent.

"Hey, what's this I hear about Jock Kornfeld?" asked Rick, leaning close to the talk hole in the glass.

"It's true," said Gabe. "He was murdered. Or so the cops seem to think."

"Jeez!" exclaimed Rick. "I thought those things only happened on the boob tube—oh, well, that's life." He shrugged and started to leave.

"By the way, Rick," Gabe suddenly called to him, "how did you hear about it?"

"Hear about what?" asked Rick, suddenly looking flustered.

"Jock's murder."

"Oh . . . well . . . I . . ." He started to stammer. "I'm not sure . . . I . . . I guess someone told me."

He turned and left in a hurry.

"What do you make of that?" Gabe asked Jenny as soon as Rick was out of earshot. "He couldn't have seen it on the bulletin board. He just got here."

Jenny didn't seem bowled over by that information. "Maybe his father told him. Dr. Reeves is a member of the board. And you phoned all the board members as soon as you opened the club this morning."

"That's right, I did." But there was still something about Rick's expression when he surprised him with that question that made Gabe wonder.

Jenny spent the rest of the day trying to get someone to answer the phone at the White's, but no one picked up. Either they were out of town or in such deep mourning that they were unwilling to talk with anyone.

"I'll try them again tomorrow," promised Jenny, as she was closing up the office at six P.M.

"And I'm still trying to track down Marty Engels," said Gabe. "I tried his house and his office. He wasn't home, and his office said he'd taken off for New York to try to secure more financing to shore up his ailing company. So until he returns—and his secretary refused to tell me where he was staying in New York—I guess I can forget about questioning him." He looked at her imploringly. "Maybe you'd like to go out again tonight and get drunk. I can't get Randall's place, but we could find a motel."

She gave him a squeeze in a most intimate place, laughed, and said, "Not tonight, Josephine. I'm pretty bushed."

That night, after dinner alone at the Hard Rock, Gabe returned to his apartment, picked up a pencil, and started to jot down on a pad all the possibilities about both deaths. There were six of them, he figured.

(1) *Danny's killer*. He was by far the one with the strongest motive. If he killed to prevent his petty thievery from being known, he'd certainly kill to cover up a murder.

(2) *Phil Neer*. From what Gabe could tell, Neer hated Kornfeld for conspiring to kick him out of his cushy job and replace him with a younger, more glamorous pro. If he were a psycho, he

could have killed Kornfeld, but Gabe didn't think he was that maladjusted. He was just a little punchy from standing in the hot sun too long and having his brains fried every day.

(3) *Rita Kornfeld.* If she suspected Kornfeld of cheating on her, she might have felt like killing him at times. But since she was home all evening, she could hardly have done it, unless she'd hired a hit man, which seemed unlikely. Besides, she probably wasn't the murdering type; she took out her rage by getting drunk, not killing.

(4) *Aaron Wexler.* If he was aware he was being cuckolded, he, too, had a motive to kill Kornfeld. But he seemed like too pragmatic a person to commit murder over a mere wife.

(5) *Ed White.* Possible that he killed Kornfeld, but unlikely that he would kill his own son. And somehow Gabe was convinced that a single killer was responsible for both deaths. As far as Gabe could see, White had no motive for killing Danny.

(6) *Marty Engels.* Of all the suspects on Gabe's list, Engels was the only one who had a motive to commit both murders, provided he was the locker room thief. And so far, the only thing linking him to the locker room thefts was his cash-flow problem and his card debts. Not much to go on there, either.

After mulling over all the possibilities, Gabe

decided that his original theory held up the best. Both murders were committed by the same person. That person was probably a man, because a woman wouldn't have the strength to strangle someone as large as Kornfeld. And that man was probably the locker room thief. He first killed Danny to silence him and then killed Kornfeld to silence him as well, after discovering that Kornfeld knew he'd faked Danny's suicide.

Unfortunately, there were no real clues to prove Gabe's theory. The only tangibles he had to go on were (1) the datebook, and (2), the anonymous note.

But if he could at least find out where the note came from, both clues would be more meaningful. Which gave him an idea, and a place to start.

Since he didn't believe Judy was going to act on his suggestion to check out the typewriter in Kornfeld's office, he decided to handle the matter himself first thing in the morning.

No, first he gave Jenny a "good morning" kiss, then he turned his attention to the business of the day.

"Dig out the address of Giverny Cosmetics for me, will you, honey? I think I'll run over there and do a little sleuthing on my own."

She punched into the computer, a Century City address came up on the screen, which she jotted down on a slip of paper and handed to Gabe.

"Thanks, Jen," he said, sticking it into his pocket. "If anyone wants me, don't tell them where I am."

"Does that include Judy Trump?"

"Especially Judy Trump."

Jenny sighed and said, "I'm afraid it's too late. She just walked in the door, and she's heading our way."

Glancing into the lobby, Gabe saw Judy Trump thumping towards him in her Adidas.

"'Hi, Judy, what's cooking?" asked Gabe affably.

"If this were an electric-chair state, I could say 'you might be.'" She laughed, which sent a chill up Gabe's spine. That laugh boded no good.

"What are you talking about?"

"Mind if I sit down?"

"Be my guest." He waved her into a chair.

"On a hunch, when I was here the other day, I took the liberty of asking Jenny to give me a sample of the typewriting from her machine," said Trump, swinging her Adidas up on the edge of Gabe's desk. "And just this morning I got the results from Carrothers." She paused for a hell of a long time before finally delivering the zinger. "The anonymous note was typed on the machine in the next room," she said, pointing through the door at Jenny's IBM Selectric.

"No kidding!" exclaimed Gabe. He studied her in dismay, worried at what she might be reading into her discovery.

"I kid you not," she replied.

"What made you think of looking at our typewriter?" asked Gabe.

"*Cherchez le obvious.*" She smiled triumphantly and exclaimed, "The veteran detective who broke me into this line of work once said to me, 'Never look for the esoteric when you're solving a case. Look for the obvious. You'll usually find your answer there.'"

Having recovered from her surprise, Gabe asked, "So now that you've found the obvious, what exactly do you know?"

"Again, I say look for the obvious," she said, shooting him a playful smile. "And the obvious thing is that you typed it, Mr. Steele."

"That's stupid, not obvious," snapped Gabe. "If I killed Danny and made it look like suicide, why would I write a note to make it look like murder? And if I intended to make it an anonymous note, why would I use my typewriter?"

"So you could say to me what you just said to me. Or maybe you wanted to get caught."

Gabe sighed impatiently. "Has it ever occurred to you that *Kornfeld* could have typed it on our typewriter here? He had access to the office anytime he pleased."

"Well, the way things are going, we're never going to be able to ask him, are we, Mr. Steele?" Standing suddenly, she headed for the door, then turned back to Gabe again. "As I said before, I wouldn't leave town if I were you."

"It's hopeless," Gabe complained to Jenny the moment Judy Trump's Peter Pannish figure disappeared through the entrance to the street. "That stubborn lady is going to go right on looking at *le* obvious until three or more people wind up in their coffins."

"You really think there are going to be more murders?" asked Jenny, furrowing her brows in concern.

"Only if I let it be known that I'm out to catch the bastard. Then maybe he'll make a run at me."

"Why'd you have to bring that up?" asked Jenny.

"Because I was thinking it's about the way now to catch this guy."

"And you're going to risk getting killed by being the bait?"

"Until I think of a better way."

"I don't believe I like that," said Jenny, with a shudder.

"Frankly, my dear, I'm not crazy about the idea myself," said Gabe. "But as long as you like me enough to worry about me, I can live with it."

"Like you? I'm nuts about you, you dumb schmuck!"

"Schmuck!!!" He started to laugh. "Jenny, you *have* made the transition from Hula-hula land to Beverly Hills. And you know what?" he added, pulling her into his arms in spite of the fact that two members were passing by on the other side of the glass partition, "I like it!"

Sixteen

Until Jock Kornfeld's funeral, which Gabe learned later that day was to be held at the Wilshire Sinai Temple Friday morning at ten o'clock, it was business as usual at the Racquet Club. The ball machine broke down. A fifteen-year-old boy had to be suspended for making himself a martini at the bar and failing to sign a chit for it. Kim Randall continued playing his "customer's" game with potential film investors. Joan Harrington complained that the ladies' locker room was a mess, and no one cared enough about the plight of the women members to correct the situation. And Joe Harris had a mild coronary in the cardroom, and nobody in his gin game stopped to pick him up until they'd played out the hand.

There were a couple of exceptions to the usual routine: (1) Jan Wexler canceled her tennis lessons on Wednesday, Thursday, and, of course,

Friday, the day of the funeral; and (2) the flag was flown at half-mast.

But Jock Kornfeld's regular four o'clock doubles match went off on schedule, the only difference being that Gabe had been drafted to take his place.

On Thursday Max Weber showed up to begin installing the combination locks. Gabe didn't know whether Kornfeld had gotten approval from the board for this unusual expense, so he had to place another call to Bob Gilmore at Vero Beach to see if it was all right to go ahead with the work.

Bob Gilmore assured him it was okay; he'd take the responsibility. "And give my regrets to Rita," he said. "I'm not going to be able to make the funeral. This Chicano pitcher I'm dealing with is giving me a little Mexican static."

Gilmore's reference to Rita Kornfeld started the wheels grinding in Gabe's mind again concerning what she had told him about Ed White. Far fetched as it seemed, it was possible that it was White who had enticed Jock down to the club in the middle of dinner. Possible, but almost impossible to prove without getting White to admit where he was that night. And so far no one was answering the phone at the White's.

On a hunch Gabe decided to pay them a surprise visit. As a reason for dropping in on them, he'd use the pretense that he felt bad that they held him responsible for their son's death and that he wanted to reiterate that he had not driven Danny to it with any loose-cannon accusations. If they'd listen, he might even tell them his theory of what really happened that night. Maybe he could get them on his side if he was convincing enough. If not that, maybe he could say something that would trigger a slip from White regarding *his* activities Tuesday night. Just what he could say Gabe wasn't sure. He'd just have to play the scene by ear when he was face to face with White.

The Whites lived in a modest ranch-style yellow bungalow, with a picket fence around it, a few doors south of Sunset Boulevard on Glenroy in West Los Angeles. It was about a ten-minute drive from the club, which Gabe managed to cover on his Honda in thirty minutes because the Department of Water and Power had one lane going west on Sunset Boulevard blocked off due to repair work they were attempting.

A black Mercedes sedan, with a personalized license plate on it that read MEDIC was parked at the curb in front of 114 South Glenroy. Behind it was a white Toyota Corolla that seemed about five years old. Gabe didn't recognize either of the cars, but he hoped, as he parked his bike between them, and let himself in the White's gate that whomever was visiting them wasn't going to get in the way of his mission.

He walked up the tulip-lined path to the front door and with some trepidation pressed the bell. He hoped to God there wasn't going to be another scene like the one at the funeral home.

Expecting one of the Whites to answer his ring, Gabe was surprised to see the door being opened by a stern-looking middle-aged lady in a white nurse's uniform who smelled of disinfectant.

"Isn't this the Whites' residence?" asked Gabe, fearful that the club's computer had come up with the wrong address.

"Yes."

"I'd like to speak to Mr. White. I'm a friend of his from the tennis club."

She shot him a deprecating smile. "I'm afraid that's impossible, sir. Mr. White had a stroke, and he's unable to speak."

"Oh, my God, I'm sorry," said Gabe, slightly stunned by the news. "When did this happen?"

"Tuesday night."

"Do you have any idea what time?"

"I really couldn't say, sir. I wasn't called on the case until four in the morning."

"How do things look for him now?" asked Gabe. "I mean, what are the chances for his recovery?"

The nurse shrugged. "Hard to tell. Probably

not good. The doctor's in there with Mrs. White now discussing whether or not to move him to a hospital. Would you like to talk to Mrs. White?"

"No, don't bother her," said Gabe hastily, starting back down the walk. "Just tell her the members of the tennis club send their regrets."

"So much for that theory," said Gabe as he finished telling Jenny about his visit to the Whites'.

"Isn't it possible," asked Jenny, "that he killed Mr. Kornfeld first and then went home and had the stroke from all the excitement?"

"Possible or not, we're never going to find out now, I'm afraid," said Gabe. "So for now we might as well cross him off our list of suspects."

"Back to Square One again?" said Jenny, with a sigh.

"Afraid so."

The first real break in the case came around six o'clock on the eve of Kornfeld's funeral.

Gabe had just finished filling in for Jock in his four o'clock doubles match, and, after showering, was sitting naked, except for a towel around his middle, on the wooden bench in front of his locker, when he suddenly felt the presence of another human being close by.

Glancing up, he found himself staring into the friendly face of Manuel, Danny's replacement.

"I found this in the utility closet when I was cleaning up in there just a little while ago." He handed Gabe a gold miniature tennis ball with the letters "U.S.T.A." engraved on it. The U.S.T.A. stood for the United States Tennis Association; and the gold ball was of the kind given only to the winner of a U.S. national championship, whether it be the National 13-and-under girl's or the U.S. Open.

"I guess one of the members lost it," said Manuel.

"Yeah, I guess so," said Gabe, studying the gold ball thoughtfully. "I'll put a notice up on the bulletin board."

As Gabe stared at the gold ball, it suddenly occurred to him that only two people out of the 150 who belonged to the club had ever won a national title—Rick Reeves and Mike Flanagan. As unlikely as it seemed that one of them had killed Danny, it was a train of thought that had to be pursued.

"Hey, Manuel!" Leaping off the bench, Gabe ran to the shoe-shining alcove. "Manuel, show me exactly where you found this."

"Sure thing, Mr. Gabe." Manuel unlocked the door to the utility closet. Then he dropped down to his knees and pointed to the corner farthest from the door. "It was back there behind a bucket."

The significance of Manuel's find excited

Gabe. What if, in the struggle with the man who killed him, Danny had yanked on the gold chain around the man's neck and broken it, causing the gold ball to tumble to the back of the closet, unnoticed by its owner whose fingerprints were probably all over it? Hoping that they hadn't already been smudged beyond recognition by Manuel's and his own prints, Gabe pulled a Kleenex from the dispenser on the wall and wrapped the ball in the tissue. Then he walked up to his locker and put the priceless little package in the pocket of his jacket.

As he dressed, he could hardly wait to go downstairs and show the gold ball to Jenny. Of course, the gold ball didn't necessarily prove its owner killed anybody or stole valuables from lockers. Even if confronted with the gold ball, its owner could simply admit that it was his and say that somehow the chain had broken unbeknownst to him when he was in the locker room, allowing the ball to fall to the floor. But could he explain what the gold ball was doing in the utility closet? He could, thought Gabe, but only if there was room between the bottom of the door and the tile floor for the gold ball to have rolled through after he'd dropped it.

Deciding he'd better check that out before doing anything else, Gabe kneeled down in front of the utility closet door and tried to roll the gold ball under it. He was relieved to find that it couldn't be done. The door bottom was practically flush to the floor.

Rewrapping the gold ball in a piece of Kleenex, Gabe carried it downstairs to the office and unwrapped it on Jenny's desk, being careful not to touch it with his hands.

"I think I'm finally onto something," he told her while she was studying it. "Only two people in this club have won national championships—Mike Flanagan and Rick Reeves.

"Don't forget Phil Neer," Jenny reminded him.

"Oh, yeah, I forgot about him." He thought about Neer a moment, then added, "But somehow he's last on my list of possible murder suspects. He's a harmless old codger."

"Somehow I can't see Mike Flanagan or Rick Reeves doing it, either," said Jenny. "Flanagan's a millionaire, and Rick has a rich father."

"Well, the sons of the rich aren't necessarily rich themselves," observed Gabe. "Besides, money doesn't necessarily have anything to do with it. Some of the most affluent people in the world have been kleptomaniacs."

Jenny sighed. "Sounds like a long shot. That Judy Trump is pretty skeptical."

"I wouldn't dare go to Judy at this stage," he said, wrapping the ball in Kleenex again and replacing it in his jacket pocket. "My case is too flimsy. First I have to find out if anyone's lost a gold ball."

"How do you do that?" asked Jenny.

"We'll have to keep our eyes open. Maybe tomorrow at the funeral. I doubt if Flanagan will be there, but Rick probably will. Let's try to sit next to him if we can."

"One thing I don't understand," said Jenny. "Supposing Rick's ball is missing? I can understand why he'd kill Danny—to keep him from talking. But why would he kill Kornfeld?"

"The same reason I've said all along."

"But how did he know that Kornfeld knew or at least witnessed the scene on the exercise porch?"

"Now you're beginning to sound like Judy Trump." He smiled thinly. "If I knew the answer to that one, baby, this mystery would be solved."

It was standing room only at the Wilshire Sinai Temple the next morning, but Gabe and Jenny drew a blank with respect to any new clues. The service by Rabbi Gladwin—Hollywood's top funeral mavin—was so well attended, in fact, that they were lucky to find two seats together, much less a place where they could observe what Rick Reeves was wearing around his neck.

They were pretty sure he was there, however, for they had noticed a red Ferrari tailgating them when they were driving through the Miracle Mile on their way to the temple.

"Try to stay close to him," suggested Jenny. "So we can know where he's seated in the temple."

But her Volkswagen Rabbit was no match for the powerful Ferrari once it whizzed past them, cutting dangerously in and out of the heavy midmorning traffic until it disappeared from sight.

There was no sign of either Rick or the red Ferrari when they left the Rabbit in the parking lot behind the temple and walked up the sidewalk to the entrance to Rabbi Gladwin's home stadium.

Thinking possibly Rick had parked farther away and would show up after them, they waited on the front steps of the majestic-looking stone edifice for about five minutes and watched the other mourners arrive. But as the time for the service approached and the last-minute crowd started to thicken and pour through the temple doors with the same enthusiasm and aggressiveness you'd expect to find at a funeral for a rock star who'd ODed on heroin, Gabe told Jenny they'd better go inside and grab some seats for themselves before they were all taken.

They were fortunate to find two aisle seats in the fourth row of pews from the rear of the cavernous place of worship. However, despite the fact that Jenny had twenty-twenty vision and Gabe's eyes weren't much worse, all they could see from where they sat were Jock's magnificent bronze casket, banked on all sides by a display of flowers that would have put the Rose Parade to shame, the bulbous-nosed Rabbi Gladwin holding forth at the podium, and a sea of yarmulke-covered heads.

Kornfeld's family—Rita, her father, her daughter Jane, and her husband—were curtained off in the alcove reserved for the survivors of the "loved one."

Rabbi Gladwin spoke for about an hour, for once he warmed to a subject, he was a hard man to stop. His talk was divided into three sections: Kornfeld the Family Man and Loving Husband; Kornfeld the Sportsman; and Kornfeld the Charitable Good Neighbor, "who loved everyone, both Jew and gentile." (You can say that again, reflected Gabe, especially if they were half his age, blond, and stacked.) At times Gladwin went for laughs, at other times for tears. What he never seemed to go for was an ending.

When he didn't seem able to come up with one, many of the mourners grew restless and started squirming in their seats. At this time Gabe got a chance to pinpoint some of the people who were there. About half the audience were members of the Racquet Club, Kim Randall included; the other half were distant relatives and business associates of the deceased. Gabe also spotted Judy Trump, trying to hide behind dark glasses, and not fooling anyone, because her pointed elfin ears blew her disguise.

Jan Wexler, looking ravishingly beautiful in a black dress, her eyes hidden behind large dark sunglasses, and her natural blond hair in stark contrast with the rest of her mourning clothes, came in just after the services began, but because she was alone and very stunning even in black, one of the husbands made room for her next to him in a row of seats in the middle of the house. Aaron Wexler was conspicuous by his absence. Either he knew about the affair Jock was having with his wife and didn't wish to be a hypocrite by showing up and pretending to be saddened by the death of the man who was cuckolding him, or else he was already hard at work on Jock's estate taxes.

Gabe didn't see Phil Neer among the mourners, either. That in itself seemed to eliminate him as the guilty party, decided Gabe. If he'd killed Kornfeld, he'd have been cagey enough to show up at the funeral so that nobody would think there'd been any bad blood between them.

When the service finally ended, Gabe and Jenny were the first out the door. They wanted to be on the sidewalk in front when the other mourners filed out. But if Rick Reeves had attended the services, he'd either left before they did or departed through a side "fire" exit. They saw and said "hello" to Rick's mother and father, who was making a date to play doubles later that day with Merrill Karp, the club's top orthodontist, but Gabe didn't think it judicious to ask them where their son was. He didn't want to tip Rick off to anything.

"Well, maybe he'll come to the club today," speculated Gabe, as they waited in vain for Rick to come down the steps. When it was apparent he wouldn't appear, Gabe took Jenny's hand, and the two started off in the direction of the parking lot.

Considering how warm and smog-free the weather was, the Racquet Club was relatively empty when Gabe and Jenny got back there a little after noon. Only one court was in use—Phil Neer was giving a lesson to an eight-year-old pigtailed girl tennis prodigy. But there was no one in the dining room except the help, the maitre d', and a uniformed policeman who freeloaded at the club in exchange for looking the other way regarding the big-money gambling that went on downstairs in the cardroom. There wasn't much more activity on the terrace: a retired airlines pilot and a used car salesman were playing backgammon for a dollar a point; a furrier with his leg in a cast, having broken his leg skiing, was taking a snooze in the hot sun; and Ricardo Montoya, a Mexican star of the silent picture days, dressed in white, with a red sash around his waist, was dictating his memoirs into a Sony tape recorder.

"The place is like a morgue today," commented Jenny, when the two of them were back in her office.

"I wish you wouldn't use that simile," said Gabe. "It makes me nervous." He shivered.

"Sorry about that." She laughed.

"Jock was very popular around here," said Gabe. "They're probably all over at Rita's house having one of those Jewish wakes."

"Jewish wake?" There was a bewildered expression in her lovely almond-shaped eyes.

Gabe grinned. How would a girl with a Japanese mother and a Hawaiian father know what he was talking about?

"Yeah, it's the *in* thing these days," he explained. "A lot of booze, corned beef and pastrami sandwiches from Nate and Al's, and coffee cake from Bailey's. It's kind of like a bar mitzvah only you don't have a bunch of noisy kids running around to spoil the fun."

"Speaking of noisy kids." Jenny nodded in the direction of the front door. "Look who just breezed in."

Glancing into the lobby, Gabe was pleased to see Rick Reeves strutting in.

"Thanks, Jen." He gave her a little hug and whispered into her ear, "Wish me luck."

"Hey, you two messing around again!" exclaimed Rick, grinning at them with his nose pressed against the glass. "You know, you two are setting yourselves up for a little blackmail."

He threw back his head and laughed raucously; he was a great audience for his own jests.

Gabe ignored the dig. He was absorbed in studying Rick's throat. To his complete frustration, Rick had on a white cashmere turtleneck sweater. If he was wearing the gold ball, it would have to be underneath.

"What are you looking at so hard, Old-timer?"

Gabe jumped with a start; he realized Rick had caught him staring, and not very subtly, at the throat of the turtleneck, wondering how to get it off him without creating suspicion.

"Just admiring your sweater," said Gabe.

"You have good taste," said Rick, pointing to his high collar. "Three hundred big ones at Ralph Lauren's."

"That's out of my league," said Gabe.

"Where is everybody?" asked Rick, looking around.

"Probably over at the Kornfeld's. Surprised you're not there."

"I don't dig death."

"Hey," Gabe suddenly exclaimed, "how about some tennis?" He didn't know if he was up to singles with Rick, but it was the only way he could think of to get him out of that turtleneck.

"With you, Old-timer?" He peered at Gabe as if he were Methuselah.

"I think I can handle you, for a couple of sets, anyway."

"You really think so," said Rick. "Well, I'll play you for lunch."

"You're on. Let's get dressed."

"Let's eat first," suggested Rick. "I'm starved. I didn't have any breakfast."

"Eat first?" Gabe was surprised.

"Sure, we can always tell Henri to hold the bill until after I cream you," grinned Rick.

Gabe wasn't crazy about playing hard singles on a full stomach with the sun nearly straight overhead. So he just ordered a glass of orange juice and a couple of pieces of melba toast. But Rick, obviously feeling he was going to have no trouble handling the ancient manager, ordered split pea soup, a steak sandwich ("blood rare"), and asparagus hollandaise.

"By the way, what'd you want to talk about that day we were interrupted?" asked Rick while they were waiting for their food.

"It's probably none of my business," said Gabe.

"No, I want to hear it."

"Well, if you promise not to get mad, it's actually something your father asked me to talk to you about. Some advice, really."

"Yeah. What?"

"Frankly, he'd like you to go back to med school and forget tennis. He says there's a better future in it."

"Are you kidding?" Rick grimaced. "It takes eight years to become a doctor. I mean, look at the money Mike Flanagan's making. And he didn't even have a D average in high school."

"But he's on the verge of being Numero Uno in the world," Gabe reminded him. "You're not in the first hundred."

"Well, I just need a couple of breaks." He squirmed uncomfortably in his seat, as though the subject were unpleasant to him.

"That's what I thought when I was your age," said Gabe. "I wound up neglecting my studies."

"That's you," said Rick, irritably. "I'm me."

"Don't get your back up," said Gabe. "I'm just trying to give you some good advice."

"Well, I don't need any advice from a failure like you."

"Don't be such a smart aleck," said Gabe, raising his voice in anger, "I've made a damn good living at TV up until now."

"Okay, okay. Sorry. But, if you're such a good writer, why did you have to take a job managing the club?"

"Unfortunately, I've run into a situation I can't do anything about. It's called age discrimination."

"Age discrimination?"

"Yeah, some executives at the TV networks decided all the older writers are hacks. So they're mostly hiring young kids fresh out of college."

"Christ, that doesn't make sense." For the first time, Rick seemed to have some empathy for Gabe's position. "I'd think writing would be the one thing you could do until you're eighty. My pop's still operating, and he's over seventy."

"Try telling that to these hotshot kids running the entertainment industry these days."

"How can they tell how old you are?" asked Rick. "What do they do before they hire you—ask to see your birth certificate?"

"They haven't gone that far yet. But they seem to have a pretty good idea of who's over forty. I've heard there's actually a list of those they'll hire and those they consider ready for the scrap heap, though no one's ever seen it."

"So why don't you old-timers do something to fight it? Sounds like antitrust or whatever you call that shit."

"Don't think we wouldn't like to. Trouble is, nobody can find any proof. If there is a list, the network bigwigs are being damn careful to keep what's on it to themselves. Meanwhile, many of the town's most experienced writers are standing in the unemployment line."

"Well, I didn't know any of this." Rick appeared genuinely concerned. "Sorry I called you a failure. I was just trying to defend myself, because I guess maybe that's what I think I am—a god-damn fuckin' failure."

Suddenly Gabe couldn't help feeling sorry for the guy. "You're not a failure. You're too young to be put in that category yet."

"I hope you're right," said Rick, with what seemed a grateful smile. "Thanks, Old-timer."

"Anyway, I'm sorry I told you to quit tennis. It's none of my business. It's between you and your old man."

"Yeah, you're right." He thought that over for a moment then stood up suddenly, at the same time pushing his chair away from the table. "Speaking of tennis, let's grab the Terrace Court before someone else gets it. If I'm going to whip your butt, I want somebody to see me do it."

Until that last remark, Gabe found himself almost liking Rick. But his challenging manner got Gabe's adrenalin rising again.

"That'll be the day," he said, following Rick to the door of the locker room and entering behind him.

Actually Gabe was indifferent about the outcome of the match; all he was interested in was seeing whether Rick was wearing his gold tennis ball, or not.

Rick, however, held Gabe's game in such contempt that when they walked on the court, he was wearing a heavy warm-up suit, despite the eighty degree weather, and the jacket was zipped right up to his Adam's apple.

Gabe's work was cut out for him; he'd have to run the cocky kid around until he was so boiling hot, he'd be forced to remove his jacket.

Fortunately, Gabe was on his game, and Rick wasn't. In order to prove that he was world class caliber and that Gabe was just another over-the-hill club player, Rick started out by trying to make put-aways of every shot. As a result, he made a lot of unforced errors, and before he knew it he was down 4–1 in the first set. The way he was playing seemed made to order for Gabe, because the points were short and Gabe wasn't a bit tired or feeling his age.

Realizing he wasn't getting anywhere trying to blast Gabe off the court, Rick started playing more sensibly. He resorted to a softer game and tried keeping the ball in play longer before going for a winner. But by then it was too late to save the first set.

Gabe ran it out 6–3, much to Rick's chagrin, for a crowd was beginning to gather on the terrace, and they applauded enthusiastically when Gabe served an ace to close out the set.

As both men stopped to towel off while they were changing courts, Rick, who was sweating profusely, suddenly unzipped his jacket and tore it angrily off his body. Gabe, his eyes riveted on Rick's neck, was happy to note that the gold ball wasn't adorning it.

"Now that I'm warmed up," muttered Rick grimly, "I'm going to whip your ass, Old-timer."

In his elation at not seeing Rick wearing the gold tennis ball, Gabe barely heard the dig at his age. Or cared. The absence of the gold ball was all that mattered.

However, he decided to wait until after the match to bring it up to Rick. As a result he could hardly keep his mind on the game, and Rick trounced him 6–2 in the second set.

Gabe was tempted to give Rick the third set without going through the motions of playing it, so that he could get on with his detective work.

"You want to play it out, Old-timer, or sign the lunch check right now?" asked Rick, with a supercilious smirk when they were toweling off.

Gabe's competitive spirit suddenly overpowered his desire to play detective. "Hell no, I'm not going to give it to you," he said. "Let's play. And to make it interesting, let's throw another ten bucks in the pot."

"Why not?" said Rick, picking up his racket and striding cockily to the base line.

"Go get 'em," he heard Jenny whisper through the fence behind the bench where Gabe was still drying his face and the handle of his racket. "You're playing like a champ."

"And that's not all," Gabe whispered to her through the chain link. "Sneak a look at his neck, if you get a chance."

She smiled approvingly and pulled up a director's chair to watch the completion of the match.

With his lady fair rooting him on, Gabe refused to concede an inch to age in the third set. Giving it everything he had, he hung in there until he was leading five games to four, with Rick about to serve. But winning his own serve at four-all had really taken its toll on Gabe's forty-year-old legs. He was badly winded when the two of them stopped to towel themselves off on their way to change courts. Frankly, Gabe didn't know how he was going to break Rick's serve again. The kid had a big top-spin delivery, and he was following it into the net now on every point, forcing Gabe into numerous backhand errors, errors made more from exhaustion than Gabe's inability to handle a top-spin serve.

As he sat on the bench, wondering if he shouldn't just concede the match and stop being a hero for Jenny's sake, something made him say to Rick, without waiting for the match to be over, "Hey, what happened to your gold ball—the one you got for winning the national 16-and-under?"

Gabe wasn't sure if Rick was startled by the question—he thought he noticed a slight quiver of his lower lip but wasn't certain.

"Beats me," he replied as he reached up with his left hand and felt the section of his neck where the gold ball generally hung from a chain. "I must have left it home."

"I thought you always wore it," Gabe reminded him.

Rick shrugged and, sounding annoyed, said, "Do you want to play tennis and let me finish whipping your ass, or do you want to talk about junk jewelry."

For some reason, the mention of the missing ball disturbed Rick's concentration. He served doubles on the first point; his first serve on the second point was so ineffectual that when he followed it into the net, Gabe easily passed him down the line with his backhand; he netted an easy volley on the third point; but he served an ace on the fourth point, making the score fifteen-forty. Gabe didn't care for that; with Rick's powerhouse serve, he could easily get back to deuce from fifteen-forty with a little luck.

But Gabe's mention of the gold ball had done its work. Rick served another double fault at fifteen-forty, to lose the match.

"Boy, was I stinko today!" exclaimed Rick, giving Gabe's hand a perfunctory shake across the net.

"Give me a break. I wasn't too bad for an old man," grinned Gabe, watching Rick sweep up his jacket and tennis rackets from the bench and stalk off the court.

"You were marvelous," said Jenny, sneaking a kiss behind the referee's stand. "I'm glad you creamed him."

After he doffed his wet tennis clothes in the locker room and was sitting on the bench for a moment, cooling off before going into the shower, Gabe wondered again about the gold ball. From every indication, it belonged to Rick. Of course, it was possible Rick had left his home and that the one in Gabe's locker belonged to someone else. Mike Flanagan, perhaps. He was the owner of at least a half a dozen miniature gold balls. But somehow Gabe didn't believe it was Flanagan's. More than ever, he was convinced the gold ball belonged to the doctor's son. Which raised a number of interesting questions in his mind. Should he mention to Rick that Manuel had found the ball in the utility closet and try to see if his expression revealed any guilt? Should he wait until he showed up on another day without it and then spring the question on him? Or should he take the gold ball to Judy Trump today and throw the whole thing in her lap? But why should he expect any satisfaction from her? No, he'd have to have further proof of Rick's guilt before he went out on a limb again.

Before going into the shower room, Gabe stopped off at the urinals to relieve himself. To his surprise, Rick was in the stall next to his.

Noticing Gabe beside him, Rick said, "I wonder what it is about asparagus that makes your piss stink so?"

Gabe shrugged, for it was not a question that was uppermost in his mind.

"Guess I'll have to ask my father the doctor sometime, if I ever see him." Rick laughed and headed for the showers.

When Gabe returned to his office, he dropped down into his chair, feeling that he could go right to sleep.

As he closed his eyes for a moment, Jenny stole up behind his chair and started massaging the back of his neck. "So, he wasn't wearing the famous gold ball?" she said.

"How about that?" exclaimed Gabe.

"Did you mention it?"

"Yep. And he said he'd left it at home."

"Did you tell him you had it?" asked Jenny.

"Boy, you'd make a rotten detective," said Gabe. "If I told him I had it, he'd ask for it back. I'd have to tell him why he couldn't have it, and that would give everything away."

"But you just can't keep it to yourself," pointed out Jenny. "That's not going to solve anything."

"But if I take it to Judy Trump, she'll just tell me again it's circumstantial evidence, even if the fingerprints on it do prove it belongs to Rick."

"So where does that leave you?" asked Jenny plaintively. "Square one again?"

"No, I'll have to confront Rick with it myself. I've just decided. Maybe he'll give himself away or lose his temper and try to throttle me."

Jenny shuddered. "I'm worried about you. He could kill again."

"As I told you before, honey, I'll have to take that chance."

Seventeen

When Rick didn't show up at the club for the rest of the weekend, Gabe started to grow restless. He didn't like the idea that a possible killer was roaming around the club—especially since he felt he could be the next victim. Twice he made up his mind to stop playing detective himself and take what evidence he had to Judy Trump. But twice something held him back. Obviously it was the fear of more rejection.

More important, if he turned the gold ball over to Judy, he'd never be able to confront Rick with it.

One bright note to the weekend. Jenny's folks went to a flower show in San Diego, and Gabe was able to spend two delightful nights with her.

On Monday Rick finally turned up at the Racquet Club to play a match with Jimmy Turrel, one of the promising youngsters on the UCLA tennis team.

Gabe decided to have his confrontation with Rick in the locker room. When Rick was undressing, it would be easy to determine whether or not he was wearing the gold tennis ball, especially since their lockers were in the same section of the room.

Because Gabe didn't want to be obvious about it, he decided to change into his tennis clothes, even though he didn't have a match.

"Oh, hi, Rick." Gabe feigned surprise at seeing the naked Rick standing in front of his locker. He was not surprised at discovering that there was no gold ball around his thick neck.

"Hi." He didn't seem too friendly.

"Find your gold ball yet?" asked Gabe.

"Find it?" Rick said nervously. "I never said it was missing."

"Well, I figured it must be because I found this in the utility closet." Gabe unlocked his locker and took out the gold ball.

Rick glanced at it with what Gabe considered feigned indifference. "That isn't mine," he snapped. Turning away, he started to put on his jockstrap.

"I wonder who it could belong to?" mused Gabe aloud.

"Well, I'm not the only one around here who's won one of those," said Rick. "Why don't you ask Mike Flanagan or Phil Neer?"

"Good idea," said Gabe, feeling the wind go

out of his sails again. "Thanks for reminding me."

With Mike Flanagan playing a tournament in Tokyo that week, Gabe decided to take a shot at Phil Neer. Not that he considered him a serious contender for the title of club murderer, but as long as anything was possible, he'd better cover that angle before sticking his neck out and accusing Rick.

He found Neer in the tennis shop, stringing a racket, a chore he didn't ordinarily take on.

"Hi, Phil." He nodded toward the racket in the vice. "Picking up a little mad money on the side?"

"Just doing a patch job for one of my kids. You know, that little girl I discovered down at Poinsettia Playground?"

"Molly Martin?"

"Yeah. She looks like a real winner. But her father's as poor as a church mouse. Can't afford a whole restring. So—" he shrugged helplessly "—old Phil here is helping them out."

"Glad you found a new protege." Gabe dropped into a chair and pretended to be studying the framed eight-by-ten glossies of Phil Neer's tournament days that decorated one wall of the tennis shop. Pictures of Phil, in the long white tennis trousers, posing with some of his contemporaries also in long white tennis trousers—Don Budge, Gene Mako, and Ellsworth Vines—and one of Phil in action on a center court somewhere, hitting an overhead smash and looking very young and agile. Awful what age does to a man, thought Gabe, comparing the fragile, white-haired Neer of today with his robust image in the photo.

"I guess you didn't get around to talking to Kornfeld before he kicked the bucket," said Neer, pulling the racket out of the vice and hanging it up on a hook.

"Unfortunately not."

"So how do you think I stand with the board without him?"

"I would say your status is about *quo*. But with everything that's happened, they might be too busy to worry about getting rid of you. Just don't make any static, and your troubles will probably go away."

"From your mouth to God's ears."

"I'm on pretty good terms with Gilmore, our new pres. I thought if he brings up the subject of your status here, I'd give him a little of your background. You know, impress him with your tennis credentials. Like what your national ranking was when you were playing—"

Gabe paused and looked up at him questioningly.

"I was number ten in 1933. I would have been nine, but I lost to Walter Senior at Newport."

"Hey, ten's real good."

Neer smiled as his mind flashed back to the glory days of his youth. "And I don't have to tell you I won the U.S. National doubles in '30. That's a big one. If it'd been today, I could have won a fistful instead of just a gold ball."

"Do you still have it? I thought maybe you'd let me hang it up in the trophy case. It'd give all of your doubters a chance to see how really good you were."

"Have it? After all these years?" Neer laughed.

"You mean, you lost it?"

"Who knows where the fuck it is? I probably gave it to my mother. Or maybe I pawned it when Molly was sick. I really don't remember."

Gabe couldn't decide whether Neer was being deliberately evasive or just had no memory for such trivia.

"The reason I asked, I found this up in the locker room." Gabe unfolded the Kleenex and showed the gold ball to Neer. While Neer examined it, Gabe stared at him, hoping his expression would reveal something.

"That's not mine," declared Neer.

"You're sure?" Gabe wondered how he could be so positive.

"Sure I'm sure." Neer pointed to the engraving on the gold tennis ball. "This one has 'U.S.T.A.' on it. In my day, it was the 'U.S.L.T.A.', for Lawn Tennis Association."

Schmuck! Of course Neer's gold ball would have had to have the old logo on it. It wasn't until a few years ago, when they stopped playing the U.S. Open on grass, that the association dropped the "lawn" from its name and became the U.S.T.A.

Well, at least he knew Phil Neer hadn't been in the utility closet. That narrowed the field down to two again.

"Guess I have to get back to my desk," said Gabe, standing suddenly and heading out the door into the warm sunshine.

But he didn't go straight back to his desk. He took a detour upstairs to his apartment, where he hid the gold ball in a bottle of Bufferins in the medicine cabinet in his bathroom. No use taking any chances that Rick would steal it from his locker, figured Gabe. If Rick really were the locker room thief, and he now had every reason to believe he was, there was nothing to stop him from taking the ball out of Gabe's locker, once Gabe had given away its hiding place.

"Square One again?" asked Jenny, after Gabe finished reporting the results of his talks with Rick Reeves and Phil Neer to her later that day.

"Not quite. Something positive's come out of all this: you and me," he said, sitting down on the edge of her desk.

"I just hope we both live to enjoy it." She sighed and stroked his hand lovingly. "You know, I was just thinking, Gabriel. Maybe you should stop trying to be Perry Mason. Maybe there won't be any more trouble here at the club. Mr. Weber tells me all the locks should be changed over to combinations by the end of next week. So that ought to eliminate any more monkey business in the locker room."

"I have to solve it, honey," he said, his voice filled with resolve. "Aside from the fact that I don't feel too secure with a murderer among our ranks, I have to clear my own somewhat tarnished name. The way Judy Trump's been acting, I have a feeling she's about to spring a warrant for my arrest on me."

"That's ridiculous!" exclaimed Jenny. "They can't put an innocent man in jail."

"Why not? Look at all the guilty people who are running around free!"

"I won't let them!"

Gabe laughed at her innocence. "And even if I can stay out of the cooler, I have my job to save. I hear Bob Gilmore's back in town, so that means there'll be a board meeting pretty soon. And who knows what that group—"

Gabe was interrupted in mid-sentence by Carter Blackman's appearance on the other side of the sliding glass panel. With a scowl, he rapped sharply on the glass with his knuckles to get their attention.

The TV executive looked angry enough to commit murder as Gabe slid the glass open and asked him what he wanted.

"God damn it," Blackman exclaimed explosively. "It's happened again."

"What's happened again?" asked Gabe.

"The thief—the fuckin' thief broke into my locker when I was playing tennis a little while ago, and this time he stole my Vuitton attache case. Damn, I had over fifteen hundred bucks in it."

"Shit!" said Gabe. "I guess yours is one of the lockers they haven't gotten around to replacing the locks on yet."

"That's a clever piece of deduction," snarled Blackman, "but it's not getting my case back."

"Maybe your homeowner's insurance policy will cover it," said Gabe, hoping to pacify him.

"It's not the case I'm worried about or the money either. It's the rest of the contents. There's some confidential network papers in there I was taking home to study tonight."

"Sorry," said Gabe. "Maybe it'll turn up somewhere."

"So what the fuck is the club going to do about it?" shouted Blackman. "You just going to stand there and tell me you're sorry? Why don't you call the police?"

"The police won't bother with a petty thing like this. They're still trying to find out who killed Jock Kornfeld."

"Jock's dead—it doesn't matter. But I can't have those papers floating around—they're important."

"Sure they are—probably the first draft of 'Married with Children,'" Gabe couldn't help retorting.

"Don't I wish it were only that," said Blackman with another snarl. "God Damn It!" He glared at Gabe for a moment then said, "Well, if it should turn up, give me a buzz."

And with that he whirled around on Gucci heels and exited through the door to the street, slamming it loudly as he went.

"One good thing," said Gabe, leaning back in his seat. "Now we know the thief isn't Danny, as if I hadn't known that all along."

"What about Rick?" said Jenny.

"I think he left before Blackman came in. But I didn't notice him leave, did you?"

"Yes, I did, and it was just a few minutes ago. But he wasn't carrying a Vuitton attache case. Just his tennis duffel bag."

"Well, he's not stupid enough to walk past the office with stolen property," said Gabe.

"He could have left it in his locker."

"Yes, he could have. But unfortunately I don't have a search warrant. So we'll never know."

Jenny's face suddenly brightened. "Then what about your other suspect—Marty Engels?"

"He's in New York, I told you."

"Not anymore he isn't. I forgot to tell you in all this excitement. He came in when you were talking with Phil. It totally slipped my mind until now."

"Really? Is he still here?"

"As far as I know."

"Then he's probably playing cards," said Gabe. "I think I'll have a little talk with him."

As Gabe meandered into the cardroom trying to look as if he had nothing in particular in mind, a six-handed gin game was in progress under a dense cloud of foul-smelling, bluish cigar smoke. Marty Engels was one of the players and was busy playing a hand. But Herb Gross had already thrown his cards down and was waiting for the others to come up with something better to beat him with, if they could.

"Can I talk to you a minute?" Gabe whispered in Herb's ear. "In private?"

"Sure thing, Gabe," answered Gross, following him into the next room. "Got a problem?"

"Just checking to see if you and Marty are okay again?"

"We're fine—so far," he added with a grin. "As a matter of fact, before the game started he made good all his IOUs. He must have robbed a bank in New York."

"Must have," said Gabe, wondering if that was all he had robbed.

"That's it?" asked Gross impatiently. "I've got to get back and protect my interests." He jerked his thumb in the direction of the card table.

"Just one more thing?" asked Gabe. "How long has Marty been in the game?"

"All afternoon."

"Did he ever leave the table?"

"Just once—to go to the john."

"How long was he gone?"

"Ten minutes at the most."

"I see. Well, thanks, Herb."

Gabe followed Gross back to the table, where the game seemed to be breaking up, and tapped Marty Engels on the thickly padded shoulder of his plaid sport jacket.

Marty looked startled as he eyed Gabe suspiciously from beneath shaggy gray eyebrows.

"Something on your mind, kid?"

"Just a little club business. Would you mind stopping by the office before you leave?"

"I guess not."

He must have been as anxious to get the talk over with as Gabe was to talk with him because his burly figure caught up with Gabe just as he was putting his hand on his office doorknob.

"If it's about my bill, kid, I'm ready to settle up right now, so please don't post me," he pleaded, making a move to reach into his pocket.

"That wasn't the main thing," said Gabe, "but the club'll be happy to take your money, too."

Engels suddenly looked concerned. "You're not going to kick me out on account of the other day?"

"No, we're not taking any disciplinary action as long as you promise to keep out of trouble in the future."

"Oh, thank God." He wrapped his arms gratefully around Gabe and pulled him into a bear hug that almost broke his ribs. "I promise. I just couldn't help myself that day. I'd just got word I was losing my business." He started to sniffle. "You know how it is?"

"I understand," said Gabe, embarrassed by this hulk of a man's sudden display of emotion.

"Here." Engels was fumbling around in his jacket pocket for something which he seemed to have trouble locating. "I've got you a check right here."

As he pulled a crumpled personal check out of his pocket, his hand became tangled up with a key ring full of keys that he unintentionally pulled out simultaneously and which dropped to the parquet floor with a loud clatter.

Engels appeared flustered as he suddenly bent over to retrieve the keys. But Gabe, realizing they were the missing set of master keys that had been taken off Danny White's belt the night of his death, bent over and grabbed them first.

"What are you doing with these?" asked Gabe, dangling them in front of Engels' nose. "These belonged to Danny White."

"They did?" Engels looked bewildered.

"That's right. They've been missing since he got killed."

"Well, I just found them on the walk when I came in. I stuck them in my pocket meaning to turn them over to the office, but I forgot I was in such a hurry to get to the card-room."

Gabe couldn't tell if he was lying or telling the truth. "You sure about that?" he asked. "It's a pretty important piece of evidence for you to be carrying around in your pocket."

Marty's face suddenly turned ashen. "Hey—you don't think that I—I—had anything to do with it?"

"It's pretty coincidental," declared Gabe. "The first day you're back Carter Blackman's locker is robbed, and then you turn up with Danny's keys to the lockers which you may or may not have found and intended to turn in."

"Believe me, kid," said Marty. "I may be going bankrupt but I'm not a killer and a thief. I'm telling the truth. You've got to believe me. I got enough *tsuris*."

Gabe studied him, trying to assess his expression, from which he couldn't tell much. In all likelihood, Engels wasn't the killer. Still the keys were a pretty damning piece of evidence.

"Okay, I guess I believe you until I find out otherwise," Gabe assured him. "But I'm going to have to turn these keys over to the detective on the case. She'll want to check them for fingerprints. She may even want to talk to you."

"Well, do what you have to do but don't push it. As I say I've got enough *tsuris* without being a murder suspect."

With Danny's keys and the gold tennis ball in his possession, Gabe finally felt he had enough evidence, along with what he read in Kim Randall's appointment book, to present a rather strong case to Judy Trump. But before he did, he decided, he'd first have to get his hands on Randall's datebook and copy it so that he'd have something more tangible than talk to back up his murder and cover-up theory.

Striding into Jenny's office, Gabe quickly filled her in on what had just transpired between him and Marty, then told her, "I think you and I are going to have to have another assignation in Randall's apartment. I have to get the infamous datebook before I can go to Judy Trump. Tonight all right?"

"What do you think?" she grinned.

"So get me Randall on the phone," said Gabe.

She plugged into the switchboard, dialed the number, and handed the phone to Gabe. Unfortunately, only the answering machine was at home.

"Hello, Kim isn't home right now. I'm in San Francisco all this week. Have a nice day!"

"*Have a nice day*, my foot," grumbled Gabe, putting the phone down dejectedly. "Jenny, I guess we'll have to put off our date till next week."

As luck would have it, Jan Wexler came to the club the following afternoon to take a tennis lesson from Phil Neer, and Gabe, while wandering around the grounds, happened to notice her.

As he stood outside the fence watching the sexy blond go through the agony of learning how to serve, an idea started to take root in his mind. If Jan were actually the girl Kornfeld had taken to Randall's apartment the night of Danny's murder, maybe Jock mentioned to her what he saw from the porch. But how could Gabe broach such a delicate subject to Jan without disclosing that he suspected she'd been messing around behind her husband's portly back.

After agonizing over it, Gabe decided on an approach. He "accidentally" bumped into her when she walked off the court after her lesson.

"Oh, hello, Mrs. Wexler. How was your lesson today?"

"I'm a klutz. I ought to give up this game and take up knitting."

"Oh, come on. You have to be improving."

"How can I tell? I never get to play in any games."

"Why not?"

"Well, all the wives around here have their set games, and they don't seem to want anyone new to join them. And I'm not good enough to play with the men."

"I'll play with you," offered Gabe.

"You're too good."

"I have two different games," he grinned. "One for the men and one for pretty women." As she laughed, obviously flattered, he said, "Go get some balls from the tennis shop, and I'll meet you on Court Seven after I change my clothes."

If Jan hadn't been such a sexpot, Gabe would have found it painful to play tennis with her, because she was a little klutzy. In the beginning she could hardly keep a rally going for more than one time over the net. "Oh, I'm so bad," she apologized after she netted ball after ball. "I'm embarrassed."

"Look, no one gets to be Monica Seles overnight. Just don't be nervous, get your racket back as soon as you see what side the ball is coming to you on, and look at the ball. Those are the most important things to remember."

Jan's figure in a short tennis dress, with a little bit of her tush showing whenever she bent over to pick up a ball, did wonders for Gabe's patience. And eventually, after feeding the ball back to her forehand and backhand in exactly the right place for her to stroke it correctly without having to do much running, he got her into a rhythm that enabled her to maintain a few sustained rallies.

"I wasn't bad, was I?" exclaimed Jan after Gabe had worked out with her for about thirty minutes and she was sitting on the bench, her face dripping with perspiration.

"You're getting there," he said, handing her a towel.

"Thanks." She smiled a sheepish smile. "I guess my face is a mess. Did my mascara run?"

"Yes," he said, taking the towel from her and wiping the black streaks off her cheeks. "But you still look better than Martina."

"You're very sweet."

"Just telling it like it is, Ma'am," he said in a kidding tone. "Would you like to play more?"

"No. Right now I'm too thirsty for tennis. Come on," she said, grabbing his hand. "I'll buy you a drink."

Upstairs on the terrace, she ordered a vodka and tonic, and Gabe asked for an ice tea.

The terrace was empty—even Dr. Reeves wasn't around scrounging for garnish—so Gabe figured this was a golden opportunity to broach a delicate subject. However, he waited until she was on her second drink and feeling as relaxed as a poodle puppy.

"I have to ask you a question, Jan. I know that you and your husband were good friends of the Kornfelds. Do you have any idea who could have killed Jock?"

"Not really." She looked disconsolate suddenly. "Maybe Rita."

"You don't mean that?"

"Not really. But he did play around quite a bit. A wife who loves her husband can get pissed off enough to kill."

"You know that for sure? I mean, that he played around?"

"Don't all men?" From the cynicism in her voice, it was obvious she was an expert on the subject. "But why do you want to know that? Do you think it had something to do with his murder?"

"In an oblique way, yes. I received an anonymous note after Danny's death, tipping me off that someone killed him. I deduced from the note that that anonymous person saw Danny being carried out to the exercise porch and being strung up. I also deduced, after doing some checking, that the only place a person could see that action from was from Kim Randall's apartment." Gabe noticed Jan stiffen slightly, so he knew he was onto something. "And I know for a fact that Jock was the person using Kim Randall's apartment that night, so I figured he sent the note anonymously because he didn't want anyone to know what he was doing there, and that the person who killed him thought Jock knew he killed Danny."

"How do you know it was Jock?"

"Because when I was searching Kim's apartment, I found Kim's appointment book, and Jock was down for that Wednesday night."

"My God, my name wasn't in it, was it?" It slipped out before she realized it.

"No, just Jock's."

"Thank heavens," she said with a sigh.

"Then it was you?"

"Yes," she admitted, her face turning crimson down to the V of her beautiful cleavage.

"I thought so."

"Why?"

"Because you hadn't been home that night, either. I know that, because your husband called the club from San Francisco early Thursday morning trying to locate you. So I just put two and two together."

"You're almost as good a detective as you are a tennis player."

"I'm doing my best," said Gabe.

"Why not just drop it?" It was evident she didn't want to be implicated. "Jock's gone. We can't bring him back."

"I'm trying to save my own skin. For some reason, the police think I might have killed Jock, so I have to find out who did."

"Why would you want to kill him?"

"Because my job is in jeopardy. Now try to think hard. I need your help. Did anything strange happen that Wednesday night when you were at Kim's?"

"Now that you mention it, yes. After we'd made love, Jock strolled out onto the porch to smoke a cigarette. I was still on the bed when I heard him exclaim, 'Holy Shit!' And when I ran out to the porch to see what he was holy shitting about, he just snapped at me to forget it. But he turned white and started acting very nervous."

"Now you know what was bothering him. But I still have to catch the murderer."

"Are you going to the police now?" She looked concerned.

"As soon as I get my hands on that appointment book. And for that I have to wait until Kim comes back from San Francisco."

"You want to get in there now?"

"I'd like to, yes."

"Well, if you promise to keep my name out of all this, I think I can help you." Opening her purse, she pulled out a key with a little white tag on it. The tag read: "Randall's apartment."

"Where'd you get that?"

"Jock gave it to me the night we last met. I won't have any more use for it."

She put it in Gabe's hand and smiled sadly.

"You're a doll," he said, leaning over and kissing her cheek.

"Just be sure to keep me out of it," said Jan, as Gabe stood up and hurried down the terrace.

Eighteen

Within the hour Gabe had retrieved the datebook from its hiding spot atop the armoire, had it copied at his Xerox place on Doheny Drive, replaced the original in Randall's apartment where he had found it, and brought the copy back to the Racquet Club.

"Well, that's done," he told Jenny as he passed through her office on his way to his own. "Now I just have to find Judy Trump."

"You don't have to look far, my dear." Jenny nodded in the direction of Gabe's office. Through the doorway he could see Judy Trump sitting in a chair, with her Adidas resting on his desk—her favorite way to relax evidently.

"What does she want?"

Jenny shrugged. "More questions, I suppose."

Judy swung her feet off his desk as Gabe entered.

"New developments?" he asked, dropping into his own chair.

"Frankly, I've come up with nothing."

"That what you're here to tell me? Seems like a waste of taxpayer's money."

"No, I'm here to substantiate your story."

"I told you the truth."

"I'll need some names to go with it if you expect me to believe it."

"No problem," said Gabe.

"I thought it was." She seemed surprised.

"That was a couple of days ago. Since then the situation's changed. I may have something that'll break open the case. Some names may be necessary."

"I'm listening."

Gabe dropped the datebook down in front of her on the desk top and flipped open the pages to Wednesday the ninth of May.

"What's the significance of this?" she asked.

"Can you keep this between ourselves? What I'm about to tell you might embarrass quite a few people."

"Depends on what you have to tell me. But if I buy it, I'll do my best."

Gabe felt encouraged. Judy seemed almost grateful now for any crumb of evidence that might lead to a break in this frustrating case.

"Okay. You remember my theory of the murder? That Danny was strangled in the locker room, hidden somewhere when I came back to look for him, and later that night his killer carried him out and strung him up?"

"It's such a fairy tale I couldn't possibly forget it," she said with a mild grin.

"You won't think it's such a joke when you hear the rest of this."

Judy studied him with a quizzical expression.

"I now know for sure that the killer hid Danny in the utility closet," he announced triumphantly. "And I even think I know who it is."

"How?"

"I'll tell you after you hear who sent the anonymous note. You see these initials in the datebook?" Gabe pointed to "J.K." on the May ninth page. "Who do you think that is?"

"I guess it won't take Sherlock Holmes to figure that one out. Jock Kornfeld. But what does it mean?"

"That he was in an apartment across the street from the Racquet Club that night."

"Whose apartment?"

"A member of this club's. His name is Kim Randall. He's a movie producer."

"What was Mr. Kornfeld doing there?"

"This is the part I hope you can be discreet about."

"I told you I'd try. In this business we can't make promises."

"Okay. Randall was loaning his apartment out

to certain married members of the Racquet Club."

"You mean, it's a nookie pad?"

"Yeah." Gabe had to smile at her raunchy phraseology. She was proving to be a real police officer after all. "Well, Mr. Kornfeld was there that night with another member's wife. By accident he happened to witness the scene on the exercise porch. But if he told the authorities about it, he'd have had to say what he was doing there and with whom. His affair would be exposed, which was the last thing he could afford, both for his marriage and his job."

"What's his job have to do with it?"

"His father-in-law owns the company he was president of—Giverny Cosmetics."

"You mean, 'Give her Giverny and she'll love you forever'?"

"You got it. If his father-in-law heard about it, and a messy story appeared in the headlines, it would have been the end of Kornfeld as president of the company. So rather than risk that, he sent the anonymous note, hoping that would alert the police enough to continue with the investigation."

"It's a pretty tall story to have to get an indictment on," commented Trump.

"Here's part of the evidence, right here." Gabe tapped the entry in the datebook with the end of a pencil.

Trump shrugged. "Who was he with that night? You wouldn't by any chance know that, would you?"

"No, I wouldn't," lied Gabe. "But I don't think that's necessary to swing it one way or another. What's important is that Kornfeld was there."

"So who did he see?" asked Trump. "And why didn't he put that in his note?"

"Evidently he couldn't see *who* it was from that distance and in the murky light, or at least he wasn't sure. But I think *I* know *now*."

"All right. Who?"

"Rick Reeves," announced Gabe proudly.

"And who is Rick Reeves?"

"The son of Dr. Reeves, one of our members."

"You mean, the surgeon to the stars?"

"Yeah. He has a son who's nineteen years old and one of our best tennis players. He won the National 16-and-under, and up until a point was Mike Flanagan's doubles partner."

"What's his motive?"

"Well, in my uneducated opinion, he killed Danny to keep him from telling anyone that he was stealing from the lockers."

"You trying to tell me that this ranking tennis player and the son of a high-priced scalpel pusher is a thief?"

"It's not so farfetched," said Gabe. "I could tell you the names of several big name tennis stars of the past who got drummed out of the game for rifling lockers."

"But why?"

Gabe shrugged. "Could be that he's a kleptomaniac. But my hunch is, he probably needed the dough."

"Are you trying to tell me that this boy committed the Kornfeld murder, too?"

"If the rest of my story hangs together, yes. Kornfeld had to be silenced."

"That's the part I just can't buy," said Judy, after mulling Gabe's theory over for an agonizingly long while. "How would Rick know that Kornfeld knew?"

"If I could tell you everything," said Gabe, "I'd have your job, and you'd be home changing diapers." It was a sexist crack he realized, but she bugged him so he couldn't help making it.

She shot Gabe a jaundiced glance. "All right. let's forget that and move onto something else. How did you link Rick Reeves to any of this?"

Gabe had been waiting for this moment. "Our new locker room attendant found something in the utility closet that belongs to him. My hunch is it was ripped off in the struggle between him and Danny White."

"What is this mysterious object you're talking about?" asked Trump impatiently.

"It's a little gold tennis ball he used to wear on a chain around his neck. He got it for winning the National-16-and-under."

"Is his name on it?"

"They don't usually put names on tennis trophies," Gabe told her.

"Then couldn't it belong to someone else?"

"Not likely. Only people who've won national titles are entitled to one, and there are only two of them at this club. Rick and Mike Flanagan."

"How do you know it's not Flanagan's?"

"Flanagan never wears his. He's too important now to show off small potato prizes like that. He's into major money. But Rick used to show his off all the time. It impressed the girls. However, in the last couple of weeks since Danny's murder, he hasn't been wearing it. Anyway, after we found the ball in the utility closet, I asked Rick why he wasn't wearing his, and he was very evasive. I deliberately didn't tell him I had found his because I wanted to see what he'd say that might give himself away."

"And what did he say?"

"He told me he'd left it at home on his bureau. The next time I met him, I told him I'd found a gold ball and asked him if he'd found the one he'd lost. He looked scared and said he hadn't lost it. He insisted it was home."

"So where is this gold ball now?" asked Trump.

"Upstairs in my apartment."

"Well, trot it out."

"I also have Danny's keys. I think if your fingerprint man checks them out, he'll find

Rick's print on them somewhere. That should put the final nail in his coffin."

"When did the keys turn up?"

"Yesterday. One of our members found them on the front sidewalk and turned them into me."

"Does this member have a name?"

"Yes. Marty Engels. You might want to question him."

"I just might. Where are the keys now?"

"Upstairs with the gold ball."

"Well, turn everything over to me, if you will. There could be some prints on them that'll prove interesting."

As Gabe inserted his key in the lock and turned it, he thought he heard a sound on the other side of the door. But when he pushed the door the rest of the way open and stepped into his cheerfully decorated parlor, everything seemed to be in order.

Must be my imagination, he thought, heading straight for the medicine cabinet over the sink in his bathroom and taking out the Bufferin bottle that contained the gold ball.

He hurriedly twisted off the cap, and was relieved to see the gold ball still inside among the white pills. He rolled it out into the palm of his hand, carefully wrapped it in his handkerchief, placed the handkerchief in the pocket of his jacket, and stepped out of the bathroom.

As he turned toward his desk, where he had hidden Danny's keys in one of the drawers, he felt sudden movement behind him and then a heavy instrument landing on the crown of his head with the force of a mule's kick.

That was the last he remembered until he came to approximately ten minutes later with an aching head and the room spinning.

Opening his eyes with some difficulty, he realized that he had a very sore spot on the top of his head. He reached up and touched the tender place with his finger. He found a lump the size of a walnut from which blood was pouring profusely.

Fearing he might still be in danger, he staggered to his feet and glanced around the room. At the same time he reached into his pocket for the gold tennis ball knowing in his heart he wouldn't find it. And he was right. The gold ball was, of course, gone, and so was his attacker, who'd also made off with Danny's keys as well, which Gabe discovered when he went to look for them in his desk drawer.

Feeling sick to his stomach, he staggered back into the bathroom to wash the blood off his head and face before going downstairs to tell Judy the good news. He also took two Bufferins, which he was in the midst of swallowing when he felt someone come up behind him again.

Wheeling and ducking his head suddenly to

avoid another blow, he almost choked on the Bufferins going down.

"Oh, my God, what happened to you?" asked a familiar voice.

Seeing that the intruder was only Jenny, Gabe let out a relieved sigh. "I just got waylaid by the locker room bandit," he explained. "At least I'm pretty sure it was the locker room bandit. Who else would clobber me with a blunt instrument just to get a gold ball and a set of keys?" He rubbed his wound gingerly.

"Oh, you poor thing," exclaimed Jenny, examining the bloodied spot.

"Not poor—stupid. If I'd had any sense I'd have turned the gold ball over to Trump when I first found it and stopped playing detective myself." He grimaced and said. "Tell her I'll be right down."

"That's what I came to tell you. She got tired of waiting and left. She said if you have something to show her, she'll be in her office.

"Just as well. She probably won't believe what just happened to me anyway. What have I got to show her now?"

"Show her your lump. She can't think it's a mosquito bite."

Judy Trump was back, in her austerely furnished office in the bowels of the Beverly Hills City Hall when Gabe finally caught up with her later in the afternoon and sheepishly related his unfortunate story.

She wasn't exactly sympathetic. Amused was more like it. But she did show a certain amount of professional compassion by sending for one of the department's paramedics and ordering him to dress Gabe's wounds properly while she questioned him.

"If that gold ball was so necessary to prove your theory," asked Trump, "why in heavens didn't you put it in a safer place? If there's a locker room thief who also kills on the loose, you of all people should have been more wary."

"Because I'm a damn fool, that's why," replied Gabe. "I meant to put it in my safe deposit box in my bank in Beverly Hills, until I got ready to show it to you, but I've been so busy around here the last couple of days between running the club and attending funerals that I just didn't get around to it."

"You're sure now that this gold ball isn't just a figment of your imagination?"

"You don't have to take my word for it," said Gabe, completely frustrated as he tried to control his temper. "Jenny saw it. So did Manuel, our new locker boy who found it and gave it to me."

"Look, a first-class defense attorney could punch a big enough hole in that kind of testimony to drive a 747 through. Jenny's your girl, and the other guy—"

"Wait a minute," complained Gabe. "How do you know Jenny's my girl?"

"I'm a detective," grinned Trump. "I've got my sources." She winked. "You're not much of a policeman, but you have good taste."

Gabe just stared at her.

"As I was saying, Manuel works for you, so any testimony from those two has got to be self-serving. But even if I believed it, it proves absolutely nothing without his prints, to identify it as Rick's gold ball. So where does that leave you—with a datebook that also proves nothing except how rotten most men treat their wives."

"What are you getting at—that I'm making all this up to throw suspicion on someone else?"

"I still say you have the strongest motive."

"Oh, come on. You think I'd make this up about the gold ball if I didn't have it. That would just make me look like a fool."

"Well, who's to say you aren't. Only a fool would have kept such an incriminating piece of evidence instead of turning it over to the authorities."

"With hindsight, I guess I should have. But at the time I didn't have the datebook. I didn't believe the ball alone was enough evidence to convince you of anything."

"You know," said Trump, studying Gabe thoughtfully, "It's a felony just to withhold evidence, especially in a capital case like this. You could go to the slammer for that alone."

"Well, if I never had it, which you seem to believe, how could I have withheld it?"

"Touche," smiled Trump.

"Besides," added Gabe, feeling he was on a roll now, "how could it be a criminal case if Danny knocked *himself* off?"

"Someone still had to kill Kornfeld," Trump reminded him.

"You're right," admitted Gabe, suddenly feeling depressed again.

As he turned to go, Judy called to him. "By the way, Mr. Steele, if you get any more pertinent evidence, why not pass it on to me? It might help us solve this case. And at the very least, it'll keep you from getting any more bumps on your noggin."

From the unexpected sincerity in her voice, Gabe was fairly certain she believed he'd been telling the truth about the gold ball, and that she didn't really consider him a murderer—just an idiot for being so careless. That was a couple of points in his favor, but he still felt as he walked out into the late afternoon sunshine sporting a large white patch of gauze and adhesive tape on his head as if he were down five-love, point game in the deciding set.

Nineteen

Jenny invited Gabe to have dinner at her folks' home that evening, and Gabe, of course, accepted. But he was afraid he wasn't very stimulating company. All during dinner, when Mrs. Ho was discoursing on the various kinds of flower arrangements she was going to enter in the Japanese Cultural Exhibit at the Convention Center, Gabe's mind kept harking back to one thing Judy Trump had always thought was a flaw in his own theory of the murder: how did Danny's murderer know that Kornfeld knew the truth about his death?

If Gabe could figure that one out, he'd not only know that Rick Reeves killed Danny, but also Jock Kornfeld. He may not be able to prove it to the satisfaction of a grand jury, but it would at least be a logical answer to that one nagging question that had bothered him, too.

He was still thinking about it after dinner

when he was lying on the couch with his bandaged head on Jenny's lap, feeling the firm, gentle touch of her fingertips on his forehead and temples as she tried to massage away the headache that refused to quit since he had blown the gold ball caper.

It wasn't until he had kissed Jenny goodnight about one in the morning and was getting on his motorcycle in front of her house that something Detective Trump had said to him earlier in the case hit him like the butt end of a mugger's pistol.

"Look for the obvious," she had told him. "I learned that from a veteran detective who broke me into this kind of work."

Look for the obvious, look for the obvious, look for the obvious!

What was the obvious way to hear something? Right from the horse's mouth. Or in this case, the ass's mouth. Of course. Jock Kornfeld must have told Rick Reeves that he knew he was the killer! But why would he have done such a stupid thing? To protect himself. Probably as a counterpunch to something Rick Reeves had told him. Rick obviously had had something to discuss that he knew was important to Jock, otherwise he wouldn't have had the nerve to phone him in the middle of dinner. And obviously it was important to Jock or he wouldn't have left his dinner and rushed over to the club to meet a jerk like Rick, and without telling his wife what this meeting was all about. Or with whom. It all seemed so clear now, he thought as he gunned his Honda along a practically deserted Sunset Boulevard, traveling east towards Beverly Hills in the ghostly light of a half-moon. Clear, that is, if you kept in mind what kind of a person Kornfeld was dealing with. Rick had stolen, he'd murdered. So why wouldn't he commit blackmail? He'd even kiddingly threatened to blackmail Gabe and Jenny one day when he'd caught them necking in the club office. Obviously, his mind worked that way. And if he needed money badly enough to steal petty cash, why wouldn't he eventually go for larger game by blackmailing Jock Kornfeld? Maybe he needed big bucks to make the down payment on that red Ferrari. But what would he have to blackmail Kornfeld about? Again, look for the obvious. The scenario as far as Gabe saw it, was this: Somehow Rick knew about Jock's affair with Jan. And in need of some heavy cash, and finding his access to the lockers cut off by increased security, Rick phoned Kornfeld, got him over to the club the night of his death, and threatened to go to his father-in-law and possibly even Aaron Wexler with the story of his affair with Jan unless Kornfeld came through with ten or twenty grand or maybe even a million in cash. Panicky, Kornfeld defended himself by doing some blackmailing of his own. He probably told Rick that he was prepared to go to the police and tell them that Rick killed Danny, if Rick didn't forget about blackmailing him about Jan. Frustrated at not getting the money he needed, Rick flew into a blind rage, grabbed Kornfeld, and in their struggle, strangled him and threw him in the pool.

It was so obvious that Gabe was surprised no one had thought of this chain of events before. It all made so much sense that he might even be able to persuade Judy Trump that he was right. Which would be some kind of a victory, for even though the evidence was still circumstantial, it would keep her digging for some hard clues, and, not incidentally, get her off Gabe's back for a while.

The sense of elation that swept over Gabe when he realized that all of the pieces of the puzzle finally fit gave him a heady, almost drunken feeling—more so than the sake he'd imbibed at dinner.

Just as suddenly, he had a feeling that he was in terrible jeopardy. He sensed, without turning around, that some kind of a powerful vehicle was tailgating him. Glancing over his shoulder, he was practically blinded by the headlights of a car coming up on him hard. He pulled to the right to let the creep pass. But the car stayed on his tail. Because the bastard didn't seem to want to pass him, Gabe gave his Honda more throttle. The cycle leaped forward, but it wasn't fast enough to shake the powerful vehicle on his tail. It, too, leaped forward, closing the gap between them to about ten feet.

Realizing that the car's driver was determined to run him off the road, Gabe made a sudden U-turn and started driving west again under full throttle. But that move only gave him temporary relief. The car behind made a surprisingly tight U-turn, too, and almost immediately was in pursuit of him again. Sixty . . . seventy . . . eighty miles an hour, read the needle on his speedometer. Gabe started to panic, for now it was perfectly clear that the driver of the vehicle was out to get him. And there was also little doubt who the driver was, though Gabe couldn't see him.

Having few options, Gabe glanced around for a sidewalk to drive his small vehicle onto, believing the car wouldn't be able to follow him there. But there were no sidewalks at all along that section of Sunset Boulevard west of the San Diego Freeway, Gabe realized as the lush residential neighborhood flew past him in one huge blur. Moreover, there didn't appear to be any policemen around at that time of morning, either.

So what now? A driveway perhaps, but Rick Reeves could follow him into a driveway, too.

As he approached Bundy and Sunset, he knew his only chance of surviving was to head for the West Los Angeles Police Station at Purdue Avenue, several miles south of Sunset.

Glancing in the mirror, he saw that the headlights were closing the gap on him again. No more than five feet separated the two vehicles now.

Hanging grimly onto the handlebars and crouching low in the saddle in case the madman had a gun, Gabe made an abrupt turn south onto Bundy Drive without daring to slow down from the daredevil speed he was presently traveling.

He didn't see what happened next. Nor did he hear the sound of the car crashing into his rear wheel at eighty miles an hour.

He sensed he was flying through space, a deadweight without any wings, for an endless period of time. And then everything went black, as if all the lights in the world had been turned off simultaneously.

Twenty

Jenny Ho was just inserting her key in her front door lock when she heard the telephone ringing imperiously inside the house.

Throwing open the door, she ran into the living room and grabbed the receiver. "Hello," she said nervously. She was afraid it might be some bad news from the hospital about Gabe.

"Jenny Ho? Trump, here."

"Oh, hi," said Jenny, in a dispirited voice.

"Sorry to buzz you at midnight," apologized Trump. "I tried to get you earlier at the hospital, but they wouldn't put me through."

"Gabe had a bad day. A lot of tests and X-rays. I had the phone blocked so he could get some rest."

"How's our boy doing?" asked Trump.

"Well," she said with a deep sigh, "he's out of intensive care today, but he's not going to be playing tennis for a long time, I'm afraid. His right leg is broken in three places. His left foot is fractured. He had three broken ribs, a sprain in his left arm, and he's just now getting over the effects of the brain concussion. But Doctor Reeves told me he's going to live and be playing tennis again someday."

"Thank God for that," said Trump sincerely. "Well, say hi for me when you see him next."

"I will."

"I have some interesting news from the lab," announced Trump. "There's some red paint on your boy's mashed-up motorcycle."

"You mean, he was hit by a red Ferrari?"

"It would seem so, but we haven't been able to check the other vehicle. The car has dropped out of sight."

Jenny shivered. "I'm terribly frightened for Gabe—alone in that hospital."

"He's not alone. There's nurses all around him on the orthopedic floor, and pretty good security in the building at Cedars-Sinai, from what I understand."

"Not from what I understand," shot back Jenny. "There were three arson attempts there last year. And whoever did it hasn't been apprehended yet. I'd feel better if you'd send a bodyguard over."

"Out of my jurisdiction," explained Trump. "Cedars-Sinai isn't in Beverly Hills. You'll have to get a private guard company to handle that."

"Well, I don't know who's good," said Jenny. "Could you possibly arrange to get one for us? And right away."

"I'll have to wait till morning, honey. Nobody's home in the administration office at this hour."

"Jeepers!"

"I'm sure he'll be all right until then."

"Let's hope so," exclaimed Jenny, with another deep sigh.

"Anyway, I just thought you'd like to know the good news about the red paint," said Trump, before signing off.

"Yeah, real good news," said Jenny glumly. Hanging up, she thought about Gabe alone and helpless in his hospital room, and wondered where Rick Reeves was at that moment. Up to no good, she imagined.

Nurse Gladys Westinghouse, who had the duty on the orthopedic floor at Cedars-Sinai from midnight until eight A.M., was sitting at her desk in the reception area filling out reports and wondering how she was going to stay awake for six more hours, when she heard the elevator door open and someone get out.

Glancing up from her writing, she saw a blond, bespectacled young man in a surgeon's green operating outfit, and a stethoscope around his somewhat thick neck, step out. He nodded curtly to the buxom redheaded nurse as he started briskly up the hall.

Nurse Westinghouse didn't recognize him, but concluded he must be one of the new interns. The older doctors wouldn't be on the floor at this hour unless called there on an emergency.

With a shrug, she watched him disappear around a bend in the corridor, then tilted back in her chair, deciding to get a few winks. It had been a tiring night, even before she went on duty. Three times Dr. Shavelson had insisted on *shtupping* her in the nurse's recreation hall on the seventh floor.

Pushing open the door to 433, the young "intern" tiptoed in, then quietly closed the door behind him.

Like every room at Cedars-Sinai, this one contained but one patient, and a helpless-looking one at that, he was pleased to note. The patient, his head swathed in bandages, was asleep, and he had one leg in a cast from foot to hip. The leg was suspended in midair in a sling by some kind of a pulley contraption, making the man an easy target.

Reaching into the pocket of his surgeon's greens, the doctor pulled out a scalpel and tiptoed to the edge of the bed. As he raised it, poised to plunge it into the man's heart, his lips curled into an ugly smile, and he hesitated in his downward motion of the scalpel to gloat over his good fortune at finding the prick alone. Well, this would teach him to mind his own business.

In the surgeon's moment of hesitation, the inert figure in the bed suddenly opened his eyes. "You know, you look lousy in glasses, Rick!" At the sound of Gabe's voice, Rick froze into immobility, his weapon held in midair. "Okay, Rick drop the knife," demanded Gabe.

Rick found himself staring into the muzzle of a snub-nosed .38 caliber Smith & Wesson. Assessing the consequences of not doing as he was ordered, Rick frowned and dropped the scalpel onto the white blanket cover.

"Thanks, Rick." Keeping the gun trained on the mesmerized Rick, Gabe's free hand shot out and picked up the scalpel in a piece of Kleenex drawn from the box beside him and moved it out of Rick's reach.

"Okay," said Gabe, his finger on the trigger. "Now you're going to give me a complete confession, and I'm going to record it on my Sony."

With the gun muzzle, he pointed to a small Sony tape recorder on the nightstand. "Give that to me!" he ordered Rick.

Rick shot an apprehensive glance at the Sony but didn't make a move to get it.

"You can't do this to me," he snapped. "I know my rights. I don't have to tell you a fucking thing without a lawyer."

"That's when you're talking to the cops," said

Gabe. "I'm just an ordinary citizen, wanting to get some information. Now hand me that thing and start talking before I put a bullet in your tennis hand."

Rick glared at Gabe then handed him the Sony.

"Now start talking," ordered Gabe, waving the gun at him with his right hand and pushing the record button with his left.

"I'm not afraid of that thing," said Rick, but his expression as he looked down the gun barrel belied his words. "You wouldn't dare shoot me. You'd be in more trouble than I am."

"All I'd have to do is claim 'self-defense' after I pump you full of lead," Gabe informed him. "Your fingerprints are all over this scalpel, and I think you'd have a hard time explaining what you were doing in my hospital room at two in the morning dressed as a doctor, especially after you tried to kill me with your car."

That seemed to take the bravado out of Rick's attitude.

"Okay, what do you want me to say?" snarled Rick. "Where do you want me to start?"

"In the beginning," said Gabe. "Tell me about the robberies in the locker room. Why'd you do them?"

"Because I needed the dough."

"A kid like you? From a good family? A good future—if you weren't so lazy."

"You know my old man. He's tighter than a virgin's pussy. I couldn't stand it any longer." He was starting to whine. "I didn't want to steal from my friends at the club. But how would you feel? Everyone over there's got money to burn, and your best friend is suddenly a millionaire. I'm as good a tennis player as he is. I just got some bad breaks, some bad calls when I was on the circuit. It only takes a couple of bad calls or a little lousy luck to sideline you in the qualifying round." From the demonic look in Rick's eyes, Gabe hoped he wasn't going to freak out before he got a complete confession. "I couldn't take it any longer. Every week seeing my best friend on TV picking up checks for fifty and seventy-five grand. While all I was getting was some shitty allowance from my father. I needed money, so I could be in Mike's league, too. How could I ever pick up a check? I felt like a nerd watching him pay for me all the time, and all those chicks falling all over him. This stinking world, it only likes a winner. It doesn't matter that there are only maybe a hundred and fifty people out of the whole world who can cream you on a tennis court. You're still a nothing-burger if you can't even qualify for the big ones." He started sniffling. "I don't want to be a nerd. I had to start getting money somewhere in order to hold my head up. I couldn't help it."

As the emotional Rick broke down now and

started sobbing like a naughty child caught with his hand in the jelly bean jar, Gabe could almost understand what had motivated him. He didn't approve, but he could understand.

It wasn't the first time that some stupid kid's life had been derailed from a worthier goal by the unrealistic anticipation of quick monetary rewards in the big wide world of sports. You could almost blame two deaths and nearly a third on the lost innocence of a sport that had originally been played purely for fun and exercise on the manicured lawns of Newport and Southampton estates. But you couldn't ascribe his treachery entirely to that, or absolve him from guilt. Most also-rans had to cope with the similar disappointment, but somehow they got on with their lives without resorting to murder and stealing. Gabe ought to know. He'd coped with it himself.

"Okay, now I know *why* you were stealing," said Gabe, when Rick had finally turned off the tears and was standing there red-eyed and embarrassed and angry. "Now tell me why you knocked off Danny and Jock Kornfeld."

"Don't you know?" He stared at Gabe defiantly.

"Yeah, I know, but I want to hear it from your lips."

Reluctantly, Rick made a complete confession. To Gabe's surprise, it was remarkably similar to his own scenario of the crimes. He killed Danny to quiet him, he said, and he *had* hidden with his body in the utility closet when Gabe surprised him by coming back. He had remained there until Gabe left the locker room, whereupon he strung Danny up on the gravity bar. As for Kornfeld, he killed him after unsuccessfully trying to blackmail him about Jan. He knew about Jock's affair with Jan Wexler because he'd seen them entering Randall's apartment building the night he killed Danny. Kornfeld *had* told Rick he'd seen him carry Danny's body out of the locker room and string him up, and he threatened to go to the police with that tale if Rick didn't call off his blackmail threat. Realizing he couldn't let Kornfeld live knowing what he did, Rick strangled him, too, and threw him in the pool.

"Well, I guess that takes care of everything," said Gabe, so engrossed in Rick's confession that he'd forgotten that his broken leg was paining him dreadfully and that his head still hurt like he'd done a dive into an empty swimming pool.

"You're pretty smart to have figured all that out," said Rick. "I've got to hand it to you." As far as Gabe was concerned, that tone of admiration in his voice was strictly an act to get him to lower his guard. From the way Rick was staring down the gun barrel, there was obviously some scheme being formed behind those cold, shifty blue eyes of his. "Just tell me one thing: when did you know it was me?"

"The day I played you tennis. I knew you wouldn't have lost to me if I hadn't upset you so by mentioning the gold ball. And then later, when we were standing at the urinals, that clinched it."

"What clinched it?"

"That remark you made about the smell of your urine after you ate asparagus. I remembered then that I'd smelled a similar odor the night I came back to the club and found Danny missing. I remembered the big deal you had made about ordering 'asparagus hollandaise' for lunch that day."

"That'll teach me to eat asparagus," snarled Rick.

"Well, where you're going," Gabe reminded him, "they probably won't have it on the menu."

"Ha, ha!" In a sudden whirlwind of movement, Rick picked up a pillow and clamped it over Gabe's face, shoulders, and arms. In the seconds it took Gabe to shake him off his gun, Rick grabbed the tape recorder and broke for the door.

"Stop!" shouted Gabe.

He aimed the gun at the back of Rick's head as he yanked open the door and started to run out into the hall. But he suddenly loosened his grip and let the gun drop to the bed. He could never shoot a man in the back, even if the son of a bitch deserved it.

Twenty-one

"You say he made a complete confession that you taped?" asked Judy Trump, sitting down opposite Gabe's hospital bed the next morning.

"Complete. Everything I've been telling you he confessed to: the locker room thefts; killing Danny first and making it look like suicide; then Kornfeld, to quiet him. And then trying to get rid of me because I was on to him."

"Then why didn't you hold him? You had a gun."

"He just surprised me completely by making a break for it, with my recorder. And I didn't have it in me to shoot a man in the back."

"You'd make a lousy cop," said Trump. "Dirty Harry would have shot first and worried about scruples later."

"Not so lousy," said Gabe, unwrapping the Kleenex from around the scalpel. "I still have this, with Rick's fingerprints all over it. He forgot to take it."

"Yeah—that'll help some in putting a case together. But I still have very little else except your word to get an indictment on. Your story all seems so pat. Even the fact that you just happened to have a tape recorder at your bedside. You certainly didn't expect him to show up and be taped, did you? I can understand the gun Jenny's father loaned you—you needed some protection. But not the Sony."

"Well, there hasn't been much to do in this bed while I'm recovering," explained Gabe, "unless I want to watch 'Geraldo' or "As the World Turns.' So I started working on an idea I have for a mystery novel. But with all my broken bones, I'm in no shape to type, so Jenny brought me a tape recorder to dictate into. I could kill myself for letting that bum grab it with all that evidence on it."

"Don't kill yourself. It wouldn't have been admissible as evidence anyway," said Judy. "Especially when he confessed under gunpoint."

"No, but at least *you'd* have believed me," said Gabe. "And if you're half the woman I think you are, it would have inspired you to pursue Rick and not pin it on me."

"Oh, I'm going to pursue him," she replied with determination as she carefully rewrapped the scalpel in the Kleenex and dropped it into the pocket of her khaki shirt. "If these prints check out, and I believe they will, you'll be off the hook, and I'll try to nail Rick for attempting to knock you off."

"Well, there's more than just the scalpel," pointed out Gabe. "What about running me down? Can't you nail him for hit-and-run driving? You said there was red paint on my motorcycle, or what's left of it."

"First we have to locate a car of that description. We have an all-points bulletin out on it, but so far no luck."

"Maybe it's back at the Ferrari dealer's."

"We checked that one out already." Judy shook her head. "The poor salesman who loaned it to Rick is a wreck. If he doesn't get the car back, he's responsible for a seventy thousand dollar loss."

"It couldn't just disappear," said Gabe. "A flashy-looking automobile like that, with some fender dents on it, ought to be a cinch to spot."

"If it's not in somebody's garage or over the border." She shook her head, as if it were all too much for her. "Rick could be in Mexico by now. It's been almost ten hours since he tried to finish you with his old man's scalpel."

"You think it belonged to his father?"

"That's the logical assumption. I'm going to call Dr. Reeves as soon as I get back to the office and ask him if one of his is missing. I'm also going to ask him if he has any idea where his son is." She stood up suddenly and headed for the door. "I'll be in touch, young man. Hope you get out of here soon."

"Yeah, this is a little confining," grinned Gabe, rapping on his cast.

"By the way," said Judy, turning back to Gabe, "what's the name of this book you're writing?"

"Murder at the Racquet Club."

"Pretty mundane," she said. "You can come up with something better."

"I didn't know you were a literary critic, too," said Gabe.

"Oh, yes. I majored in Elizabethan literature when I went to college."

Judy laughed, started to leave again, then turned around a second time. "By the way, Mr. Steele, I'd watch your step if I were you. If that kid tried to get you twice, who's to say he won't try it a third time?"

"How do I watch my step in this contraption?" asked Gabe, pointing to his suspended leg.

"Keep your gun handy," advised Trump, "and don't be afraid to shoot him in the back the next time. Remember Dirty Harry."

Twenty-two

As Gabe suspected, Rick didn't make any further attempts on his life during his last week in the hospital. He knew that if Rick had any brains, he'd flee the country, or at least lay low for a long, long while. As a precaution however, Gabe kept the gun close to his side but out of sight of his private nurse.

On the morning of his release, Gabe's nurse got him up early, dressed him, and put him in a wheelchair, where he dozed off while he was waiting for Jenny to arrive and take him home in her car.

"Wake up, sleepyhead! Time to start living again."

Gabe stirred at the sound of her voice.

"I must have dozed off after breakfast," he explained, opening his eyes and gazing into Jenny's.

"You must have." She kissed him on the lips,

sticking her tongue mischievously into his mouth and wiggling it around.

"Hey, that's nice," said Gabe. "I've missed that."

Jenny tapped the cast on his right leg with her index finger. "Well, when you get this off, we'll be able to go all the way again."

"Now you're talking." He laughed, and looked at his watch.

"Eight-thirty! Who's letting in the Early Birds?"

"Tony. He's done very well filling in for you until you're back on the job."

"You mean I still have a job?"

"That's one of the things I have to tell you. The board had a meeting last night and voted you in for as long as you want to stay. They're so grateful for what you've done that you can write your own ticket."

"What have I done? Rick is still at large."

"But they know now that you put your own life on the line because you didn't accept Judy's suicide theory."

"How do they know that?"

"I got Judy to attend the meeting and tell them everything that's happened—including Rick's confession. After that, they voted Rick out of the club."

"Honey, you just made my day," he said, grabbing her from the wheelchair and kissing her. "Now let's get the hell out of here and back to the club."

"You think you're up to managing the club now—with this leg still in a cast?"

"I can sit at a desk with both legs broken—as long as I have you to look at in the next office."

"There's just one thing that worries me," smiled Jenny. "How are you going to get up those circular stairs on crutches?"

"I've been thinking about that, too."

"Maybe you ought to sleep at our house. It's all one level."

"Your folks going to object?"

"I thought maybe we could get married first."

Gabe pulled her onto his lap. "You know, I just may take you up on that." He squeezed her to him. "Of course, I don't know if I'll be able to afford a wedding ring after I get my hospital bill."

"Don't worry about that," Jenny assured him. "I've already checked. Your Writers Guild insurance is covering most of it, the club's employee medical insurance plan will cover the rest, and I have enough money in my account to pay whatever those two don't cover."

"In that case, I'll have to marry you," he said as the nurse came in to prepare him for departure. "If I don't the business office downstairs will never let me out of here."

Gabe and Jenny were sitting on the club terrace later that day, having lunch together for the first time since their boss-secretary relationship began. They were unconcerned now whether or not the rest of the membership knew they were lovers.

Gabe's crutches were leaning against the railing, his cast-encased leg resting on a chair. He was no longer just a manager; he had become something of a hero in the other members' eyes. Everybody, both young and old, was stopping by to congratulate him on cracking the case. No matter that it wasn't officially over; Rick's crime binge had ended, everyone believed.

The food at the hospital had been awful—"no, worse than awful"—despite the enormous daily tab, so Gabe felt no guilt about eating two orders of the apple pancake with sour cream and chicken livers, which Tony had prepared especially for his homecoming. However, he momentarily lost his appetite when he noticed Judy Trump at the top of the stairs, craning her neck as she tried to spot him among the diners.

Gabe waved, catching her eye, and she sauntered over to their table. From her expression, it was more than just a social visit.

"Talk to you a minute?" she asked, dropping into a chair.

"Of course. I've missed our daily schmoozes," said Gabe pleasantly. "What's up?"

"Something happened last night that caused me to rethink your murder mystery theory. Our prime suspect is dead." As they looked at her in disbelief, Judy continued: "The West L.A. police found Rick's body on Wilshire Boulevard early this morning. It was splattered beyond recognition all over the pavement."

"Oh, how dreadful!" exclaimed Jenny. "A car?"

"No," replied Judy thoughtfully. "He took a nose dive off the Crown towers—that's one of those high rises along the Wilshire corridor, and one of the few with an open balcony. We don't know what he was doing there—or whether he fell or was pushed. No one in the building, including the girl at the switchboard on the night shift, remembered seeing him come in."

"Suicide?" conjectured Gabe aloud. "He doesn't seem like the suicide type."

"I don't think so either," said Trump. "Why would he kill himself? He knew we don't have enough hard evidence to convict him of anything, except possibly petty theft, even if we did catch up with him."

"I wonder what he was doing in the Crown Towers," speculated Jenny. "He didn't live in an apartment. He lived with his father in a house on Rexford Drive."

"Maybe he was hiding out in a friend's apartment," suggested Gabe. "You said his father didn't know where he was."

"The same thought occurred to me," said Trump. "Which is why I'm here. I'd like to see a list of all your members along with their home addresses. Maybe between the three of us, we can spot a connection. You have a list handy?"

"Sure thing," said Jenny, jumping up from the table. "I'll go get it."

While Jenny was getting the list, Tony brought Judy a cup of coffee and a toasted bagel, which she munched on thoughtfully.

"Rick's father know about this?" asked Gabe.

"Yes, he was informed shortly after they found the body. He's the only one who could make a positive identification, Rick's face was so smashed and bloodied."

"How'd he take it?"

"Very stoically, according to Lieutenant Shaw at the Purdue Precinct. Almost as if he were relieved to hear it."

Jenny was gone about fifteen minutes. When she returned she was carrying a computer printout of the members names along with their addresses. "Sorry, I took so long, but I ran off a copy just for you. You can keep this one for your investigation," she said, putting the list on the table between them.

As Gabe scanned the list, the name of "Carter Blackman" popped out at him.

"Hey, this is interesting," he said. "This may be something. Carter Blackman lives at the Crown Towers."

"Who is he?"

"He's a big wheel at World Broadcasting. One of the yuppy group who've replaced the old guard."

"You know him?" asked Judy.

"Not well. He's not my cup of tea. A little too smooth and eager to conquer the world. Has *two* phones in his car. But I have nothing against him. We say hi when we meet, and we've played tennis together occasionally."

"So what's so interesting?" asked Judy. "Was he a friend of Rick's?"

"Not that I know of. But there's something strange here. Blackman was the last person to my knowledge to have his locker broken into. About two months ago, shortly before my accident, Blackman came to the office and said someone had stolen his attache case while he was playing tennis. He was quite upset about it, too, because he claimed it contained some important papers."

"You think he knew that Rick had taken it? That couldn't be a strong enough motive for murder, say he was murdered," Judy said, wiping some jam off her chin with a napkin.

"Probably not, but we'll never know until we ask him. Why don't you go see Blackman and find out if Rick was at his place last night? It's a shot in the dark, but at least you'll find out if they were friends or not."

"He probably wouldn't admit it."

"You're pretty perceptive, Judy. Maybe you can read a reaction on his face. I mean, if he's being devious or not."

"Yeah. I'll go have a talk with him. But I want you to come along too to make the introductions. With you, it'll seem less like a police investigation."

Twenty-three

Carter Blackman was unexpectedly cooperative when Gabe phoned him at his office at World Broadcasting a little while later to set up an appointment. He didn't even ask what they wanted to meet him about, which in itself was suspicious. He must already have known, even though there'd been nothing about Rick's death in the papers or on the radio yet.

"How's two o'clock?" suggested Blackman. "I'll leave a drive-on for you at the gate."

The World Broadcasting Company was in the Valley, near the intersection of Ventura Boulevard and Coldwater Canyon. In the days of silent films, it had been the Mack Sennett lot. But now the old sound stages had been torn down and replaced by an ugly contemporary structure of black glass and cement blocks four stories high.

When they reached Blackman's office on the fourth floor, a pretty young secretary with pouty lips and one of those extremely "fit" bodies in a tight skirt that quit just below her crotch, ushered them right into the inner sanctum.

Blackman's office was a typical network office: large contemporary desk, framed posters of all of World's hit prime-time programs on its stark white walls, two visitors' chairs of real leather, and white shag carpeting.

When they walked in, Blackman was at his desk, with his suit jacket off and his French cuffs rolled up, being given a manicure by another pretty young lady in a mini skirt up to her thighs.

He shot them a fatuous smile and said, "Well, what can I do for you two? But if you're here to sell me a cop series, forget it. We're up to our ass in cop shows."

"I'm here to investigate a death at your building last night," explained Judy Trump. "A young man named Rick Reeves—a member of your tennis club—was found splattered on the pavement this morning on the same side of the Crown Towers as your penthouse balcony."

"And you think I did it?" said Blackman, his handsome face expressionless.

"Did what?" Judy jumped at him. "I didn't say anybody did anything. I just said his body was found after some kind of a fall. And since he didn't live there, we thought maybe he was visiting a friend there, and—"

"So what do you want from me?" asked Blackman. "He was no friend of mine. Why would he be in my place?"

"We just took a chance that you might have known him, since you're the only member of the Racquet Club who lives in the Crown Towers."

"I've seen him play tennis, but I don't know him. Why don't you check the other ninety tenants in my building? Maybe one of them knows who pushed him off."

"I intend to," said Judy. "I just started with you first because there was a possibility you knew each other, and if that turned out to be correct, it would save me a lot of legwork."

"Well, it's not correct," he said crossly. "Now if that's all you want to know, I've got to get back to work."

"Yeah, sure," said Judy, standing up. "Thanks for your help." She started to shake his hand, then pulled her hand back. "We'd better not shake, sir. I don't want to mess up your new polish job."

She waved, started to leave, then turned back, as if doing an imitation of Columbo. "By the way, Mr. Blackman, I never said anyone *pushed* Rick off the building. Do you know something I don't?"

His face turned ashen and for a moment he

lost his cool. "No, no," he blurted out suddenly. "I—I just assumed the obvious. How could a good athlete like that *fall* off a balcony without a little help?"

"You're right about that," said Judy. "He probably was given a little help. Well, keep your eyes and ears open when you're at the Crown Towers. Maybe you'll see or hear something that'll help us get to the bottom of this."

She dropped a business card on his desk. "There's my number if you have something to tell me. Have a good one, Mr. Blackman."

She waited at the door for Gabe to negotiate the distance from Blackman's desk to the door on his crutches then followed him into the reception room.

"What do you think?" asked Gabe when they were riding back to Beverly Hills over Coldwater Canyon in Judy's police car.

"I think he was lying through his capped teeth," said Judy, "but there's not a way in the world we can pin anything on him unless somebody at the Towers happened to spot what went on, and the chances of that are between slim and nothing. Since he lives in the penthouse, there's nobody above him who could have witnessed the scene."

"Except God."

"And he's exempt from testifying."

"Back to Square One?" Gabe felt depressed again.

"I'll spend a few days questioning the other tenants, but I don't expect it to lead to anything." Judy's expression suddenly brightened. "But at least one good thing's come out of all this. Whoever pushed Rick off saved the taxpayers one hell of a lot of money in not having to prosecute Rick. We had a pretty shaky case against him, to be perfectly frank."

Twenty-four

Gabe and Jenny decided to hold off their wedding day until the doctor removed the cast from Gabe's left leg. That way they'd be better able to enjoy the water—and bedroom—sports on their Hawaiian honeymoon.

Meanwhile, things settled down to normal at the Racquet Club. The only changes were that Doctor Reeves resigned, from the humiliation of it all, and Gabe felt it safe to remove the locker room signs warning members not to leave valuables in their lockers when they went out to play.

After all, the thief was six feet under.

There was one aspect of the case, however, that was still troubling Gabe.

Why did Blackman kill Rick?

And then one day, about a week after Rick's funeral, Gabe stumbled upon the answer, thanks to Rick's father.

Gabe was just opening the club in the morning when he received a phone call from Dr. Reeves, asking him to empty out Rick's locker for him. He said he just couldn't face the chore himself.

"I understand," said Gabe. "Be glad to do it for you."

Armed with a laundry bag and the club's passkey to the lockers that still hadn't changed over to combinations, Gabe flung open the steel door of Rick's locker and started pulling out the dead tennis player's belongings.

At first he found nothing unexpected—a half a dozen rackets, some clean tennis clothes, a pile of dirty tennis clothes, a jockstrap, some shaving gear, swimming trunks, and a copy of *Penthouse*. But then, lo and behold, he hit pay dirt.

Beneath a pile of towels he found Danny White's set of keys to the club, a men's Cartier wristwatch, fourteen hundred dollars in cash, and Carter Blackman's Vuitton attache case.

Although it was after the fact, this cache of stolen loot, plus Danny White's key ring, proved beyond a shadow of doubt that, (a) Rick was the locker room thief, and that (b), he had killed Danny to keep from being exposed by him.

But it did nothing towards solving Rick's mysterious death, though for some reason Gabe had a hunch that the answer to that might be found in Blackman's Vuitton case.

For a moment he debated whether or not to open it. After all, it didn't belong to him. But using the excuse that he didn't know who the case belonged to until he did open it, he flipped up the lid and examined its contents.

It wasn't very full. It contained an American Express platinum card, an electric razor, a small dictating machine, a package of multicolored condoms, and some official-looking papers on World Broadcasting Company letterhead.

He wasn't going to bother reading the documents, but something on the top one caught his eye.

MEMO TO ALL PROGRAMMING HEADS
HIGHLY CONFIDENTIAL
SUBJECT: Acceptable writers

Beneath the heading was a long list of writers, some of whom Gabe recognized from their TV credits, some from meetings at the Guild, and some he didn't know at all.

On another sheet of paper, also marked "CONFIDENTIAL," was another list. This one was labeled:

"NEW UPDATED GREY LIST"

"The following names, regardless of credits or reputation, are not acceptable because they don't fit into our youth concept."

Glancing down the list, Gabe saw the names of many of his contemporaries, including his own.

At the end of the grey list was the following: "For obvious reasons, it is imperative to keep the contents of these memos out of the hands of nonnetwork executives. Although our present hiring practices are not actually illegal, we and the other major networks could be targets for class action suits by veteran members of the Writers Guild of America on the basis of unfair age discrimination under the antitrust statutes."

Well, I'll be god-damned, mused Gabe. So there really is a "grey list." And all the while the majority of agents, producers, network brass, and executive writers in Hollywood have banded together in denying that such a thing existed.

Suddenly it flashed through his mind why Blackman was so upset about losing his attache case and what Rick was doing at Blackman's penthouse. If he knew Rick, he'd been trying to blackmail Blackman, too—by threatening to show the "grey list" to the Writers Guild. But he'd taken the precaution of leaving it in his locker in case Blackman tried to grab it from him.

That had to be it. Rick had a penchant for blackmailing. He had tried to blackmail Kornfeld. He admitted that to Gabe in his confession in his hospital room. And now here was a chance for him to make some really big dough—enough to pay for the red Ferrari.

But evidently Blackman wouldn't cooperate. So they had a violent argument, which turned physical and culminated with the TV executive pushing Rick off the balcony.

All of which was pure conjecture, of course. There wasn't a chance in a million that anyone could pin a murder rap on Blackman unless it could be proven that Rick had been in his penthouse.

"I agree with you," said Judy Trump, after she had carefully examined the contents of the Vuitton attache case in Gabe's office later that day and listened to his explanation of what he thought had happened. "It makes a nice story—all the pieces of the jigsaw puzzle fit neatly together—but it's still as circumstantial as it could be. So I might as well close this case right now. I'm never going to be able to hang that TV fellow."

"Now that the case is officially over," said Gabe, closing the Vuitton attache case, "what do you plan to do with this?"

Trump thought it over a moment and said,

"Well, it's stolen property, but there's no use my hanging onto it. The person who stole it is dead so I guess I might as well return it to its rightful owner."

"Do me a favor, Judy? Let me return it, I've got something I'd like to say to the guy."

Judy thought it over, then said, "Why not?"

Twenty-five

Once he got Judy's permission, Gabe wasn't sure how he wanted to handle the situation.

He mulled it over the rest of that day and evening. And by the following morning, he had worked out a pretty good plan.

He phoned Blackman at his office and told him he had found his Vuitton case and would like to return it to him.

"I'll send a messenger for it," offered Blackman.

"No, I want to personally put it in your hands and have you sign for it," said Gabe. "Can't I bring it to your office?"

"It's not a very good time for that. I'm just going into a series of meetings that will last all day."

"How about tonight?" suggested Gabe. "Why

don't I come over to your apartment, say around seven?"

"I guess so," he replied, not sounding overjoyed about the prospect.

Since he couldn't drive a car with his leg in a cast, Gabe had Jenny drop him off at the Crown Towers at the appointed hour.

"This shouldn't take too long," he said, as he struggled to get out with his plaster-encased leg. "But if you don't want to wait, I can take a cab to your folks' house."

"No, I'll park here in the drive. I can't wait to see how this turns out." As he leaned over and kissed her on the cheek through the car window, she said, "Be careful. I don't want the same thing to happen to you that happened to Rick."

Gabe hobbled into the glitzy thick-carpeted lobby on one crutch; in his left hand was the Vuitton attache case.

"I have an appointment with Carter Blackman," he told the girl at the switchboard. "The name's Gabe Steele. Want to announce me?"

She did and then told him, "You can go up now. It's the penthouse."

The penthouse was by itself on the twenty-first floor.

Gabe pressed the bell, and the door was opened almost immediately by Carter Blackman, with a drink in his hand and a smile of welcome on his face.

He had on slacks, Gucci loafers, a blue-and-white-striped shirt with French cuffs and gold cuff links, but no jacket, for the weather had turned warm and he was relaxing.

"Well, well," he said with false heartiness, as he eagerly yanked the Vuitton case from Gabe's hand. "I never expected to see this baby again. Where'd you find it?"

"In Rick Reeves' locker." He studied him to get a reaction, but he remained deadpan. "Evidently Rick was the locker room thief."

"No, kidding?" His cold blue eyes twinkled in amusement. "Quite a yarn to be spinning at our quaint little tennis club."

"Better open it up and see if it's all there," suggested Gabe.

"Don't worry." Blackman set the case on a marble-topped credenza in the entrance hall, opened it, and made a quick check of its contents. "Everything's in order." He seemed quite relieved as he put the cover down quickly and snapped the fasteners.

"How about a drink?" he said, "as long as you're here. Got to repay you some way."

"Good thought," said Gabe. "A vodka and tonic would hit the spot."

"Coming up." Obviously wanting to keep an eye on the Vuitton case, Blackman put it on top of the bar while he was preparing Gabe's drink.

"Nice place," said Gabe, crutching his way

into the living room, which was tastefully furnished with a mixture of Country French antiques, and contemporary sofas, and some very good modern art. "Mind if I look around?"

"Help yourself," grinned Blackman.

"Great view," said Gabe, hobbling out onto the terrace which overlooked Wilshire Boulevard. He peered over the railing, at the long drop below.

"Hope I made this strong enough," said Blackman, loping out onto the terrace and handing Gabe his drink.

"It's fine, I'm sure," replied Gabe, holding up his glass. "Well, cheers."

"Cheers to you." Blackman dropped onto a chaise. "Have a seat, Gabe. You look uncomfortable leaning on that crutch."

"Thanks, but I prefer to stand. My gimpy leg gets a little stiff if I spend too much time sitting. I'll just sit on the railing here."

"Suit yourself."

"By the way," said Gabe, "as long as I've got your ear, and my agent doesn't seem able to get me a meeting, would you mind if I pitched an idea I have for a movie-of-the-week to you?"

"Why not?" said Blackman, mellowing from the effects of his third drink. "My network is always open to fresh ideas."

"I didn't know that," said Gabe. "My agent tells me you people won't listen to ideas from anyone over forty, that there's some kind of an age list."

"Pure fiction, pure fiction," said Blackman sharply. "I'd buy an idea from Methuselah if it was any good."

"Then you ought to be crazy about this one," said Gabe. "It's really high concept. The background is a tennis club like ours. And it starts with a series of locker room thefts. One of the things stolen is a Vuitton attache case owned by an important executive at the fourth network. When the thief looks inside, he discovers a list of writers who are being blacklisted by all four networks because of their age—not how well they write. Just like the McCarthy era. Armed with this he calls on the owner of the attache case in his high rise building and threatens to expose him if he doesn't come through with some big bucks. Well, the network guy balks at being blackmailed. At the same time he is so scared of being exposed that he loses his temper and pushes the blackmailer over the balcony to his death."

Gabe paused while he looked into Blackman's eyes to see if he could read what the man was thinking. Blackman glared back at him silently. "Well, what do you think so far?" asked Gabe. "Does it appeal to you?"

Blackman suddenly leaped to his feet, his eyes flashing anger. "What is this?" he shouted.

"Some kind of a joke? That story couldn't happen because there is no list. It's pure horseshit. I didn't kill Rick."

"Oh, yes, there's a list," said Gabe. "I saw it in your attache case, and I've already turned it over to the Guild."

"You what?!!!" As if not believing Gabe, he sprinted into the living room and came back with the attache case, which he threw open. "You're lying. You're a fucking liar. It's all here," he said, riffling through the papers.

"Those are just copies," grinned Gabe. "The originals are in the hands of the president of the Guild, who's turning it over to their lawyers. You network assholes could be in big trouble when this hits the media."

In a sudden loss of control, and looking quite apoplectic, the normally smooth-acting Blackman leaped at Gabe with both hands open, as if intending to strangle him.

"You god-damn fucking blackmailer!" he shouted, coming at him like a tackle on the Rams. "You're as bad as Rick."

Gabe jumped aside, then took the heavy end of his crutch and swung it at his assailant like a baseball bat. It was a perfect hit. The crutch smacked Blackman in the face, stunning him and throwing him off balance. He staggered against the railing, and somersaulted backwards over the side. As he hurtled to his death on the concrete below, he let out one eerie blood-curdling shriek, and then all was silent.

Gabe watched Blackman hit the pavement, and then with a shrug, he hobbled over to the phone and tapped out Judy Trump's number at the police station.

"Hello, Judy? This is Gabe. No, he didn't like my movie-of-the-week idea. In fact, he hated it so much he tried to kill me to keep me from telling it to anyone else. But luckily he lost his balance and fell over the railing and killed himself. Yeah, it is too bad. But what the hell, he won't be missed. There are plenty more like him at the networks." Despite the solemnity of the occasion, he couldn't hold back a laugh. "Anyway, I'm in his penthouse, if you want to skip over here and finish wrapping up this case."

Also by Arthur Marx

FICTION

The Ordeal of Willie Brown
Not as a Crocodile

NON-FICTION

Son of Groucho
Everybody Loves Somebody Sometime (Especially Himself)
Goldwyn
Red Skelton
The Nine Lives of Mickey Rooney
My Life With Groucho

PLAYS

The Impossible Years
Minnie's Boys
My Daughter's Rated X
Groucho: A Life in Revue